Jeremy!
Party like it's
1999!

Also by Joe Prosit

Machines Monsters and Maniacs Volume 1

Bad Brains

7 Androids, Book Two of the "From Order" Series

Zero City, Book Three of the "From Order" Series

And coming soon…

Machines Monsters and Maniacs Volume 2

99 TOWN

BOOK ONE
OF THE "FROM ORDER" SERIES

JOE PROSIT

Copyright © 2023 by Joe Prosit
All rights reserved.
No part of this book may be reproduced or copied in any form without the written consent from the author. This is a work of fiction. Names, characters, businesses, places, events, locales, and incidents are either the products of the author's imagination or used in a fictitious manner. Any resemblance to actual persons, living or dead, or actual events is purely coincidental.
Author Photo by Cadence Porisch, on Instagram @cadey_photography
Book Cover by Nabin Karna
1st Edition 2023, ISBN 9798862210644

Prologue

A contraband drone hovered over the alley in the sky that night. A cat cried in the dark. Four blocks over on Fifth Street, police sirens came and went, the whine contorted by the Doppler Effect. A cool wind cut through the backstreets.

Nancy threw open the back door of Rogue's Tattoos, spilling light, noise, and warmth into the night. She stormed through the trapezoid of light on the pavement, sloshing a mostly empty bottle of whiskey as she went. The door, having slammed against a dumpster, narrowed the band of light as it swung shut. Before it did, Nancy turned over her shoulder and let him know how she really felt.

"You know what? I'm glad your mom fucking died. You deserve it. I'm going to dig that bitch up and throw her dead body on your front lawn."

The door shut before she'd gotten out all of her peace. It didn't matter. The alley was dark again, but the black sky speckled with diamonds was fading to a deep blue canvas. Under the soft light of the coming dawn, Nancy saw her gleaming white 1970 Dodge Challenger R/T. She staggered, drunk, but had too much pride to throw the small plastic bottle of whiskey before draining it dry.

The last drops burnt her tongue. Nancy hocked it over her shoulder and the bottle bonked and bounced against the pavement. She fumbled for the keys, fumbled for the door handle, and fell behind the wheel. Once there, the nest of leather seat and wood steering wheel and shifter comforted her. Her hands landed on the wheel and the shifter as they had a thousand times before. She could drive in her sleep. She could drive maybe better drunk than sober. She cranked the ignition and the 440cc engine rumbled to life like an earthquake.

Nancy reached out for the door and slammed it shut. The sounds outside the alley, the cry of the cat, the whirl of some contraband drone overhead, the chatter of her friends inside the tattoo shop all went mute. All she heard was the ballad of the idling V8.

When she pulled the car keys from her pocket, another key landed in her palm with it. This one was attached to a rubber fob with the number nineteen printed on one side. She toyed with it as the engine idled. Her mind strayed to what the key could open, and to the terabits of encrypted data waiting inside, and what that data could open once it was exposed. She should go there now, to the locker, then to the woman in Chicago, and then…

"Home," she mumbled to herself and reached to put the Challenger in drive. "I want to go home."

Before she could, another engine roared. Two steel lions in a pre-modern savannah. Headlights popped and blinded her from her left side. She held up a hand and squinted against the glare. Tires squealed. A steel front bumper slammed into the driver's door of the Challenger and Nancy smacked her head against the top of the concave door. Her brain lit up like a slot machine. Glass shattered into bits of popcorn. The Challenger slid ten feet sideways. The key on the "19" fob tumbled into the passenger seat.

The other car backed up, dislodging itself from the crumpled side of the Challenger. The headlights blinded Nancy again. She was still conscious and now angry. She heard the other car's transmission grind as the driver shifted from reverse back into first gear.

"Not again, motherfucker," Nancy said through drunk lips. Her hands and feet knew their tasks. Off brake. On clutch. Shifter up into drive. On the gas.

The Challenger roared and lurched ahead. The other set of headlights charged forward and clipped the rear fender, twisted the Challenger ninety degrees, nose towards the exit of the alleyway. Nancy kept her foot on the gas and barreled between two buildings towards the street. She was in second gear by the time the car jumped across the gutter and onto 10th Street.

She turned hard to the right, leaving trails of black rubber on the asphalt as she steered and counter-steered. The car shifted side to side on its suspension as she brought it on course down the center of the lane. Her hand stayed on the shifter and was instinctively ready to throw the car into third gear, but Nancy was never one to run. She threw it back down into first, cranked the wheel hard left, and hit the brakes.

The Challenger skidded sideways to a stop, perpendicular to the yellow center line. As soon as it came to rest, Nancy reached under the seat and grabbed her old friend. She popped open the door, the bent metal groaned but obeyed, and put one foot down on the blacktop. Nancy stood up and steadied the .38 Special in her right hand by holding her wrist tight with her left hand. She aimed the barrel towards the alleyway leading out from Rogue's Tattoo. She waited.

The city was quiet. The slow sunrise still an hour away made no noise. About every other streetlight was working. The ones that did buzzed and crackled. The rumble of the Challenger blotted out everything else. There was no other traffic yet. The two and three-story buildings on either side of 10th Street were still dark. The residents inside still slept. She'd wake them up.

That drone she'd heard coming out of the tattoo shop, it was back again, buzzing above her. Didn't matter. She'd plug this asshole in the middle of the street right under its lens. Not like that evidence would be admissible in court.

The other car, its make and model still hidden behind a pair of round headlights, pulled out of the alley, slow and deliberate. She wanted to know whose car it was, wanted to know who'd smashed up her baby, who she was about to kill, but she still couldn't make out so much as the shape of the vehicle. It turned towards her, slow and steady, coasting in neutral once it was on the street so the driver could pump the gas and rev the engine.

"Oh, you're an arrogant cocksucker," Nancy said. "How 'bout you suck on this."

She squeezed the trigger of the .38. The cylinder turned and the hammer snapped. No neighbor-waking bang. No recoil. She looked through the cylinder and saw the glow of the flickering streetlights through the six empty chambers.

"Motherfucker," she said and threw the gun onto the passenger seat. She slid back into the driver's seat and slammed the crumpled car door.

The other car came rushing towards her again, but her hands and feet did their thing. The Challenger's fat tires squawked as they bit into the blacktop and launched the car straight toward the other.

There were two seconds when both cars were locked on a collision course like two trains riding the yellow center line instead of a set of tracks. Those headlights, round and set wide on the front of the other car grew larger and brighter. At the last moment, Nancy swerved to the right. The other car swerved in the opposite direction. Her side mirror caught the other car's A-pillar and snapped off.

Nancy ignored it and shifted the transmission into second and then third gear. She checked her rearview mirror and saw the other car burn its tires around a U-turn. By the time its headlights were back in her mirror, she was in fourth gear and the Challenger was doing sixty miles per hour. The V8 was just getting warmed up.

The other car, still nothing but a shadow behind two headlights, was quick on the accelerator. Nancy glanced from the roadway to the vibrating rearview mirror, checking the other driver's slow but steady gain on her.

"Who the hell are you?" she asked no one. Whose car was fast enough to match her Challenger, and why did they suddenly want her dead bad enough to smash both their cars to pieces?

Ahead, 10th Street came to a T-intersection. A thick brick storefront stood across the intersection. Nancy pumped the brakes, downshifted, and took the turn at forty miles per hour. The other car matched her moves but was still a good quarter mile behind her. That was until she slipped the transmission, and the engine redlined in neutral before she found third gear.

A chump mistake. A drunk mistake. A mistake that cost her about a quarter mile in lead space. The other car was coming up right on her rear bumper.

"Who the fuck are you?" she yelled inside the car.

The other car veered into the oncoming lane, to the left of the Challenger. They were going for a pass. Nancy steered in front of the other car, denying them an edge in whatever game they were playing. The other car swung back to the right. Nancy swerved back, following the other move for move.

She watched the rearview mirror more than the road, trying to anticipate her stalker's next move. At the first glance of another swerve to the left, she veered left harder. Only it was a feint. The chaser gunned it and put their front fender next to her rear fender. One more swerve and the mystery car caught her rear bumper and pushed it sideways.

The Challenger twisted into the clip. The sides of the wheels bit into the asphalt. Nancy counter-steered, but it was too late. Before she could brace herself, the Challenger barrel rolled sideways. Everything was centripetal force and broken glass. Without a seatbelt, Nancy banged off the roof and the bucket seats and both doors. She lost count of how many times the car turned over. All she knew was when she finally came to a stop, the car was upside down and everything in her body hurt.

Nancy saw an exit, one of the smashed-out windows, and crawled through the crushed and collapsed opening rimmed with glass teeth. Her fingernails clawed as the asphalt and pulled her torso free. As she did, it became obvious that the bones in her right forearm were shattered. Blood ran in a thick stream down her nose and to the blacktop. It hurt to breathe.

She was half out of the Challenger when she looked toward the blinding headlights of the other car. The driver got out and walked her way. He was all silhouette in front of those round and wide-set headlights, but she could make out what hung from his hand. It was a big thick tire iron. And the way he gripped it, she knew he wasn't coming to help change a flat.

"Who the fuck are you?" she managed to eke the words out of her crushed rib cage.

No answer. The silhouette with the tire iron walked closer. Confident. Patient, but eager all at once. He set his feet over her shoulders and raised the tire iron against the deep blue morning sky.

Chapter One

I wasn't there when my wife jumped a hundred stories out of our apartment window. I wasn't there when she rigged an android to bust out the glass. I wasn't there when she decided life was worthless and she'd rather be dead.

The next day, sifting through dozens of pictures of her corpse, I felt bad for not feeling worse.

My name was Federal Investigator Chuz Alawode, and that was the morning before I left for 99 Town. I stood at my workstation, fixated on the images. In the still pictures, her torso was compressed and thin. Her head and chest cavity had burst from the impact of the fall. Dried blood looked black against the white pavement. The clichéd thing to say would be that the scene looked like a Jackson Pollock painting, but the pictures lacked the color and joy and serendipitous fun of Pollock's long looping continuous swoops. No. She looked more like one of those Ralph Steadman drawings as if her blood were big drops of Indian ink plopped on paper, surrounding some clearly-insane character in the middle of the composition. Only difference was that the central character in this composition was Maggie.

The images shined in high definition on my digital workstation. I shuffled through the photos in silence, sometimes swiping one still away or zooming in on another, either gesturing with my fingers or sending mental commands through my implant to the workstation to manipulate others. I hardly recognized her. Was it even really her? Was this mess on the sidewalk my Maggie?

I zoomed in. Zoomed back out. Brought another image to the front. Tossed that image to the side with the flick of a wrist to bring another shot to the top of the virtual pile. Limbs were twisted in ways they shouldn't bend. Her torso seemed flatter and emptier than I'd memorized it with my fingertips back when she was more than just still photos. Even after rotating the 3D images, I wasn't sure if this was because of a condensed torso or a crushed sidewalk. It didn't matter, but I couldn't stop looking all the same. In each picture, my wife of twelve years was laid out on a sidewalk. Parts of her body I'd known so well were transformed and alien. Twelve years of marriage and it all came to this. A corpse.

I had to stop myself. Emotions were creeping into my thoughts and clouding my judgment. Emotions were selfish distractions. Besides, this was just data. Nothing more; nothing less.

"Chuz," someone called my name. It took me a moment to pull myself out of the mental tar pit I had wallowed into.

The open-air office of the Anomaly Investigations Department inside the Chicago Federal Building was quiet and peaceful. A dozen other investigators, all clean-cut and dressed in our white uniforms of the Order, were toiling away at the grid of identical workstations. The department was quiet, orderly, and pleasant. The windows surrounding the shared workspace gave a clear view of the peaceful streets of the city around us. The buildings were clean and white, their lower levels decorated with green flowering vines with red blossoms. The plaza outside was adorned with lush trees and an orange steel sculpture that despite its media, made me think of a goldfish swimming through water. Sun came through the windows.

"Hey, Chuz," my boss moved through the dress-right-dress rows and columns of workstations. Phom Bramstedt, the Senior Chief Investigator of the branch. He was always a cheerful guy. "Hey, you found some new simulation you haven't told me about? What's got you so enthralled this early on a Monday?"

His smiles came easy and often, always on the verge of turning into a laugh. Phom was well-groomed to the point of shining but still came off casual. Shorter than genetically optimal, his body fat composition flirted with breaking federal regulation. But he was a good boss and an even better friend. Still, I issued a mental command,

and the images of Maggie's corpse laid out on the sidewalk vanished as fast as my neurons could fire.

"Sorry. Just a distraction," I told Phom. "Nothing you'd be interested in."

I felt the influence of Phom's good mood trickle into my implant and wash away some of the melancholy. No doubt, Phom could feel some of my detached despondency too. The implants shared everything through the Network.

Phom gave me a hesitant glance before responding. "Huh. If you say so, bud."

"Yeah. It's nothing. Really," I said, and I meant it.

"Well, I have something for you. A new case."

Relief replaced the morose. "I could use a new case." I resolved and corrected the last anomaly I'd investigated yesterday, and the lack of a project left too much room in my brain for… less productive mental exercises. "What is it this time? Another malfunctioned android or maybe something a little more challenging?"

"Think of it more as a malfunctioned human," Phom breathed in. "I'm sending you out to 99 Town."

"99 Town? I've heard of the place." Heard of it, but never thought much about it.

"Haven't we all," Phom said.

He gave his implant a silent command, and my workstation lit up with images. A map of an old city stretched from one edge of the desk to the other. Grid streets. Train tracks. A river cutting through the middle. Towers near the city center, the skyline sloping down to smaller and smaller brick buildings near the outskirts. Above the map were suspended images highlighting specific locations. A brick storefront. A dam along the river. A bridge crossing a stream in a wooded park. Tire marks on an asphalt street. Everything looked dirty and broken. A tighter shot showed us a car wreck and a pool of blood on the pavement. More work influenced by Ralph Steadman's hand.

"Well, let me tell you something, Chuz. Whatever you've heard doesn't do it justice. An absolute zoo. These Luddites… Sure, their technology is just a hundred years old, but their brains are locked in the caveman days. And like cavemen are wont to do, every once in a while, they off one of their own in such a manner that necessitates our involvement. I was sent there a few years back. I could tell you about it, but you wouldn't believe me. 'Sides, you'll find out soon enough."

"Okay. So who expired this time? And why do we care?"

"Little Miss Navatny Meade. A runaway from here in Chicago. Her parents live over on the North Side up in Glencoe. Father's an old war hero. Mom's some hoity-toity philanthropist. Both politically connected. Big donors to local charities. Pillars of the community. That sort. They've asked us to get involved." With a thought, Phom cleared away the aerial images and brought up headshots of three individuals. These images were from Chicago; I could tell because they were short 3D video loops. Two registration shots of a pair of well-to-do seniors, smiling and nodding. The third, a school ID photo of a young girl, maybe fifteen years old at the time. Red hair. Lots of freckles. Her cheeks blushed as she pushed a strand of loose hair back behind her ear.

"Looks like a nice kid," I said.

"I'm sure she was. Till about two years back when Little Navatny felt she needed a taste of life on the other side of the tracks. She ran off to 99 Town and started calling herself 'Nancy.' Parents begged her to come home, but she dug in her heels. They figured it was a phase and she'd eventually come back to her cozy home in the suburbs. So there she stayed, and for a while, everything was copasetic."

Phom flicked those images away. The next stills weren't as nice. "Two nights ago she gets herself drunk and goes for a joy ride around four in the morning. Non-autonomous cars and booze are legal there in 99 Town. Inevitably, she wrecks. Totals the car. A beauty by the way. The car, I mean. A Nineteen-Seventy Dodge Challenger. And you might think the story ends there. Another 99er killed by her own recklessness. Tragic, but too common for anyone to care. However, when local law enforcement investigates the scene, they don't find her body. Instead, they find blood splatters consistent with a bludgeoning. They also find a tire iron in the gutter wiped clean of fingerprints but still covered in bits of brain matter and blood. Nancy's blood."

"A tire iron?" I asked.

"From what I gather it's a wrench they use on their cars. Big believers in manual labor these 99ers," Phom said. "At any rate, the local authorities can't find the body, but their rudimentary forensics team is able to determine from the DNA and the brain matter it was Nancy, and she is most certainly deceased. They notify the next of kin."

"That's insane. How does a body just go missing?" I asked.

Phom tapped the small device behind his ear. "No implants in 99 Town, Chuz. No implant means no GPS locator, no biometrics reported to the Network, no nothing. Until we physically dig up a body, we're really just trusting twentieth-century forensics to know she's even dead. The 99 Town cops tell Mister and Misses Meade all these gory details, and naturally, they're traumatized. Hysterical. The Network does what it can to level out their biochemistry, but they've been persistent. They're demanding we take action. So, here we are.

"The locals already have a kid in custody on murder charges. As soon as they have the body, they'll try him for Murder One and execute him the same day. Old fashion lethal injection. Crime and punishment are different in 99 Town. You'll see. So the thing is, the Meades want to know the right 99er gets the big needle. It just might be that the kid they're ready to execute is a witness rather than the perpetrator. We let them have their way, it's gonna be awful hard to interview that witness after he's expired. So I need you to go there, poke around a bit, find the body, and make sure the kid they have is the kid who killed poor little Nancy. Bring the Meades closure. You're the best investigator I got. You're thorough. Relentless. If anyone can sort out truth from fiction in that cesspool, it's you."

I was beginning to see the shape of this assignment. Nodding, I summarized what Phom was telling me, "Go to 99 Town. Confirm her expiration. Confirm or correct local law enforcement's findings and ensure a proper conviction. That should be easy enough." It felt good to have business to concern myself with.

"Don't be so confident. Chuz, you're the best I got, and there's still no guarantee we'll ever find out what really happened. Like I said, crime and punishment are different there. So's their investigation methods. You'll be in a dead zone, and the Network won't be there to do the heavy lifting for you. It's going to take you a couple of days, maybe a week."

A week. In 99 Town. Away from the Network. I had to take a step away from the workstation and let the complications stir around in my head for a moment.

"Hey," Phom said and put a hand on my shoulder. "Listen. I hate these filthy 99ers. They're violent, careless, self-destructive ingrates. They could have peace and safety. Instead, they put a fence around their town and spit on what the Order has done for them. And it wouldn't be so bad if they could keep their chaos to themselves. But then you get what we have here. So I understand if you don't want to go there and hold their hands through what should be a simple investigation. I get it. But Chuz, I felt your emotions across the whole office. I saw what images you were looking at before I came to you."

And just like that, my stomach sank, and my thoughts returned to what I'd been looking at earlier. Phom would feel that too.

"No. No, I'm okay. Really, Phom. It's no big deal," I said and felt my own face grow hot and flushed. How long had I been hypnotized by the images of my dead wife? How long did I have the files open for anyone in the office to notice?

"You and your wife, Maggie. You two were close. She took her own life, and I'm sure you have all kinds of questions swirling around in your head. How did it happen? Why'd she do it? It's distracting. It's got to be."

"Phom, really—"

"And it's against regulations. It's not your case. You know your access is unauthorized. And as for this sadness I felt inside you, you know more than anyone what can happen when folks don't allow the Network to moderate these sorts of emotions."

"No, Phom. I promise—"

"How long have we known each other? Listen, I'm not going to report you. I'm doing you a favor. This case will be good for you. Get out of the city. Go. Get some fresh air. Focus on something as far removed from her expiration as possible."

"You know, I think she may have been cheating on me?" I admitted, the first time to anyone. "She was hiding things from me. Before she died. I could tell she was keeping things—"

"See?" Phom interrupted me. "That's the kind of thinking you should avoid. Let your thoughts stew like this and you'll come up with all sorts of nonsense to worry and stress about. Take the case, Chuz. Put your energy into the case."

He was right. I knew he was right. Phom was a good friend and had an objective cool-headed perspective I envied. All I could do was listen to him. So, I pulled off my wedding ring, set it on the workstation, and solidified my intent. Phom sensed that through the Network and slapped my shoulder.

"Case files are uploaded. You can review the details on your trip out there. Go home, pack up, and have an autocar pick you up at your apartment. Pack light. You're going to want to pick up some clothes when you get there. They don't wear a lot of white in 99 Town. You'll want to blend in. And when in Rome..." Phom pulled an item from behind his back and set the black chunk of metal on the workstation. It looked vaguely like a direct neural inhibitor but cobbled together from bits of machinery. It was covered in levers and buttons and sharp edges, thick and heavy, telling by the clunk it made when Phom set it down. All black. All metal. "It's a firearm. A Ruger nine millimeter. Standard issue to any federal agent sent into one of these Luddite enclaves. Neural inhibitors might not do you any good there. No Network. No implants. Most don't even have the port or the internal hardware a neural inhibitor needs to work. Hit someone like that with a neural inhibitor and you might as well be aiming a toy's remote controller at them... I'm telling you, pal, going to 99 Town is like stepping inside a time capsule."

"99 Town, huh?"

"99 Town," Phom said.

I stepped out of the Chicago Federal Building and into the daylight. The sun shined down, and a light breeze cut through the streets and swirled around the trees and that goldfish-like sculpture in the plaza. The glistening smooth white towers of downtown Chicago surrounded me on all sides. To the east, the Network erased buildings from my view so I could see Millennium Park, the Art Institute, and beyond that Lake Michigan. Those buildings were there, just as gracious and unmarred as all the others in the city, and if I wanted to see them or if the Network detected a need for me to see them, they'd reappear. In the meantime, skyscrapers were to my north, west, south, and a view of the lake to my east.

People were coming and going, stepping in and out of autocars along Dearborn Street. Timely, efficient, peaceful, and happy. This was life under the Order, and I was about to leave it for the chaos and crime of a hundred years into the past.

The noise of traffic was muted by ambient music coming from everywhere and nowhere. The music was nothing I recognized but was soft and ideal for my mental well-being. It could have come through speakers hidden in the landscaping about the plaza, but more likely, the Network was pumping it directly into my auditory cortex through my implant. I couldn't tell the difference and didn't care. It eased my concerns, as did the peaceful and orderly people moving across the plaza, so I accepted it.

But all these pleasantries were a double-edged sword. While the city itself eased my worries about the new case, the truth was that I was about to leave this place, and that truism left my levels unbalanced and my mind ill at ease. I queued my implant, and it released a micro-dose of serotonin. That was better. The discomfort washed away like a smudge wiped off a mirror. I'd miss Chicago for everything it was, but there was no point dwelling on unpleasantries.

Maggie and I had an apartment on the hundredth floor in a high-rise not far from downtown. I walked through the door and our household android turned to greet me. "Welcome home, Mister Alawode."

I didn't acknowledge her. She looked perfectly human. Pretty, even. Her face and skin covering her steel frame were customizable, interchangeable, and passed for human to anyone without a microscope. Her voice and personality were customizable too, but we'd never changed it from the flat but pleasant and reassuring default attitude of the Network.

"Schedule an autocar to bring me from here to the border of 99 Town," I told her. "Pick me up in thirty minutes."

"Thirty minutes, sir. Your reservation is confirmed," the android said. "Anything else? A meal, perhaps?"

"No. Thank you." Despite knowing it was a robot, I found my eyes lingering on her. Her features were welcoming, enticing, tempting in a way they'd never been before... before Maggie left. I was uncomfortable with how the machine drew me in with her smile, so subtle and indistinguishable from a human's. I turned away and walked to the wall of windows running the length of the apartment. I ignored her reflection in the glass. The view, digitally altered to erase the other Chicago high-rises, gave me a clear view of the restless waves of Lake Michigan pounding the concrete shores.

Thirty minutes ought to be enough time to get ready. The case files would be available on the Network at any time. I'd need to pack clothes, a hygiene kit, the firearm, and the holster Phom gave me. I wore that on my left hip, even though the holster was right-handed. The pistol grip stuck out forward that way, but it would have to do. I wore my direct neural inhibitor on my right hip at all times. That'd come with too.

Neural inhibition was crucial to the peace we'd chiseled out of the chaos following the Event. Every citizen wore an implant, a small device plugged in behind the ear. Among many other features, the implants allowed law enforcement officers and federal agents to temporarily paralyze any individual on the verge of committing a crime or disturbing the peace with a shot from a direct neural inhibitor. It was a line-of-sight tool similar to the firearms of previous generations. A last resort failsafe. In the vast majority of cases, the Network itself detected elevated heart rates, increases of testosterone and blood pressure, and other biometrics that coincides with the build-up to a criminal act. In all but the rarest anomalies, the Network would stop any would-be criminals with indirect neural inhibition as soon as they thought of acting out. For the remaining few, well, that's what folks like me and Phom were for.

So why didn't they use neural inhibition on Maggie just before she jumped?

The Ordered Assembly of Individuals and Collectives presided over the entire North American continent, and since its creation, the Order sought to rid the populace of this sort of brutality. The Order strived to improve and extend life. Upon seizing control of the implants and application of the Network, the Order achieved a comprehensive peace. Through the Network, the Order could paralyze any citizen instantaneously to prevent crimes and accidents. It was the first line of defense against chaos and violence. Tampering with the Network was illegal. So was re-programming androids. So was ordering an android to cut a hole through the glass one hundred stories up in the air. So was suicide. Why didn't they zap her as soon as she got started? Or at least before she jumped? Why had the Order failed her?

It was all under investigation. They'd find the source of the anomaly and fix it.

"Trust the Order, Chuz," I whispered to myself.

The window was repaired within hours of her expiration. Federal Investigators, agents from another branch I'd never worked with, came even faster than the window crew. They reprogrammed the faulty android, gathered the evidence, and saw to the removal of the remains. They did a good job, too. They were efficient. Thorough. Still, for reasons I couldn't quite grasp, I hated them for it.

They should have completed the investigation already. How was it her implant history was erased as soon as she expired? I didn't believe for a second she had a dead man's switch installed. She had nothing to hide.

Dead man's switches... illegal without special authorization from the Order. They wiped all the history and records from an implant upon the user's expiration. Government secret keepers and corporate intellectual-property holders were authorized dead man's switches. The only other way to get one would be through the resistance movement.

Maggie was a journalist, not a spy or a member of the Underground. I was convinced the investigators failed to access her implant correctly. They botched the job. It was their incompetence, not my wife's secrecy that was the problem. If I were investigating, there would be none of this... deceit. I was good at sniffing out lies of omission and commission, of half-truths and withholds. I had a nose for them, like a bloodhound. Somewhere, someone was clouding the truth.

"Stop," I told myself.

I was questioning the Order. I shouldn't question the Order. I knew that sometimes the Order operated in ways that didn't initially seem logical from an outside point of view, but there was always a reason behind the method. It was wise of the Order to send investigators from a different department. If I had to work with those gentlemen every day it would be... a distraction.

A distraction...

Why didn't I stop her? Why wasn't I here for her? What did I do—

Get a hold of yourself, Chuz. These things didn't matter. People didn't matter; it was the system that mattered. If we took care of the system, the system would take care of the people.

Coming out of the swamp that was my own undisciplined thoughts, I found myself in the middle of our living room. No. It was just *my* living room now. It was a nice space. A sitting area with a beautiful view of the lake, digitally perfected with no other buildings or structures to block the view. A few clouds were rolling in from the north. The sunlight poked through in rays. The waves glittered like a blue sequined ball gown. My eyes focused on somewhere between the window and the lake, hovering in that non-space between clouds and lake and living room.

Would they stop me?

I had a position in the Order. I was a valued investigator. This assignment to 99 Town proved as much.

Maggie was a journalist. An investigator in her own right. If they let her go...

I sleepwalked through the sitting area, past the overstuffed chairs, and put my hand on the glass that wasn't there two days ago. Wasn't there, and then was there again an hour later. It was cold to the touch. It chilled the nerves in my palm and sent a chain reaction through my core all the way to my feet.

A hundred stories below, cars passed by. Soft music played. People walked over the repaired sidewalk. She'd stood here where I was standing now, just before the fall, just before interrupting all those people going about their business of moving to and fro with such urgency and purpose. I closed my eyes and imagined leaning forward through an open pane, just testing out the idea to see if she was onto something I wasn't. Then, in my mind, I resisted the urge to fight the pull of gravity. I fell. The wind rustled through my clothes as I rushed to catch up with her, everything silent but the air moving past my outstretched arms.

"Your car will arrive in two minutes," the android said.

I pulled my hand away from the glass, having forgotten I'd even put it there. It was numb from the cold. My knees were locked, and I stumbled so as not to fall.

"What?" I mumbled. I couldn't have heard the android right. "How much time?"

"Approximately two minutes, Mister Alawode."

Her words seemed to uncramp my muscles, clear my head, and set me back in motion. "I… have to pack. I have to go."

There wasn't enough time. I needed a bag. The bag in the closet. An extra set of clothes. Hygiene kit. What else? What the hell happened? I'd set the car for thirty minutes. How was it outside the door already? If I missed the car, it would be inefficient. It would be noticed. I checked my hip and found my direct neural inhibitor was still there. So was the firearm on my other hip. Next was clothes. Did I need extra clothes? Phom said to buy them there. Something about blending in and not wearing white. Where the hell was my bag? If I didn't pack clothes, did I need a bag?

Forget it.

In the bathroom, my toothbrush and comb were in a cup on the counter. I grabbed those. That would do. Moving through the bedroom toward the front door, an item out of place caught my eye. It froze my hectic momentum.

There was a small slip of paper lying on the hardwood floor as if it had been knocked off a pillow the night before.

How long had it been there? I stopped, picked it up, and unfolded it. There were just a few words on the slip of paper, scrawled in my wife's unpracticed handwriting. It read,

In case you still love me.

I flipped the paper over. There was more on the back, written by the same sloppy hand.

1321345589

If the numbers meant anything, I had no clue. They meant nothing to me. Neither did the message on the front. Something Maggie wrote, maybe to her secret lover days or even weeks ago. Something the android had missed in its cleaning. A distraction. A waste of time. On my way out the front door of the apartment, I tossed the piece of paper onto the dining room table and forgot about it.

Chapter Two

The autonomous car cruised out of Chicago at two hundred kilometers per hour, carrying me west and away from the city, through the suburbs and into the countryside. Out here, towns and residences disappeared. Huge unmanned agricultural machines tended to endless fields of corn and soy. The landscape was as flat as a billiard table. Nothing to see but the slow-rolling combines and wind-dancing crops.

The Network estimated an hour-long ride. The car was equipped with a workstation and served as a mobile office. I'd use every second of the trip to pour over the case files. I didn't like going into a situation without all the details, and operating in 99 Town as opposed to under the Order created more than enough unknowns to begin with. I found hearing the details aloud helped my comprehension and retention, so I had the Network narrate the images and reports I displayed on the workstation.

"List of persons involved," I said.

The first image on the board was similar to what I'd seen in the office already. Nancy, but not the outdated animated image from two years ago. This was Nancy in 99 Town, frozen in time. Still young but worn a bit thin since they recorded that image of the young girl with the embarrassed, coy smile.

"The expired: Navatny Meade. Seventeen years of age at the time of death. Left Northside Chicago two years ago for 99 Town and has been off the Network since. Estimated date-time-group of expiration: Four May, Zero-four-thirty, Twenty-one-twelve," the

Network spoke from speakers in the car in that same pleasant, sensuous voice as my housekeeper. If I wanted, I could have the Network voice pump straight into my auditory cortex and the imaging injected straight into my visual cortex. But sometimes I preferred stimuli to come from an exterior object if it was an option. The android. The car. Better to listen to inanimate objects than disembodied voices in my head.

Navatny, or Nancy as she'd taken to be called, looked like a sweet girl. Soft smile, even in the institutional identification photo. Straight red hair. The last of her childhood freckles fading away. A tiny diamond pierced into her right nostril. There was wear in her eyes as if her two years in 99 Town had already begun to break her down, but her youth and health were still in charge. It was hard to imagine her dead.

Next up was a mugshot of a man. A boy? Patchy pubescent facial hair. Big thick earrings and another thinner ring pierced around his lip. Sunken eyes. Clearly angry.

"Primary suspect: Drex Carlsrud. Eighteen years of age. An acquaintance of the expired. Employed at Rogue's Tattoo Parlor in 99 Town. Born in Milwaukee, moved to 99 Town at the age of five. No other data is available."

I slid those two photos to the upper left of the workstation, carefully positioning them side by side. Moving those images revealed a third. Male. A sharp angular face. A head shaved bald on the sides but featuring a long limp row of hair running up the center that hung down over one side of his face.

"Primary witness: Samuel Candelario. Twenty-five years old. Owner and proprietor of Rogue's Tattoo Parlor. Employer of Drex Carlsrud and Nancy Meade. Local police have taken a statement but have not uploaded it to the Network."

"That's not much help," I said and brushed that image to the side with the others.

"Person of Interest: Eric Sinclair. An acquaintance of the expired. Nineteen years of age. A native to 99 Town. Also employed by Mister Candelario."

"And let me guess. No history or statements uploaded to the Network?" I said.

"There are limited tax filings and—"

"Next," I said and flicked that image away.

"Person of Interest: Ruby Arylav. An acquaintance of the expired. Move to 99 Town—" An ill-tempered girl. More piercings and shaved temples. I shucked that image away as well.

I'd have to speak with the local law enforcement once I arrived in 99 Town to get worthwhile dossiers of the persons involved. "Show me a video feed of the crime scene on the night in question. Aerial imagery first."

"I'm sorry. There is no live feed available."

"How is there no aerial live feed? You know what? Never mind. Show me the street views of the night in question."

"Sir, there are no video feeds available."

"You're kidding me. Stills?" There had to be some stills. I saw some photographs already back in the office. "Show me a map of 99 Town with icons of all photographic and video evidence overlaid on the map."

The photos of the missing girl and the primary suspect remained in the upper left-hand corner of the workstation. The rest of the surface flashed into a street map of 99 Town. A grid street system for the most part. North-to-south roads labeled numerically as "avenues," except where they weren't. East-to-west streets named after fauna, alphabetically, except where they were named after US Presidents. Then, as if that chaos wasn't sufficient enough, I found Xerxes Street between Cleveland and Coolidge. toward the center of town, the grid system skewed and surrendered to curves and triangles to accommodate the river that cut through the city running predominantly northeast to southwest. Freeways encircled the city to the south and east. The largest, I-29, led off toward Chicago.

Icons sat over the map wherever the local law enforcement had uploaded a photo. Most were centered on the southeast side of 99 Town. Here was the bulk of available evidence. Some of the images were repeats I'd already seen in his office. The blood splatters. The wrecked car. Others were new. Close-ups of the damage to the vehicle, its license plate, its registration number, and tire tread pattern. There were multiple shots of rubber tire marks on the old bituminous street surfaces. Another photo showed the bloody tire iron wrench lying in the ditch. A crude device that wasn't much more than an angled bar of metal. The next photo revealed an exterior shot of Rogue's Tattoo Parlor.

I committed nothing to memory. Instead, I let it all churn in my mind. Best to let the pieces of the puzzle intermix and flow until the chaos began to resemble order. Even then, I had to make sure to keep all facts and suspicions fluid, in case future evidence contradicts current findings. When my mind needed refreshing on any one aspect, I reexamined an image, the map, the sparse dossier of a person involved, the written police reports that had been uploaded to the Network, even the communiques between 99 Law Enforcement and the Order. They were all pieces to the same puzzle.

"We will arrive at the destination in five minutes," the Network said and broke me away from my thoughts.

"Fantastic," I said and gave my implant a mental command. The images cleared away from the workstation. I peered out the front window of the car and saw a distant city skyline grayed by dust and fog. "It still looks a ways away."

"The city center is approximately ten kilometers from the border. Due to 99 Town regulations, you will need to disembark this vehicle at the border. A Lieutenant Michael Andrews will meet you there."

"Huh. Okay. Thank you, Network."

The road approached and ended in a traffic circle in front of a spartan concrete building. Nothing moved outside but dust and dead leaves. Above the entrance were the words "CUSTOMS STATION" molded into the concrete. The front wall of the building was made of glass. I could see more glass walls inside the building and daylight filtered to a blue hew by even more glass coming through the back. On either side of the building was a machine gun automaton guard tower. High fences topped with concertina wire stretched out through the farm fields in either direction.

The car parked itself at the curb near the front of the building and opened the door. I stepped out of the Autocar, and the wind blew my tie. The air smelled different out here. Dank. Earthy. The crops extended on the other side of the border fence but were dried and yellowed on the other side in stark contrast to the lush green fields on this side. There were no lumbering pilotless machines keeping watch of the harvest on that side either.

"This must be the place," I muttered.

The interior of the building was bifurcated through the middle, in line with the border fence outside, by a thick glass wall that stretched from side to side and floor to ceiling. There were two tunnels of scanners that breached the wall and there were plastic bins sitting on a small table in front of the scanners. A pair of Order agents, dressed all in white, greeted me as I came inside. I could see others on the far side of the glass, 99 Town agents who wore dark blue uniforms.

"Mister Alawode?" one of the agents on this side of the border said.

I nodded.

"If you have any items on the contraband list, you can secure them with us," he said.

"Excuse me?"

"Your implant, sir. And any other networked devices," the second uniform said.

"I'd rather keep it if you don't mind," I told them.

"I understand, sir. But they won't let you through with it on your person, by order of The Keepers," the first said. "You might as well leave the neural inhibitor with us as well."

I looked these two guys over and wondered what poor performance they must have demonstrated to be relegated to this duty way out here in the middle of nowhere. Then I wondered who these "Keepers" were. Then I looked through the glass at the two 99 Town agents in blue and realized I was going to have to abide the mild incompetence of more than just these two. But I'd give them as little as I could. I reached up behind my ear, got a firm grip on the implant, and unplugged.

As soon as the jack was clear from the port, my vision went ever so slightly out of focus. Nothing I'd notice after a few minutes of compensating. What was worse was the high-pitched ringing and low-pitched muffles in my left ear. An old injury from childhood I'd forgotten about years ago. But my hearing in my right ear was fine and that'd get me by.

I hefted the tiny light-weight implant in my hand a couple times before tossing it in the little plastic bin.

"I think I'll keep the inhibitor, if I may," I told the agent.

"They're not on the contraband list. Your call, sir," the first agent said.

"Safe travels, sir," the second said as I entered the scanner tunnel.

The short walk-through resulted in no warning beeps or flashes. On the other side, I was greeted by the two agents in blue I'd seen dimly through the glass. A woman and a man. There was a third person who stood by the exit of the Customs Station. His clothes were odd and eccentric. A leather jacket, a shirt unbuttoned low enough to expose a tuft of chest hair. Blue jeans. Sunglasses on his forehead. Pale skin and hair that mushroomed out in a sphere around his head. He leaned against a concrete pillar, his demeanor as unprofessional as his attire, and chewed his cheek.

"Step this way, sir," the man in the blue uniform said.

The two agents ushered me to a wall. Yellow footprints were painted on the floor, and yellow handprints were on the wall about two meters up. I got the idea and placed my boots and hands into the yellow marks, facing the wall.

"Any contraband to declare?" the woman officer said from behind my back.

"None," I told her.

The male officer drew his firearm and watched me just above the weapon's sites. The other officer ran her two hands over each arm, quickly, aggressively. Hands went up underneath my armpits and ran over my chest and stomach, then to my waist around the inside of my belt. She found the handgun and placed it in a bin. She lifted the neural inhibitor from its holster and stuck it over my shoulder so I could see it.

"Really?" the officer smirked and then tossed it into the bin.

I said nothing. What they probably didn't know was the direct neural inhibitors didn't need an implant to work; they just needed the port, the hardware everyone born under the Order has installed as a child. Sure, nobody wore implants in 99 Town, but I bet a whole lot of them still had the port installed in their heads.

The officer frisking me didn't stop to consider this but kept on with her groping. Her hands were running down each leg, inside the lip of my boots, between my legs, and over my crotch. They came away with the only personal effects I'd brought from Chicago: my toothbrush and comb.

They finished and I stepped away from the wall, feeling violated and demeaned, but not ready to let them know it. The gun, neural inhibitor, toothbrush, and comb were in a bin. "You can keep these," the male officer said.

"Thanks," I said and snatched up my things, pocketed the bathroom items, and holstered the weapons. My clothes were jostled and out of place, so I took the time to straighten up and compose myself as I walked away.

The man in the old civilian clothes approached.

"Welcome to 99 Town," this strange man said. "Sorry for the hands-on welcoming committee. The Keepers are pretty strict with the rules around here. That neural inhibitor toy you have won't do you much good around here, but suit yourself. Not too many people have ports installed in 99 Town. You're not hiding any implants, are you?"

"No. My implant's with them," I said.

"No skeez machines?"

"What?" That ringing in my left ear...

"Never mind. Your implant will be safe there with the customs agents." The man stuck out a hand. "Name's Lieutenant Michael Andrews. 99 Town Police. Homicide. Call me Mike."

I took his hand and shook it. "Federal Agent Chuz Alawode."

"Car's this way," Mike said and led me out of the building.

We stepped outside on the opposite side of the fence, and I squinted at the bright sunlight. Normally, my implant would filter the visual stimuli for maximum visual clarity and comfort. Mike slid his orange-tinted sunglasses down on his eyes and gestured to one of three parked cars in front of the building.

Each of the vehicles had a unique shape and color and was in varying stages of disintegration. Mike's, a long black four-door sedan, was the furthest along. Bald tires. Dents and paint scrapes along the fenders. A beefy tubular steel bumper painted black. As we approached the vehicle, I saw it was also equipped with police lights hidden behind the grill and the windshield. There was a cage between the front and rear seats.

Mike opened the driver's door and sat down inside. The suspension groaned. As soon as I climbed into the passenger's seat, I noticed a long and thick-barreled gun racked there and a manila folder full of papers just as thick as the gun barrel. I picked up the heavy file folder, sat down next to the long gun, and put the papers in my lap. The driver's seat had a computer screen, a radio mic, and a million controls and indicators I couldn't identify. It was crowded inside. No workstation or desk to speak of. The dash in front of me read "Ford Crown Victoria" in decorative letters.

Mike cranked the ignition, and the gasoline engine sputtered to life. He reached over his shoulder and pulled the restraint system across his waist. "Better buckle up, Chuck. You're not in Kansas anymore."

"But we're not…" If I didn't believe it before, it was decided now. This was a strange man. "I've never been to Kansas."

Mike just snickered, put the car in gear, and backed out of the parking space. Another transmission shift and we left the Customs Station in the dust.

"Those are case files in your lap there," Mike said, eyes on the road but gesturing to the thick stack inside the manila folder.

"Why are they paper?" I asked.

Mike looked over to me, grabbed the papers, and moved them to his lap as if he were going to try to read them and drive at the same time. "Oh. I'm sorry. Let's use yours instead."

I sat there, empty-handed, catching glances from this officer as he careened down the uneven highway at what had to be a hundred kilometers an hour. My implant with all the files on it was obviously still back at the Customs Station and this Mike character knew that. They weren't going to help either of us now. And it was about then that I realized just how detached from the Network I'd become.

Mike, apparently satisfied with the discomfort he'd created, slapped the case files back in my lap.

"Now, like I was saying, these are the case files," he said. "We have one suspect in custody. Probably our guy, but we need to get some statements from some of his buddies and find the body before we can charge him and make this a done deal. His name is Drex Carlsrud. Local loser who spends most of his time at a tattoo shop called Rogue's Tattoos."

I opened the folder and started paging through the various sheets. Some were hard copy photos, glossy and smudged with fingerprints. Others were text documents clipped together by bits of metal. Most of it was just loose stacks of paper. I found a series of photos with names and dates printed next to the faces in the up right-hand corner. The faces were starting to become familiar. This one was Drex.

"What do we have for a motive?" I asked.

Mike shrugged. "Beats the shit out of me. Obviously, he had some problem with her."

"Murder is no kind of solution," I said.

"This town is full of violent solutions," Mike dismissed.

"As far as witnesses?" I asked.

"The most credible witness we have is Sam Candelario. He runs the tattoo shop and employed Nancy, Drex, and one or two other kids at any given time. Kind of a revolving door for delinquents and runaways. As much a flophouse as it is a tattoo parlor. Between me and you, Chuck, I don't think they get a lot of business there. This Candelario has money, but I don't have a hair on my ass if it's all from legit business. If you ask me, they're running contraband through the shop and making more money doing that than they'd ever make inking people's skin."

"Contraband?" I prompted him to go on.

"How much do you know about 99 Town, Chuck?" Mike asked.

He kept getting my name wrong, calling me "Chuck" instead of "Chuz." Was it on purpose? Another game of his? I ignored it for now and gave him a rundown of 99 Town as I understood it. "There's no Network here. No artificial intelligence. No androids or anything resembling robotics. You've banned nearly all modern technology if what I've been told and seen is true. The idea is that you live your life as if it's the year 1999."

"We have shit we ban. You have shit you ban," Mike said. "By law, you won't find any robots, drones, GPS-equipped tracking equipment, immersive simulations, genetic editing, cybernetic implants like the doohickey you plug into your ear... Oh. And no driverless cars. Hence, me, behind the wheel, masterfully and safely navigating us to our destination."

I was genuinely curious, so I had to ask, "How do you know where you're going?"

Mike tapped the side of his head with his finger. "Amazing what the human mind is capable of when it's not distracted by the entire collection of all human knowledge twenty-four hours a day. We do have the internet, but streaming any data of any kind is not allowed. It gets a little technical the difference between streaming and downloading, so I won't get into that. We're not here to work the Contraband Division, so I don't concern myself with the details. Did they tell you what's not banned here?"

He'd tell me, I was sure, whether I wanted to know or not.

"Of course, they didn't. The Order never mentions what they've banned. No, it's just bass-ackward 99ers who have oppressive laws, am I right?"

"Well—"

"Here's what's not banned in 99 Town, Chuck. Beer. Booze. Porno. Cars. Real cars, I mean. And guns. Now from what I'm told, the Order doesn't technically ban bad language. It's just become a dying fucking art. Is that about right?"

"I... Yes. I suppose that's about right," I said.

"What else? Gambling is legal in 99 Town. So are tattoos. Tobacco, both smoked and chewed. All the fun stuff in life, really. Drugs are banned and have been since the dawn of time, but that's never really stopped anybody, now has it? Now, I love 99 Town. Born and raised here. But I'll admit, as a law enforcement officer, my job would be a hell of a lot easier if it were all banned. Job security, I suppose," Mike said. "What about you? What keeps you busy under the ever-watching electric eye of the Order?"

"Anomalies." That was the official term for the times when things didn't go according to the Order's will. "Rare events. Things that shouldn't have happened, but due to some flaw in the system, were allowed to."

"Things like what?" Mike pushed.

"Accidents. Equipment malfunctions. Crimes, just like in 99 Town, I imagine. Not a lot of theft, but homicides. Suicides," I said, and the word stuck in my brain.

"Suicides? Not much to investigate there, is there? Somebody got tired of living, and so they called it quits. Case closed, am I right?"

"But it shouldn't happen," I said. "We've built social safeguards to keep people mentally healthy. We have physical safeguards, walls, fences to protect people from dangerous areas. Biometric parameters to alert the Network of potential suicide risks. Neural inhibitors in case the individual defeats the rest of the social, physical, and digital safeguards. Really, we shouldn't have any suicides. Zero. Yet…"

"Yet, they still happen," Mike said. "And for all our safeguards we still have contraband on this side of the fence. Sounds like neither of our bosses have it all figured out yet."

"But anomalies are extremely rare," I said, clear that he didn't understand the differences between our two worlds. "The rate of untimely expirations is at an all-time low. The average citizen will never see a crime in their entire—"

"Uh huh," Mike said.

"—lives. The system and the Network, as a whole—"

"Sure."

"—are statistically flawless. Yet…"

"Yet?" Mike said.

"Anomalies happen," I admitted.

"Job security, my brother. No system is perfect. Anomalies are what keep fuckers like us employed."

"Fuckers like us…" I tried out the word and liked it. Was beginning to like Mike's style too.

I gazed out the window of the Crown Victoria. The farm fields of stunted crops gave way to a smattering of residential housing and a few commercial businesses. Everything along the highway seemed dirty and dust covered. There was litter everywhere, or maybe it was just property that was indistinguishable from litter. Rusted metal bikes. Sun-faded plastic kid toys. Paper. So much paper. Why was there so much paper around? Then I looked down to my lap. The case files were still there, heavy on my legs.

"So tell me about yourself, Chuck," Mike said. "You got a wife and kids back in Chicago?"

"No. I just lost my wife," I said matter-of-factly. No point in thinking of it any other way.

"Ain't that some shit?" Mike said. "My old lady just left me too. Walked right out the door and didn't come back. Said I never let her talk."

I looked over at a police officer, half expecting this to be some kind of joke. But Mike's face was more serious now than since I'd met him.

Mike held up his right hand and used his thumb to wiggle a gold ring on his finger. "Divorce papers went through just last week. We're kaput. Officially now. Guess I should toss this thing into the river, huh? Means nothing to me anymore. She's dead to me."

The turn of phrase, the oblivious self-indulgence, something about Mike made me smile, despite the topic. "Yeah. I can relate." A joke I told only to myself.

"Did you bring any cash?" Mike changed the subject. "Of course, you didn't. No worries. You can make a withdrawal. We do have ATMs, you know. We're not Amish."

"What's Amish?"

"What's Amish? Christ on a cracker. You might as well be Amish. Listen. Stick with me, and you'll be fine. Capisce?"

"Yeah. I capisce." Did I?

The Crown Victoria rolled on.

I paged through the photos, most of them were print-outs of the images I'd already studied. A few were new. Some from the crime scene. Some of the cars involved. There was the white one I'd seen before in the blood splatter photos. Flecks of red on white. But these shots were of the car back upright on its wheels. One photo was of the model of that car brand new with its name and technical specifications. 1970 Dodge Challenger R/T. Curb weight. Fuel displacement data for the engine. Transmission style and number of gears. None of it meant much to me. Then there were photos of another car. Dark green, a different make and model. The promotional photo said it was a 1971 Pontiac GTO "Judge." More technical data that I glazed over.

"Sweet ride, am I right?" Mike said.

"Huh?" My left ear, the one full of cotton and a high-E violin note, was the closest to Mike.

"Nineteen-seventy One. That was a long damn time ago. You know, they only made three hundred and fifty-seven of that particular model that year? Three hundred and fifty-seven, and out of those how many do you think are still on the road all these years later? Not many, but if they are, they'd be in 99 Town," Mike said.

"This green car…"

"Looks like there was a chase. Nancy in the white Dodge Challenger, and whoever was driving Drex's GTO. Probably Drex. The GTO drove the Challenger off the road. It rolled. Then the killer finished the job by pounding Nancy's head to a paste with a tire iron. Damn shame it's all smashed to shit now. The GTO, I mean."

"Oh," I said. "Yeah." Clearly, these people had a much closer attachment to their modes of transportation than I did for each random autocar I stepped into.

I flipped back to the mug shot of Drex Carlsrud, then of Nancy Meade. Innocent-enough looking kids. Why would one kill another? And once he had, how did he manage to haul off her body and hide it from the authorities? Where was the late Nancy Meade now?

"When we get into town, I'd like to interview the suspect. Then I'd like to visit the crime scene. See it for myself," I said. "These case files, can I keep these? Without a connection to the Network—"

"Ah, so my old fashion case files aren't so dumb after all, huh?" Mike said. "You're learning, Chuck. By god, you're learning."

35

Chapter Three

    For the rest of the ride, I split my time studying the case files, knowing I would have to commit them to memory now, and studying the city as it scrolled by my window. We entered the city, and it became clear that there was as much to learn from one as the other. 99 Town itself was a suspect, witness, victim, and perpetrator.

    Mike drove past the city limits, and the farm fields were replaced by sprawls of low-income housing. The houses were made of composite materials, each with the same blueprints and design as the next, but each made unique by decades of occupation. Many of the houses were painted a dull earth tone, which seemed to be the default color. Others had been re-painted vibrant shades from one end of the spectrum of visible light to the other. A few had been turned into canvases for artists and featured murals of people and the city with a swooping and bulbous style I had never seen before. Looking beyond the paint, each house was made its own by the items gathered in and around it. A few were neat and clean, but most of the yards were a place where all the human detritus from inside the house had spilled out. Again, the piles of garbage were indistinguishable from piles of possessions.

    The lonely highway spread into a four-lane freeway. Traffic swelled around us. Mike's natural reaction to other cars on the road was to swerve and swear much more often. At one point during a lengthier diatribe of profanity, he flipped on the lights and sirens, which cleared the traffic away long enough for him to regain composure. That was enough to convince me that humans had no business operating any car of any kind.

The cars were even more eclectic than the houses. There was no uniformity of color or design. In Chicago, every car was the same and behaved the same. Here, each seemed to be a living extension of the owner. Some were big and slow. Others fast and sleek. Each a quick summation of the driver's attitude, style, discipline, and wealth. Ubiquitously idiosyncratic.

Residential zones gave way to pockets of commercial stores and industrial parks on our way toward the towers at the heart of 99 Town. One kilometer was filled with the rust and exhaust of industry. The next was lit with neon advertisements featuring partially dressed models of all genders, hawking a vast array of products for sale and consumption. The advertisements were the hardest to comprehend and process. Too many images with too many words, flashed too quickly to read unaided by an implant. If the primary marketing strategy was sensory overload, they succeeded remarkably. Chicago had its own ads and marketing campaigns, but those were measured and logical compared to this assault on the rational decision-making processes.

I broke eye contact with the ads long enough to notice the skyscrapers of 99 Town rise up around us. Some stood hundreds of meters into the air, not as high as Chicago's highest summits, but beyond the limits of what the word "town" suggested. These buildings were built in the twentieth-century style of architecture, with tall spires made of composite, glass, and steel. Closer to the streets than the sky, the modern demands of industry and function gave way to historical designs of concrete sculptures of goddesses, gargoyles, laurel wreaths, and columns. But those were often hidden behind steel I-beams, electrical cables, plumbing pipes, and layers of exhaust soot. Above the street level, the taller buildings were interconnected by a system of enclosed pedestrian bridges and walkways. There were no hover crafts drifting through the air from skyscraper to skyscraper here. Instead, an elevated train gave the city a sense of having two street levels, one level with the ground and another ten meters up. The shadows of the higher level made the lower level dark, filthy, and ridden with more crime and poverty. As Mike drove us across a bridge, I looked over the Cut Rock River that ran through the city below street level. More a canal than a river. Another layer to the three-dimensional maze.

Downtown, foot traffic became as dense as car traffic. Peddlers intermixed with legit salespeople, tourists, and business professionals. Those neon ads still hung from billboards and flashed through windows. Everyone and everything was loud. It was an untuned orchestra of humans and machines.

"Here we are," Mike said and pointed to a larger building a block up the road. "Our modern-day Camelot."

A stoplight turned from red to green, a simple traffic-control measure I had figured out after the first half dozen we'd come upon. Mike stepped on the gas. Another car seemed to have ignored the signal and sped past them, less than a meter from the Crown Victoria's front bumper. Mike erupted.

"Hey, shit for brains! I'll throw you in the clink faster than you can fuck your mom!" As fast as the car and obscenities came, they were gone. Mike's mind switched from calm to homicidal and back to professional in a matter of seconds. "This is 99 Town's Government Center Building. Police. Judges. Bureaucrats. The Keepers have their offices way up toward the top. The jail's in the basement."

The Crown Victoria rolled past the building front. The Government Center's façade was limestone steps, pillars, and lion statues, all well-worn by weather. There were a few people moving up the wide steps, but the entrance seemed more decorative than functional. As we rolled by, Mike turned the car down a narrow ramp that led to a garage door and a subterranean parking lot.

Once away from the front steps, the Government Center was much more utilitarian. The below-ground parking lot was crammed with cars as old as Mike's and a dozen or so marked police cars. The obsolete LED lights over our heads flickered. As Mike parked, a mangy cat ran between tires and shadows. He killed the engine, and we got out. The doors slammed and echoed against the concrete walls, ceiling, and floor. A few blocks away, unseen but felt and heard, a train rolled by and shook the city foundations. I tried not to look at the dripping water coming from the ceiling, the cracks in the pillars, and the rusted rivets in the I-beams. Best not to think about the millions of tons of steel and concrete over our heads.

"Come on. This way," Mike said and led the way to an elevator.

We exited the elevator on the second floor and entered a lobby for the 99 Town Police Department. Various motley citizens waited there, presumably to be helped or incarcerated by an officer. It was impossible to tell by looking at them which fate each awaited, and I got the sudden feeling of being on the wrong side of the enclosure at a zoo. At the back of the lobby, a female uniformed officer sat behind a glass pane. Mike walked fast past all of the people to a door around the side. I watched him wink at the officer behind the pane as she buzzed us in.

The large room behind the door was full of desks and officers. This room served the same function as my shared office back in Chicago, but the similarities began and ended there. In this room, telephones rang unanswered. Officers typed on computers with keyboards and screens. There was swearing and yelling and laughing, and quiet conversations on telephones. The old tile floor cracked under our feet as we moved toward a back office surrounded by glass walls. Printed on the glass were the words "Chief of Police, Captain T. Reiner." The door was open, so Mike entered, and I followed.

There was a desk with a phone and computer and more paper than I had ever seen in my life. Behind the desk was a well-over-regulations obese man on the desk phone. Behind him were various framed photos and certificates, a shelf with a few books, an uncapped half-empty bottle of gin, and a pair of dying house plants. There was an outdated but not completely obsolete workstation in the corner. The surface was blank and inert, and without an implant in my port, that's how it would remain. It was small and there was an equally aged implant tethered to it by a thin steel cable. The jack was filthy, and I dreaded having to insert it into my port at some time in the future. A window to the left spilled horizontal jail cell bars of sunlight onto the desk and across the large man.

Mike stopped in front of the desk and waited with crossed arms as the man behind the desk swore into the phone. I waited respectfully, with my hands clasped behind my back, holding onto the thick file folder. The man behind the desk prattled on about... What was it? Nothing law enforcement related; I was confident of that.

"I already have an estimate, that's what I'm trying to tell you. Well, this one is going to have to be good enough because I'm not paying for another. You're going to have to figure it out. This is on your end, not mine. What a bunch of shit. This is bullshit, that's what this is. Listen. I have to go. One of us works for a living. Yeah. Have fun. Go fuck yourself. Bye."

Mike cleared his throat. "Sir," he gestured to me. "Our visitor from the Order."

I stepped forward and offered a handshake. "Federal Agent Chuz Alawode from the Anomaly Investigations Department. Looking forward to working with you."

The chief, a sloppy man who looked like the bottle of gin behind him was emptied during this very workday, looked up but said nothing. Instead, he opened a drawer on the old oak desk and set several items on top of the stacks of paper. A badge. A set of keys. A pair of handcuffs. A cell phone.

I pulled my hand back. "What's all this?"

"That toy on your hip ain't worth for much more than a dildo around here," the chief pointed to his neural inhibitor. "The gun on your other hip, you know how to use it?"

"Of course," I told him. Did I?

"Works the same as your laser zapper there. After you shoot the poor bastards, you'll need the handcuffs to detain the sons of bitches. Use the cell phone after you fuck that up and end up getting shot by the sons of bitches instead of the other way around. The keys go to an unmarked squad in the parking garage. You know how to drive, right? Of course, you do. You're a grown fucking man, aren't you?"

I wasn't sure which question to answer first, but just like Mike, he let this uncomfortable silence do his work for him. "Yes, sir. I know how to drive." I lied and realized I could lie here, and no one could catch me.

"Fan-fucking-tastic. Congratulations. You just graduated 99 Town Police Academy and earned yourself that badge. Try not to shoot yourself in the foot as you exit Stage Outta My Fucking Face."

That meant leave. I understood that much. I gathered up the items, using the case files as a table on which to mound up the objects.

"Thanks, sir. Come on, Chuck," Mike said, not giving me much time to follow him.

"Oh. One more thing," the chief called after us. "The Keepers would like to speak to you, Special Federal Agent Alawode. Check your gun and inhibitor with the duty officer. I wouldn't keep them waiting if I were you. Mike, show him the way."

"Sure thing, boss," Mike said.

I had to leave the weapons and the case files with the woman Mike had winked at when we came in. The rest of the items I found homes for in my pockets alongside my toothbrush and comb. Mike showed me the elevator that would take me up to the Keepers but declined to go with. So, I stepped into the elevator by myself and took it up the ninety-seven floors to the top of the Government Center. The symbolism of the Keepers keeping their offices on the ninety-ninth floor wasn't lost on me.

When the elevator came to a stop and the doors opened, it was as if I'd traveled to a different city that wasn't 99 Town but wasn't anything like modern Chicago either. The floor was covered in thick burgundy carpet. The lighting was soft and indirect. The walls were stucco and decorated with twentieth-century abstract and Martian absurdist artwork. The poverty and utilitarian aesthetics of everything else I'd seen since coming to this place were nowhere to be found. In stark contrast, the penthouse lobby was more vibrant and decadent than anything else in 99 Town or Chicago. All this I saw from the view of the spartan insides of the elevator. I stepped out.

"Good afternoon, Agent Alawode," a woman behind a desk greeted me. She was pretty, youthful, and smiled in a way that told me she was hired for it. This was a growing trend: women set in places of servitude rather than positions of power. "A Keeper is waiting for you in the office to your left, my right." She gestured with her palm.

"Thank you," I said and moved to a thick oak door. I turned the brass knob and entered.

The office behind the brass knob was more of a penthouse than an office, and far more luxurious than the lobby before it. There was a large mahogany desk at the far end, but it was almost an afterthought. There was a wall of windows that overlooked the oxidized and weathered crust of 99 Town out to the border fence and the expanse of the Order beyond it. A pair of leather sofas faced each other closer to the door. A large TV mounted on the wall streamed the news feed off the Network, and another TV looked like it was playing the local 99 Town news. More artwork on the rest of the walls, a few I recognized by the artist, but couldn't name the piece. War and collateral damage by Picasso. Vaginal flowers by O'Keefe. Art so subtly offensive it only resulted in the general discomfort of the viewer. Still, offensive enough to earn their way out of the Order. In the center of the room was a healthy middle-aged man watching the news streams. He was handsome but nondescript, much like his attire. The black suit he wore was plain but clearly expensive and tailor-cut.

"Mister Alawode," the man said and strided over to meet me. He pulled a hand from his pocket, and we shook. He was gracious. Polite like a politician. "Welcome. Welcome. Can I get you something to drink?"

"Thank you," I said. "And your name, sir?"

The man moved over to a small bar along the wall of the office. His hands were smooth and practiced as they went from glass cupboard to ice bucket to unlabeled crystal bottle. He set two tumblers up with a few cubes of ice, then uncorked the bottle and poured. "No name. I'm just a Keeper. We find the anonymity keeps the focus on the position instead of the individual."

"Is that so?" I said. "Well, if you can't tell me about yourself as an individual, tell me about your position."

"Certainly," the Keeper said and came back from the bar with two drinks, one for me and one for himself. "Make yourself comfortable."

We moved to the couches. The Keeper placed the drinks down on the table and sat opposite to me. He hoisted his glass.

"To mutual objectives," the Keeper toasted and drank without waiting for me to concur or rebut.

I brought the glass to my lips. The tang of ether flooded my nose.

"So," the man began. "I am one of six Keepers, but we speak with a consensus. Together, we ensure our way of life in 99 Town is preserved. Often, that means law enforcement. Other times, it means negotiations with representatives from the Order. Today, it seems we're blending those two strategies. At any rate, the task has fallen on me to impress upon you the importance of respecting our rules and laws."

The muted TV streaming news from the Order's Network contradicted him behind his back. I wondered if the Keepers ever plugged into the Network and decided to wait for an opportunity to look for an implant or a port behind his ear.

"Life is different than where you came from, and I understand our ways can seem confounded and frustratingly backward, especially to an investigator such as yourself. But this is how we choose to live. While you're here, it is essential to our way of life that you respect the rule of law. I understand you were issued some tools necessary for your trade downstairs?"

"Yes," I said. "They're not the tools I would choose, but they'll suit me just fine."

"Excellent. I've seen your instructions as issued to you by the Order, and while none of us who Keep agree with the Order's desire to have you here in 99 Town, we have decided to allow it, as long as you abide by our laws. Outside of 99 Town, the Network is broadcast wirelessly across every square mile and to every citizen. You won't find that here, but we do have a few hardline access points here in 99 Town, necessary to liaise with the Order. There are those and other… opportunities… to violate our laws. If you break those laws, the Keepers and the Order have agreed that you will be held accountable. I suspect we won't have any issues with that," the Keeper said.

"So far, I've seen no opportunities to do otherwise," I said. "The bans seemed to have effectively removed all technological and social progress made since the Event."

"Yes. The Event," the Keeper said. "I remember it. I know I don't look that old, but I was a mature-enough youth to remember the tragedy and its subsequent effects across the continent. Terrible. So many gone insane. So many dead. And, in one regard, the Order is right: It could have all been prevented. They saw their rise to power and totalitarian rule as necessary to prevent something like the Event from ever happening again. They had their goal. They used every means available to achieve it, and they succeeded. There is peace.

There is order. They will never see another day like the Event ever again. I don't disagree with their thought process.

"See, Mister Alawode, they're keepers too. The only difference between us and them is what we've decided to keep and what we've decided to forget. The Order will never forget the Event. They live with it fixed uppermost in their minds every day. On the other hand, we've chosen to forget it, intentionally, so that we may live a simpler life. We reject control and overwatch so that we might stay free. It's anarchy compared to the environment outside of our borders. I understand that. But we've embraced the chaos and have found peace and freedom inside of it."

I considered the paradox of chaos keeping the peace and decided I'd need a drink to help wash down that nonsense. I sipped from the tumbler and nearly choked as the fluid burned down my throat. Coughing it up would be a faux pas for sure, a sign of weakness to this man, so through force of will I managed to work it down and keep my composure.

"I've read the case files for the murder I've been brought here to investigate," I said after the alcohol was in my stomach, burning hot even there. Nevertheless, I had a few of my own points to make. "Like the Event, this death should have never happened. Anywhere else it would have been too easy to prevent, and even easier to convict the attempted murderer. That girl is dead because of your rejection of the Order."

The Keeper smiled, a thing much less sincere and practiced than his receptionist's. The smile of someone eager to stab me in the back. "I'm being cordial, Mister Alawode. But don't confuse my civility with impotence. You will respect the rules of the Keepers while in 99 Town. As far as this case goes, the girl who died was a troublemaker who brought her early demise upon herself. The only reason the Order has shown any interest in her death is because she ran from a wealthy and influential family. But remember that part of the story, Mister Alawode. She ran from your Order into my 99 Town. She chose her path, as is our way here, and if her decisions led to her own death, I say so be it.

"Do I feel bad for the girl? For the girl's parents? Of course, I do. I'm not a monster, Mister Alawode. But I won't sacrifice our way of life because some street whore got in an argument with the trick she was trying to turn. Our police have already investigated the case and have a suspect in custody. Soon, they'll find the body and justice will be done. So, in essence, your job here is already done for you. I suggest you enjoy your time here in 99 Town. Partake in the many things available to you here that aren't available under the rule of the Order. This case will wrap itself up in a matter of days, at which point you can return to where you came from and go on cowering from another Event that will never come. In the meantime, why not give our brand of freedom a try?" The Keeper raised his glass to his mouth and drank.

"Why not?" I smiled and drank another sip from the cup. It was easier to mask my body's revulsion now that I knew what to expect. Besides the harsh flavor and burning sensation, I felt a bit of the alcohol's inebriating effects. It wasn't all that different than the inhibition-lowering gamma-aminobutyric acid neurotransmitters people have their implants dump into their brains to help them relax in social settings. That was good because I had some things to get off my chest. "The Order has allowed 99 Town to exist the way it does as a consolation to old ways. To ways before the Event," I said. "Unfortunately, sir, I've been assigned to this case. The mission assigned to me and the authority that I derive from the Order doesn't stop at the border to 99 Town. As a commissioned Federal Agent, I am sworn to pursue justice no matter the victim, perpetrator, or circumstance. It is my mission to find the truth, and I will accomplish my mission. So I appreciate your civility. But don't confuse your position with my authority."

"Go back to your time, Mister Alawode. Let us 99ers handle 99 business," the Keeper said.

"I think I'll stay. But I intend to interview a suspect and visit a crime scene yet today," I said. "So, I'm afraid I'll have to be on my way. Thank you for the drink. I'm sure you'll be kept informed of my progress."

"That we will. Rest assured of that," the Keeper said. "Watch your step out there, Mister Alawode. 99 Town doesn't have the safeguards you might be used to back in Chicago."

A poorly veiled threat, but at least now I knew how the game was going to be played. I raised the glass of liquor. "To mutual objectives," I said and suffered down the rest of the drink.

When I walked out of the elevator back on the second floor, Mike was waiting for me.

"Chuck, buddy. How was it? You know, I ain't never been up there. I heard you only see one of them at any one time, and that they all share the same name. Lived my whole life in 99 Town, and all this time working in the same building, would you believe I've never seen one Keeper? I mean, on TV, sure. But not in real life."

"He had a TV. It was streaming the news feed from the Network," I told him as we walked back to the duty desk to fetch my weapons and case files. "Didn't you say they ban streamed media around here?"

"You saw that, huh?" Mike said. "Guess they play by their own set of rules."

I nodded to the duty officer, and she set out my inhibitor, the gun, and the stack of papers. I holstered the inhibitor first, then a little less naturally, the firearm.

"Say, you have fired one of those before, right?" Mike asked.

I threw Mike a sideways glance.

"Sure you have. You're an officer of the law," Mike said. "So, I know you haven't eaten. Least not since I picked you up at the border. I know this Chinese place across town. Real authentic. Cook the best Border Collie this side of Beijing. Make it just like they did back around the turn of the century."

I had to step around Mike to get back toward the elevator.

"The suspect. Drex Carlsrud. He's in the basement, correct?"

"Well, yeah, but he ain't going anywhere. Why? You want to interview him right now?"

"As a matter of fact, I do," I said and stepped inside the elevator.

"He'll want his lawyer," Mike followed in after me.

"He was given a public defender, was he not? Isn't the public defender's office in this very building?"

"Not necessarily. And even if it is, that doesn't mean she's in," Mike said.

I pushed the button to bring the elevator down. The doors shut us inside.

"Hey. Slow down, man," Mike said. "You just got here. I know you haven't eaten yet. Why don't you take your time about things? Let's go get some Chinese, have some beers, you can give me the dirt on your conversation with the Keeper, and we'll interview Carlsrud in the morning."

Charming, but this stonewalling was becoming a pattern. I said nothing. Mike smirked back. The elevator doors opened. Mike put his hand on my shoulder and pulled me back, keeping me inside the elevator with him.

"Listen, Chuck. You need to realize things are different in 99 Town. You need to learn how we do things around here before you go off making a damn fool out of yourself. Let me show you the ropes. Get you acclimated. It's not like this sack of shit isn't going to still be here rotting his ass off in the morning."

And that was enough of that. I pivoted toward Mike and took two big handfuls of the collar of Mike's leather jacket. One good step and a shove, and Mike slammed against the wall of the elevator. The flimsy metal panels rattled. The orange-tinted sunglasses slid off Mike's forehead and landed crooked on the bridge of his nose. I got in close to him.

"No, you listen. I did not come here on vacation, and I didn't come here under my own volition. I am on assignment from the Order to find out exactly what happened here, and if I deem it necessary to hold an interview at midnight, then that's what I'm going to... fucking... do."

"Alright. Alright," Mike said and reset his sunglasses. "Easy, Chuck. Chuz, I mean. Have your interview. Do your thing."

For some reason, him using my actual name didn't sound right coming out of his mouth. Sounded patronizing, like another one of his jokes. The doors of the elevator opened, and another officer hesitated before coming inside. I let go of Mike's jacket and stepped out. "I will do my thing. And call me Chuck."

Mike laughed. "You know, Chuck? I'm starting to like you."

47

Chapter Four

By the time the public defender arrived, and the jailer brought the suspect into an interview room, and the lawyer finished her pre-interview with the suspect, and they allowed me into the room, I was hungry. I'd lost track of time, and without my implant, I had to rely on wall clocks to tell me the time, most of which operated by the ancient method of rotating hands pointing at numbers around a dial that didn't correspond with the twenty-four hours in the day or the sixty minutes in an hour. I knew it was getting late, and I was fairly certain my empty stomach only made me more impatient. Still, I waited in a small lobby, flipping through ancient paper magazines full of fashion advice so out of touch it was historical as it was hysterical.

"Mister Alawode?" a woman called my name.

I turned and saw a tall woman in business attire. Her face was stern and impatient, but behind the cold expression, I couldn't shake the notion that she seemed familiar to me. Her skin was darker than any I had seen before. Under the Order, humans were all a uniform bronze, but out here, skin tone varied wildly. Mike and the Keepers were pale. This woman was a rich brown. Her hair was a black nest of tight curls. Physically, she looked nothing like Maggie, but she burned with a fire the way Maggie used to. Distant and disguised, she hid a softness behind the scowl. She was an anomaly to be solved. A question to be answered. In those ways, she was very much like Maggie, a mystery that eluded me even beyond her death. I hid my thoughts; that was something I could do here I couldn't have done under the Order. I tossed the old magazine down on the table and stood up to greet her.

"Yes. Federal Agent Chuz—" I stopped myself. In for a penny, in for a pound. "Chuck Alawode."

"Sara Cohen, Attorney-at-law," she said. Her voice was meek and mouseish, but as hard as steel at the same time. We shook hands, professionally, dutifully. Her hand was cold but friendly. Still, there was something behind her eyes. "My client is ready for you now."

The client. He was who I was here to see. Not this woman.

"This way," she said and led me down a hallway.

The interview room was small and unadorned. Tile floors. Tile walls. The mirror-side of a two-way mirror. A metal table with a loop welded on top, through which ran the chains of the suspect's handcuffs.

Drex Carlsrud sat at the table, looking down at his hands he'd folded near the loop. The chain between the cuffs gave him little slack to do otherwise. He wore an orange jumpsuit with a white tank top underneath. He wore white socks and tan rubber flip-flops. All jail-issue. When I sat across the table from him, the kid lifted his head. His hair was long and hung below his brow. His right eyebrow, visible between the greasy locks, had a row of four holes in the fatty tissue where four piercings had been. His earlobes had holes that had been stretched open by big earrings that had since been removed. His eyes were tired and dark. He had deep brown irises so dark they were almost indistinguishable from the pupils, like a dog's eyes.

"Mister Carlsrud," I said and opened the file folder.

"Call me Drex. Everybody calls me Drex," he said. His language was slow and lazy. He barely moved his lips when he talked.

"My name is Federal Agent Alawode. I'm here from the Ordered Assembly of Individuals and Collectives, and I'm going to find out what happened to Nancy Meade, and who was responsible."

"She said I don't have to answer any questions if I don't want to," Drex said, nodding toward the lawyer.

"Drex, I'm here—" I said but was cut off by the public defender.

"Local law enforcement has already taken his written statement," the lawyer, Sara Cohen, Attorney-at-law, said. "We've gone over all the details of Miss Meade's disappearance. Why are we repeating all this de integro?"

"Humor me, Miss Cohen," I said.

She rubbed her temple. "I quite honestly don't know what we're doing here. My office hours are nine AM to five PM. Why again, couldn't we do this during regular business hours?"

She played the ill-tempered lawyer act well. I could tell she enjoyed it, pushing against tough-guy cops and hard-case prosecutors. This was just another stonewall in a city full of them. Every person I talked to threw up another obstacle. And for what? To defend some pathetic kid who managed to find his way into a jail cell. But I understood it coming from her; it was her job. And if she wanted to play, so could I.

"I think we got off on the wrong foot. Let's start over," I said and looked at both Drex and Miss Cohen. "I'm not here to convict you, Drex. Not if you're innocent. Every other person in this entire building, from the jailers outside the door to the Keepers in the penthouse, wants to see you charged, tried, convicted, and executed. And as soon as they find that body, that's exactly what they'll do. But I don't answer to any of those people. My only boss is the truth, and I am here to find precisely that. So make no mistake, I am the only one who can help you. *If* you're innocent. But before I can do anything, you have to convince me you weren't the one that killed Nancy Meade. And to do that, you're going to have to start talking. More than just the mumbles you've managed to let slip from your mouth so far. You're going to have to tell me everything. Capisce?"

"You don't know she's dead," Drex said, a little upset at the idea. "She's just gone missing. She could still be alive, maybe gone off—"

"They found brain matter on a tire iron at the scene of the crime. Never mind all the blood; humans don't live that long when they've had a portion of their brains removed with a steel wrench. Body or no body, they got you on Murder One, and unless you have something very interesting to say that you haven't said yet, you'll be as dead as Nancy by the end of the week. They got an empty room and a syringe full of chemicals with your name on it. Now, are you going to tell me who killed her?"

Drex turned those sullen eyes to his lawyer, who didn't tell him no. He turned back to me. "Okay. Here's my story. I didn't do it. I wasn't there. I had nothing to do with it."

I wasn't speaking this kid's language. Time to change that. "That's fuck. That's a bunch of bull fuck, and you know it."

Drex looked over to his lawyer again, this time more confused than intimidated, like I was going for. Too late to back down now.

"It was your car, Drex. They matched the tire treads to your 1971 Pontiac GTO Judge. They impounded it, and the front fender is all smashed in. White paint from Nancy's Challenger is on your car's bumper and front fender. You were there with Nancy at the Rogue's Tattoo Parlor just before she was killed. Your buddies say in their statements that the two of you had a verbal altercation that night in the tattoo shop. So please, try again. And this time spare me the bull fuck."

The lawyer's expression had changed too. Now she was just as curious or at least confused as her client. She piped in. "Um. I think what you're trying to say—"

Drex cut her off. "Is… Is she really dead?"

"Do you want to see the pictures?" I said and started paging through the files. I figured the one of the big blood pool next to the overturned Challenger should convince him.

"Okay. Fine. Yeah, it was my car, but I wasn't in it. I love that car. It's a classic. Only three hundred and fifty-seven of them made like that. Why would I smash it all to shit? And why would I do that to Nancy? I've known her since she came to 99 Town. She was like my sister. More than my sister. I loved her."

I sat back. I hadn't expected this connection between the victim and the suspect. Had I missed that in the case files? If I had my implant, I could have scanned and searched for key terms right then and there and found the answers. Instead, I was reduced to flipping through the stack of loose pages in front of me. The answer could be buried in there somewhere, but it was no use trying to find it now.

"You two were romantic together?" I asked. "You were a couple?"

"No," Drex said. He looked back down at his folded hands, his eyes examining the dirt crammed underneath each of his fingernails. "She shot me down."

I stirred the words around, trying to sort out their meaning. She didn't shoot him, not with a gun. It was slang. "What do you mean, she shot you down?"

"I asked her..." More hesitations from Drex. More digging at the dirt under his nails. "I asked if she wanted to fuck."

"For sexual intercourse," Miss Cohen chipped in.

I eyed her again. "Thanks," I said. I got it the first time. What was with this woman? Back to Drex. "And the two of you hadn't had sex before? You weren't in a relationship."

"No. I was just giving it a shot, you know? I thought maybe since, you know, we'd kind of gotten to know each other she might be interested," Drex said.

"That's what the verbal altercation was about?" I asked.

"I guess. My mom died a while back in Chicago. And she had parents in Chicago too, and we were talking about it, and she was real nice to me. So, you know, I figured she might... you know... Anyway, she told me I was gross and that I could go fuck myself," Drex said. Finally, he looked back up and made eye contact again. "But that was it, I swear. Me and her went back to the fridge to grab more beers, I asked her, she said no, and we brought the beers back to the rest of the guys. She was pissed for the rest of the night and the others heard her yell at me, but I didn't do anything back. Didn't even say anything. I just did my thing and got drunk. We all did. I woke up in the morning, and the cops are there arresting all of us. I don't know what happened."

"You fell asleep in the tattoo parlor," I said.

"We all did. It was a Saturday night, and the shop's not open on Sundays, so we all tied one on. Nancy too. She out-drank us all. I was passed the fuck out long before she left."

I sensed a lie there but continued on. "Who was with you in the tattoo parlor that night?"

"Me. Sammy, Ruby, Eric... Nancy."

"Anyone else?"

"No."

"Did anyone see Nancy leave that night?"

Drex shook his head no. "We were all passed out by the time she left. At least I was. For all I know, somebody murdered her right there in the shop and dragged her off while we slept."

"Why would she leave when everyone else stayed at the tattoo parlor?"

"Fuck if I know," Drex said. "She'd done that before, left in the middle of the night to go on some joy ride."

"Did you kill her?" I asked.

"No."

"Did you have any reason to want her dead?"

"Don't answer that," the lawyer was quick to jump in.

"Did anybody else have a reason to kill her?" I kept on.

"No, man. No. Everybody liked Nancy. She was a great girl. Always just happy to be around. I mean, if you pissed her off she'd let you know, but it was never a thing, you know? She didn't hold grudges."

"Somebody had a grudge against her," I said. I'd found the blood pattern analysis photos and spun them around from Drex to see. "Looking at these pictures, somebody had a big shitting grudge against her."

"Don't say that. Put those away, man," Drex said. "I don't want to see those."

I left the photos out on the table as I flipped through the rest of the files until I found what I was looking for. Drex leaned back and closed his eyes so he wouldn't have to see what had become of Nancy. I made a mental note of how he flexed the muscles in his jaw and clamped back the tears in his eyes. I found the photo I was looking for and set it over the blood pattern analysis photo. "Tell me more about your car. A Nineteen-seventy One Pontiac GTO. That's a nice car. An old car."

Drex opened his red eyes. "It's the Judge, man. Four fifty-five high-output vee eight. Three hundred and thirty-five horses under the hood. Can do a quarter mile in thirteen flat. I love that car."

"Ever have any maintenance problems with it?" I asked.

"Yeah, all the time. Eric's the greasy monkey of us guys. He helped me change out the alternator and helped me do the brakes and shit."

"Ever have a flat tire?" I asked.

"All the time. The car looks nice and runs like a fucking beast, but the tires are re-treads. The body is held together with JB Weld. I doubt there's a single original part under the hood. That's just how we keep them on the road, you know? Not like we can buy new cars with all the computers in them. We're always fixing shit on 'em."

"So you know where the tire iron is stored?" I said.

"Don't answer that," the lawyer spat out.

Drex looked over at her. "Of course I know where the tire iron is. But that doesn't mean anything. It's a tire iron. You keep it in the truck with the spare tire. Everybody knows that."

"Where're the keys?" I asked.

"Cops took 'em from me that morning. They probably got them in some evidence locker somewhere," Drex said.

"You had them all night? The keys?"

"In my hip pocket. The whole night, man."

"You didn't lend them out, or let them out of your sight?"

"No, man. And I want them back when this is all over and done with. They're my only set. That car is mine, and I don't let anybody else drive it. She's my fucking baby. I want her back."

"They also have the tire iron," I said.

Drex scoffed. "They have my whole fucking car, don't they?"

"Did you kill Nancy Meade?" I asked again.

"I'm telling you, no. I didn't," Drex said.

"Who did?"

Drex threw his hands up, as far as he could with them chained to the table, which was about four centimeters. "I wish I knew, man. You have no fucking idea how bad I wish I knew."

"Do you have anything else to tell me before I go?" I asked.

"Like, that's it? You're not going to ask me any more questions?" Drex said.

"That will do for now," I said, put the photos back on the stack, closed the manila folder, and stood up. "It was good to meet you, Drex. Ma'am, we'll be in touch, I'm sure."

With that, I stood up to leave. The jailer was at the door and opened it for me. I was down the hallway before the lawyer could react. I heard her shoes clack down the hallway. I let her chase after me. All part of the game.

"Excuse me," she called. "Hey! Detective!"

I reached the lobby near the front desk and the elevators before I stopped and turned to face her.

"Who the hell do you think you are?" she asked.

"Just a friend of the court," I said.

"Amicus curiae, my ass," the lawyer said. She jabbed a finger into my chest, hard enough for it to hurt. Her voice sounded meek, but the will behind it clearly wasn't. "Everybody has some skin in the game. Everybody's got an angle. Tell me yours."

"Nancy's parents. They want to be sure the 99er that takes the fall for this is the one who actually did it," I said. "I'm here on their account."

"So, now you're just going to walk out without saying a word to me? You don't seem like much of a detective to me."

The elevator door opened. I pulled away from Miss Cohen and stepped inside. She followed me in.

"You're thinking something but not saying it. I can see it on your face," Miss Cohen said. "That kind of tight-lipped strategy hasn't helped my client, and it won't help you."

"Okay. He didn't do it. How's that?" I said.

"Of course, he didn't," she was about to reach out and hit a button on the elevator panel. She stopped herself, then looked at me from the corner of her eyes. "Are you going to tell me why you think that?"

I hit the button. The elevator door closed us in together. It started its slow climb back above ground. "He didn't do it because he wasn't in the car that night. The police report shows the ignition system in the GTO was short-circuited to start the engine. If Drex was driving, why wouldn't he use his only key instead of damaging the wiring?"

"Maybe to make it look like the car was stolen, to give himself an alibi," Miss Cohen said.

"You're not much for defending your client. If he wanted an alibi, why not bypass the ignition on someone else's car? If he knows how to short-circuit his own car, it stands to reason he could short-circuit any car. And why hasn't he mentioned this alibi in any of his statements?" I said.

"He doesn't usually talk that much," she said. "You were asking about the tire iron. The cops have it in the evidence locker, covered in brain tissue, blood, and hair. Whoever killed Nancy Meade needed to get into the trunk to get the tire iron out. If they didn't have the keys…"

"He couldn't open the trunk from the inside?"

"On these older models? Maybe. Maybe not," she said.

"Then either Drex short-circuited the engine but used his keys to access the trunk, which doesn't make much sense. Or the killer, maybe Drex, maybe someone else, got another tire iron from another car," Chuck said. "I need to see the GTO. Need to get into the trunk and see if there's still a tire iron inside. If the tire iron isn't in there, then Drex probably did it. If there is a tire iron…"

"Then whoever did it is missing theirs," she said. "Listen, um…"

"Chuck. Call me Chuck."

"Listen, Chuck. I think we might be able to help each other out here. I can get you into the impound lot. We can get a look inside that trunk. See for ourselves whether or not there's a tire iron in the GTO."

I nodded, and she let a thin smile slip across her lips. For the second it stayed there, it was like she slipped on a whole different face. The face behind the one she'd worn when I first met her. A face I could swear I recognized from younger, better times. A beautiful face I'd fallen in love with years ago. The elevator door opened to the basement parking garage. We stepped into the concrete cavern with its rows and rows of cars.

"Which one is yours?" I asked her.

"This one over here," she pointed. "It's a Nineteen-ninety Six Ford Taurus."

The Ford Taurus was in worse shape than any of the other cars I had seen so far, save all but Miss Meade's totaled Challenger. It was rusted from bumper to bumper. Its latest paint job had chipped away to expose three layers below it and in some places the bare metal below those layers. When the lawyer opened the door, the hinges creaked and whined.

"Don't say anything," she said. "This car is older than you are."

"That's actually the newest car I've seen in 99 Town yet," I said.

"Yeah, well, I guess even with all the gearheads in this city, nobody cares about restoring Ford Tauruses," she said.

"Well, Miss Cohen, pleasure to meet you."

"Sara," she said and extended an open hand. I shook it. Her skin wasn't so cold this time around.

I pulled the set of car keys out of my pocket. "I'd love to show off my car, but first I have to find it. When I do, can you show me the way to the impound lot?"

"Okay," she said. "But there's only one problem."

"Besides me finding my Ford Crown Victoria in a garage full of Ford Crown Victorias?"

"The impound lot is closed. It's nine o'clock at night. No one's going to be there for another ten hours," she said. "So, see you there tomorrow morning?"

"That should give me enough time to find my car," I said.

"Good luck, Chuck," she said and looked back twice before getting into her car. The Taurus started with a struggle and drove out of the garage.

I looked at the rows and rows of Crown Victorias. Great. Now all I had to do was test the keys in each lock, find my car, then learn how to drive it.

Chapter Five

    The cheeseburger tasted like nothing I had ever eaten before. Rich, fatty, meaty... Could I die of a heart attack after just one? That had to be a joke, right? Something people said to tear down 99ers? Something to convince people they weren't missing out by not having them in the modern world. They kill people, these big, scary, juicy, delicious sandwiches. Eating a cheeseburger was a surefire shortcut to an early expiration.

    It was worth the risk. I unwrapped a little more of the burger from the slick paper and took another bite. The toasted buttery bun. The crunch and cool wetness of the pickles and tomatoes. The heat and surge of flavor from the patty. Ketchup around the corner of my mouth. Heart attack be damned.

    The drive from the Government Center Building to out here on the edge of 99 Town was challenging but uneventful. Thankfully, most of the traffic was cleared off the street by the time I figured out the basic controls of the car and the traffic control measures of the streets. What traffic was still out provided me with immediate feedback via their horns and hand gestures at the first inclination of any minute breach of driving etiquette on my part. I knew all the signs along the sides of the road and symbols painted on the pavement meant something. Some, like the signs that said STOP and the arrows on the pavement were fairly intuitive. Others, like the "55 MPH" and random pictographs of swerving cars and yellow diamonds filled with lines and hash marks... Those came with the same frequency of honking drivers. But I took it slow and even managed to steer the car to a drive-thru ATM, right before finding a drive-thru restaurant. Then I came here, to this lonely and desolate corner of town.

The Crown Victoria was now parked half-on a sidewalk, engine off and out of the way of any other drivers.

I stood in the middle of the dark street, looking for tire marks, bloodstains, anything to identify the exact spot where Nancy Meade was killed. The night was dark. No moon. Only a little ambient noise of the city. The whine in my left ear. Far off traffic. A barking dog a few blocks down. The quiet buzz of a drone flying overhead. Wind cutting through the buildings and alleyways. I folded up my collar to keep the chill out.

Looking up and down the city street, I saw no traffic in either direction. Hadn't been any since I'd pulled over to the side of the road. Still, I took note of the hazard, then took another bite of the cheeseburger. The photos in the case files didn't show any reference points to determine precisely where the murder had taken place. So before I could take anything away from the scene, I had to determine where the scene was. There had to be something still here that could act as a reference point. A datum point in the dark.

A glistening in the far gutter caught my eye.

"There," I said out loud. I'd developed the habit of talking out loud so my implant could record words to match my vision. Out here, no one was watching, and no one was listening, so I felt no need to self-censor. I walked over to where I had spotted the oddity.

The city had done a good job of cleaning up the mess and wiping the slate clean of the crime, but they hadn't gotten it all. There in the low spot between the curb and the street was a hundred bits of broken glass, sparkling like diamonds in a jeweler's display case. I turned to look back across the street.

"And here," I said and walked to a dark spot on the blacktop. A stain large enough to match the fresh red pool of blood in the crime scene photography. "This is where it happened. This is where she expired."

I stood in the middle of the stain and took another bit from the burger. Kneeling down, I saw there were two stains, one a shade lighter than the other. I put my fingers down on the first stain and felt it was dry but still oily. Petroleum product. Probably a leak from the wrecked Challenger. I ran my fingers across the porous blacktop to the second stain. This was dried out too, but the residue flaked away under my fingertips. Blood. A drop of ketchup landed in the middle of the dark spot.

Suddenly the burger didn't taste so good anymore.

Without the images readily stored in an implant, my mind conjured up memories of the crime scene photography. Unprompted and doubtfully accurate, the images morphed into a living video. They came from that way, going fast, Nancy swerving and trying to get away in her white Dodge Challenger. The killer right behind her in the GTO. In her rearview mirror, it would have been just the shape of the car and the glare of its round headlights. Then, the driver of the GTO got the best of her. She lost control. Rolled the Challenger. That had to be down the road a stretch. Going as fast as they were, it would have taken some distance for the Challenger to grind to a stop. Then...

She was trapped inside the upside-down car. Already hurt, no doubt. Broken glass. Broken bones too. The killer could have taken his time and strolled up to the wreck with the tire iron in hand. Would he have had enough time to get out from behind the wheel, get the tool out of the trunk, and then catch Nancy as she still fought to get free of the wreck? Maybe he was panicked. Maybe he was scrambling to get the tire iron out of the trunk and once he had it, he rushed up to the side of the Challenger and came down on Nancy swinging. His first swing probably didn't do it alone. No. He would have swung several times. She resisted and tried to block as many blows as she could with her already bloody hands and broken bones. But however many it took, he finished her off. He swung again and again and again until she stopped struggling, stopped reacting, became an unmoving and unprotesting target, and then finally expired.

Expired. Was that really the right word for it? Food expires. Contracts expire. People... This person was broken apart, her mind and memories split into chunks of meat and spilled over the roadway outside of a car wreck, surrounded by cracked sidewalks and ghetto apartment complexes. Her blood intermixed with oil and antifreeze.

"Expired," I said the word, and it carried away any pleasure I'd taken from the cheeseburger. I swallowed what I had left in my mouth and wanted it out of me as soon as it was inside.

I stood up, looking for a place to throw the rest of the burger. What had I come out here to learn? The 99 Police had been here and done a thorough-enough job of recording evidence, photographing the scene, and documenting the damage to both cars. What else was there to discover? Was I here just to satisfy my own morbid curiosity? If so, mission accomplished.

No. There was something else. Something to learn. Something they'd missed. Something small. A tiny, overlooked detail. There were always overlooked details.

"So..." I started but wasn't sure how I'd finish the thought.

"So you came to the wrong side of town, motherfucker," a voice called out.

I turned. There was a large man leaning up against the fender of my parked Crown Victoria. A hooded sweatshirt hung over his eyes, the streetlight above him casting a shadow over his face. His arms were folded and legs crossed at the ankles, looking comfortable with how aggressive he was ready to become.

Footsteps behind me, from the opposite curb of the man leaning against my Crown Victoria. Two more individuals stepped out from an alleyway. A man and a woman.

The man wore a limp Mohawk that hugged down over half his face. Light glistened off a half dozen rings and studs pierced into his face. The woman sauntered out, all hips and swagger. A short wooden baseball bat was slung over her shoulder like an old soldier in history would carry a gun. The quad-copter drone flew directly overhead, close enough for me to see the design of it and to know I was surrounded.

"Nice night for a walk," I said.

"Yeah. Nice night for a walk," the big one leaning on the fender called out. "Nice night for us to smash your face in too."

"Let me handle this, Eric," the one with the wet Mohawk and piercings said. "You. You're from the Order, aren't you?"

"Federal Agent Chuck Alawode," I said. I pulled out the badge the chief had given me and held it above my head for them to see. My other hand, still gripping the cheeseburger, moved aside my jacket and exposed my holstered weapon. I wanted to make sure they saw the weapon as much as the badge. "And I'll tell you right here and now, interfering with an investigation is a federal crime. Whatever good idea you think you have, I recommend you reconsider."

"That's a local-pig badge," the girl said. "You really think we ain't seen one of those waved in our faces before?"

"But you sure don't look like a local pig, dressed all pretty in white like a bride on her wedding day. Where's your hubby in his fancy tux and tails?" the big one said as he pushed himself off the Crown Vic.

This man was a distraction. While he talked, the other two were strolling closer and closer. I didn't see any guns on them, so distance was to my advantage. Every second I waited, and they closed in, I was losing it.

The big guy cracked a wide teeth-laced grin under his hoodie. "Cat got your tongue, is that it? Well, we have some questions for you, and we'll get those lips of yours to loosen up one way or another. Best start talking."

The cheeseburger was still in my hand. My right hand. My shooting hand.

"You might not like my answers," I said and dropped the burger.

"Get 'im!" one of them called out. They charged.

I drew and fired on the closest, the one with a mohawk, all in one smooth motion. The move was more a subconscious reaction than a deliberate action. Something I'd polished off the rough edges in hundreds of immersive training simulator sessions, and once or twice in real life. My muscles and nerves just waited for the initial impulse from my brain, and then they took over the rest of it. And that was the problem. The barrel was aimed at the second target before I realized the neural inhibitor had had absolutely zero effect on the first target. And why would it? Without an implant or at least the internal wiring, it had all the impact of standing next to a radio antenna.

Well-learned habits die hard. The firearm, the one I was issued for just such an occasion was still holstered, grip pointed backward on my left hip, and as long as it was there, it was just as ineffective as the neural inhibitor.

This was not the case for the thick heavy fists of my attackers. The first punch came from the side and set off a fireworks display inside my brain. The next hit caught me high on the cheek and turned off motor control to my lower body. I was halfway to the oil and bloodstained pavement by the time the baseball bat slammed into my back. That one hurt like hell. No implant to ease the pain flooding into my mind out here. By the time the fourth punch and the first kicks came, I wished they had used a neural inhibitor on me to turn me limp and compliant. But things were different in 99 Town. Much more manual. Much more brutal. I balled up and did everything I could to soften the blows to my face and head.

"He's got a gun! Get it," one of them said.

"His cuffs. Use his cuffs."

Hands were all over me now, pulling and pushing, pinning me down to the ground.

"Grab his arms."

I struggled to keep my hands over my head. If another blow landed...

They pried and yanked, multiple arms against each of mine. They wrenched my wrists behind my back and rolled me on my stomach. My swollen face was shoved into the street surface. As I felt the metal handcuffs snap on my wrists, I spotted the thick drop of ketchup on the pavement just a few inches from my face.

It was a stupid thought, but I couldn't help but wish I was still alone in the street, my mind set on the mystery of the murder, all of the violence still fiction, eating a cheeseburger, listening to the soft howl of the wind moving through the night.

"Here. Take it. Put it in his head," one of them said.

With my hands cuffed behind my back, there wasn't a thing I could do to stop them from pinning my head to the ground, I felt the jack of an implant fumble around the outside of my port. Then, like someone turning out the lights, the sight of the ketchup dollop disappeared, and everything went black.

Chapter Six

These are the people who killed Nancy, and now they were going to kill me.

The implant in my port shut off all stimuli to my visual cortex. It was as effective as digging out my eyeball. I'd never heard of someone using an implant for that before. There was nothing in the technology that prevented it from doing this, but it certainly was the intent of the device. And now they were dragging me around, probably to line me up for an execution-style gunshot to the back of the head. Hard to strategize while they did that. Hard to comprehend why they were stuffing me into the backseat of a car instead of shooting me there in the street.

With my hands bound and my eyes blind, there was little I could do to fight back. They threw me inside a car, piled in after me, and the car started to move. Where were they taking me? To a field? One of those dried-up cornfields between the city and the border where they had a hole waiting for me? Someplace where no one would ever find my body. Just like they did to Nancy.

About then I noticed the ring in my ear was gone.

So, this implant wasn't devoid of functions other than blinding my eyes.

I reached out to the Network, to the department back in Chicago, to Phom. Nothing. I sent mental command after mental command for the device to restore my sight. Again, nothing.

The car ride was short, too short for a ride to some field outside of town. When it came to a stop, I was split between relief and terror that my inevitable execution wouldn't be in a field but had come before I'd had time to make a plan.

"Be cool," one of them said. "Don't try any shit."

"Don't shoot me," I said, ashamed that I'd been reduced to begging, but what other options did I have?

"Come on, piggy. Out of the car," someone said.

They manhandled me out of the backseat. Two of them had me by each armpit. I wanted to fight them off and pull away, but with my hands cuffed and this hacked implant blinding me, even if I did break away, where would I go? If I were in a cornfield, any direction would do. I could hide between rows of corn and eventually work the implant out of my head. But my feet were on pavement. The buzz of the drone was back. So was the barking dog. I was still in the city.

A door opened. They swore at me, shoved me, and dragged me inside. Footsteps echoed off tile floor. The door shut behind me and the sounds of the city at night were cut off. They moved me to a specific spot, adjusting me left and right.

This was it. They were going to shoot me right here in some abandoned warehouse or wherever the hell they'd dragged me. But no doubt about it; this was the spot.

I was a split second from bolting, regardless of direction or walls or doors. Then someone shoved me hard in the chest, and I fell backward. A mid-air moment of reprieve. Another moment of life. Another moment of paranoia. They say you never hear the bullet that kills you. You can't experience death. By the time it happens to you, all your neurons have stopped firing. That's kind of what this was like.

Only I didn't die. I landed in a chair, still bound and blind. Blind, until they quit laughing long enough to pull the plug from my port.

I squinted away from the glare of harsh neon lights mounted to the ceiling. Someone was still laughing. I tipped my head forward and saw it was the big man who had been leaning on my Crown Victoria. The hoodie hung from his collar, and I could see his bald head. The girl, her hair buzzed up to the crown of her head, sat in a tattoo chair across from me. She didn't look happy. The other man, the one with the hanging Mohawk of hair, stood next to me with the implant between his fingers.

"I get to do that next time," the big one said between laughs. "I love seeing the look on their faces when they come to."

The man next to me held out the implant for me to see. It was old and dirty. "Don't get excited. It's not connected to the Network," he said. "Funny all the different little things these things can do when you're willing to void the manufacturer's warranty."

"Those are banned here," I managed to say.

The big guy kept laughing and said, "We just piss-pounded him in the street, abducted him, knocked him out, and he's worried about contraband laws!"

Ignoring him, I took a second to examine my surroundings. I was in the front room of a tattoo shop. Steel shutters were over the front windows, blocking the view from outside. The walls were covered in dozens of pieces of artwork. Skulls and sexy ladies and swirling black arabesque patterns. No Picasso's or Monet's here, but the skills of the artists were no less impressive. There were six stations, each separated by a short half-wall, each with a tattoo chair or table and a counter with all the tattoo guns and ink and tools of the trade. There was a refrigerator near the back of the room and next to it was the drone that had been hovering over my head. Its red standby light blinked in the dark.

The people around me who'd jumped me in the street, I knew all their faces from the case files. These were the acquaintances of Nancy Meade: The Rogues.

"Samuel Candelario," I turned to the one with the Mohawk. "You own this place. You're in charge of this whole circus."

"Oh shit, Sammy," the big one said. "He made you. You're screwed now."

"Eric Sinclair," I said, making eye contact with the big bald bastard. Dirty loose clothes. Meaty grimy hands. The greasy monkey, as Drex called him.

When I said his name, he laughed. "Yeah. I know who I am. Who the fuck are you?"

I ignored him and turned to the woman. "And you're Ruby. Ruby—"

"Ruby Louise Go-fuck-yourself," the girl said. The shaved sides of her head exposed the big round plugs in each earlobe. She had tattoos starting at her hands and working up her arms until they disappeared up her shirt sleeves. "That's the name on my driver's license."

"You were friends with Nancy. And with Drex," I said. "Listen, I'm here to help. You don't want to kill me. You want me on your side."

"Oh, well shit," Eric said. "Listen to that fellas. The pig's here to help. Why didn't you just say so? Never mind that you just pulled a gun on us. Let's uncuff him and give him a beer."

"Shut up, Eric," Sammy said. Then to me, "If you're a regular cop, how come you're dressed like some dildo from the Order?"

"Yeah. What gives with the white outfit? What are you in the navy or something?" Ruby said. Then to Big-guy Eric, "Hey, get me a beer, will ya?"

Eric nodded and went to the fridge.

"I'm from Chicago. I'm a federal investigator, just like I told you," I said. "I'm here to find out what happened to Nancy Meade. If you care one bit about what happened to her, you'll let me go right now."

Ruby laughed. "Are we really supposed to believe that? Why would some prick from the Order care about Nancy?"

"Shut up, Ruby," Sammy said and then turned back to me. "Why would some pencil-dick from the Order care about Nancy?"

This was a start. Sure, I could have gone the tough-guy route, threatened them with bringing down the full weight of the Order for them laying a hand on me. But I was betting the likes of these didn't handle threats like normal rational human beings. So I played this from the other angle. "She came from Chicago, just like me. Her parents still live there. The Order sent me to find out why one of their own died on some street in 99 Town. They want to know who killed her. Don't you want to know the same thing?"

And here was the test. Did they want to know? Did one of them already know?

I watched. My right eye was swollen and half closed from the contusion, but I watched closely and attentively all the same. There were always details that could be missed. Ruby turned her head away from me, maybe because what I said upset her. Maybe. Eric shook his head from side to side. Sammy gave no tell-tale signs but spoke first.

"Nancy may have been born in Chicago," Eric said. "but she doesn't have anything to do with that place anymore. She belonged here. This place is who she was. It's who we all are."

"This place killed her," I said. "In Chicago, she was safe. Now she's dead."

"She's still missing. How do you know she's dead?" Ruby asked.

"Brain matter found on the murder weapon. And blood pattern analysis," I said. "She lost too much blood to still be alive. I'd love to tell you different but—"

"It wasn't Drex," Sammy said. "I don't believe that for one second."

"It was the fucking cops," Eric said.

"Or maybe the Order," Ruby said. "Maybe even you."

"Yeah. Returned to the scene of the crime just like in the movies. That's what murderers do. We should be asking you questions about what happened to Nancy," Eric said. He came back from the fridge with a six pack of beer held together with plastic rings. He pulled one off and handed it to Sammy, then Ruby, then himself, leaving three still hanging on the rings. "I bet it was this cock sucker right here."

"I was in Chicago," I said. "I've never been to 99 Town before, and I'll be happy to leave as soon as my job here is done. I never knew Nancy. Why would I ever want to hurt some girl in 99 Town I never even met?"

"Great question. Maybe you're a hitman, hired by the 99 Town cops," Sammy said.

"Listen. I'm not here with the local police. I don't buy their case that Drex did it any more than you. He's a fall guy, set up to look guilty and then forgotten," I said. "For all I know, you're right. The cops did it. I don't know why they would, but for all I know, they could have."

"You pointed a gun at me," Sammy said. "Why'd you point a gun at me if you're so fucking open-minded about everything?"

I had to laugh. "You'll have to excuse me for confusing you with a pack of street thugs ready to beat me within a centimeter of my life."

Sammy looked to Ruby, then to Eric. Ruby pulled the Ruger nine millimeter Phom had given me from behind her back and set it on her lap. Eric dug out the keys to the handcuffs. Sammy turned to me.

"Listen, if you hadn't pulled the gun we probably wouldn't have beat the shit out of you," Sammy said. "So, if we uncuff you now, are you going to be chill?"

I thought about it. I could probably jump the girl and get the firearm back, fight or shoot my way out of the tattoo parlor from there, but what good would it do? This gang of misfits were the best witnesses I had. They looked like low lifes, sure, but not much like murderers. Still, I couldn't help but dream of sucker-punching the closest one as soon as they uncuffed me, just to pay him back for the mental torment of blindly waiting to be shot in the head.

"I'll be chill," I said, using their word.

Sammy gave the big bald guy a permissive nod. Eric set the three beers left on the rings in Ruby's lap and came up to me. He nearly pulled me out of the chair so he could get to the cuffs. He bumbled with the keys and the lock, but eventually, one cuff popped open, then the other. I thought really hard about driving a fist right into the man's gut. I thought about it, but that was it.

Sammy nodded to Ruby. She peeled a beer off the rings and tossed it my way. I caught it.

"Sorry about the beat down, and the trick with the implant and all that. We cool?" Sammy said.

"Cool," I said, not sure what the word meant, but knew I had to be it to get anywhere.

"Man, this is bullshit," Eric said. "You know he's going to call in his buddies to piss-pound us and haul us off to jail right along with Drex. He's got one of those brain-radio things. He's probably calling them right now."

Sammy threw the implant at Eric, and it bounced off him. "We just pulled the only implant around here *out* of his head you, fucking dummy." Then, to me, he said, "Drink up, man. We got some shit to get straight."

Yes, we did.

Sammy cracked open his beer. I examined the top of my can and the opening mechanism. A pre-scored oval and a lever. Simple, but ingenious. I cracked it open, and foam rolled out of the top.

"To mutual objectives," I said and raised up the can.

"Whatever the fuck that's supposed to mean," Ruby said.

I drank and immediately regretted it. Dear god, how did these people live? Instead of the gasoline fumes of the liquor, the beer tasted like a mouthful of dirty laundry. For as palatable as the food was, the beverages of 99 Town all seemed designed to induce vomiting. Involuntarily, I gagged and coughed.

The whole shop burst into laughter. Especially the big guy.

"This tastes like my socks," I said.

"You ain't never drank beer before?" Sammy said between laughs. "What do you poor stiffs even do for fun out there?"

The beer, the Keeper's liquor, manual cars… I was beginning to see the rationale in the Order's laws. This was insanity. Pure madness. Besides the cheeseburgers. Everyone should eat a cheeseburger before they die. If I was ever about to be gunned down execution-style in some filthy backstreet again, I knew what I'd ask for as a last request: a cheeseburger.

That thought let me crack a smile. These kids weren't going to kill me. If they were laughing at me, they couldn't be too angry with me. And if I played my cards right, there was a lot I could get out of them. I had too many questions not to earn their trust. Like what kind of cars they drove and if they had tire irons in their trunks. And where did they get an implant from, and which of them was smart enough to rig it just to blind me on demand?

I went to drink from the can again, this time prepared for the earthy taste, and it wasn't so bad. "The Order doesn't know what they're missing," I said and poured more beer down my mouth, determined to drink it down like it was fresh, cool, clean water. After it was down, I wiped the strained look off my face.

They laughed again. That was fine. Laughter was good. Now I just needed to get them talking.

"Do you really think the 99 Town police could have had a hand in her expiration?" I asked.

"Expiration?" Ruby said. "You talking about Nancy? Didn't you just say she got clubbed to death in the street? She's either missing or dead. She's not a jug of milk that sat out too long."

I had to learn faster than this. Had to drop the Order-speak I'd been taught since birth. "Yes. The murder. Do you think—" I said.

Sammy cut me off. "The cops are always harassing us. Trying to shut me down. They want to say we smuggle contraband into 99 Town. I'm sure they told you all about how we're tied to some huge underground black market. But look around. We do tattoos. That's it. Everything here is on the up and up."

"What about that little toy of yours? And the drone over there?" I said. "That's contraband, isn't it? Too close to the Network and artificial intelligence for the Keeper's liking?"

"Fuck the Keepers," Eric said. "They'd make light bulbs contraband if they had their way."

"Nobody goes to prison for flying drones," Sammy said, pretending like their hacked implant didn't exist. "But the cops want to make it out like we're part of some underground conspiracy. See, the Keepers can't keep out all the tech you guys have under the Order. And the Order can't keep out all the good stuff we have here, like beer, and porno, and whatever else they deem subversive."

There was that term again: Underground. That term didn't belong in 99 Town.

"Is it true? Is the 99 Town black market connected to the Underground?" I asked and noticed I wasn't keeping up with how fast they drank their beers, so I tipped back the can. I couldn't tell if it was from the contusions or from the alcohol, but my head swam. Nothing I couldn't handle.

"What the fuck's the Underground?" Ruby said with a smirk. "We ain't never heard of any Underground."

She knew. According to the case files, she lived under the rule of the Order until the age of ten. Whatever game she was playing, I decided to play along. "The remnants of the Independent Resistance Movement that fought the Order just before the Event. They were rebels. Dissidents. And when the war ended, they didn't disappear. They just went underground. And now they oppose everything the Order has managed to build up since. They smuggle alcohol, tobacco… Also weapons and anti-Order propaganda. If there's a black market in 99 Town, it must be tied to the Underground," I said.

"Sounds like my kind of people," Ruby said.

That was close to the truth.

"Man, we could care less what you people are up to under the Order," Sammy was quick to say. "What do we care if you people can't get booze and smut? Our lives are in 99 Town. We love it here, even if it is full of asshole cops and backward Keepers. We don't know anything about any underground resistance movements."

"Yeah. We might be customers," Eric said. "But we're not running the show."

"We do tattoos. That's it," Sammy said. "And Ruby does piercings."

"What about you?" I said to Eric. "You don't have any tattoos or piercings."

"I don't like needles, man," Eric said.

"Eric takes care of other things around here. Sweeps out the floor. Takes out the trash. Keeps the cars up and running. Those sorts of things," Sammy said. "Doesn't make him any less of a Rogue."

"Delivery boy?" I suggested.

Sammy laughed and waved a finger. "Naw, man. I know what you're thinking, and it ain't like that. Eric takes care of the shop and the cars, and that's it. What you see is what you get, man."

I let that stir in my brain while I took another drink. Never in my career had I run into a scenario where what I saw was what I got.

"But if the local law enforcement thinks you're part of the black market and maybe came to the conclusion that Nancy was your connection to the Underground, they'd be motivated to shut you down. Cut off your ties to the Underground. They'd have a motive to kill Nancy," I said. That actually made some sense. A little too much sense for comfort.

"See?" Ruby said. "Even the fucking pig thinks the pigs did it!"

But that wasn't the complete picture. The car used to kill Nancy came from this parking lot. Someone here would have had to assist them.

I watched Eric saunter over to the fridge again. No tattoos. No piercings. He seemed too obvious to be a plant. Surely these kids would have sniffed him out. Maybe it was the girl, Ruby. She played dumb, but she was obviously hiding something.

Sammy pitched his empty beer can into a recycle bin, or maybe just a trash can. Eric, still standing in front of the fridge, tossed him a new beer. Sammy caught it.

"Anyone else?" Eric said.

"Me," Ruby said, shaking the bottom of her empty can.

I drank. Big gulps. "Me too," I said when it was empty. The carbonation filled my stomach. The alcohol filled my head. That was maybe too quick.

Eric tossed each of us a fresh can. Sammy and Ruby cracked theirs without hesitation. I summoned up my constitution. I could handle this. If I played this right, I could learn things. I pried open the top and slurped off the foam that escaped from the top.

"You know what you don't get, Mister Federal Agent Man?" Ruby said. Her eyes locked with mine. My eyes had trouble staying focused on hers. "We loved Nancy. She was like my sister. For you, this is a little puzzle to solve. A game to play. To us, she's family."

"I'll drink to that," Eric said.

"To Nancy," Sammy said. "Actually, you know what? We need shots for this. Eric, grab the whiskey, will ya?"

You got this, Chuck, I told myself. I could do this. Just needed to keep my wits about me.

Chapter Seven

I woke up on a cushioned tattoo table in the middle of Rogue's Tattoo Parlor on the outskirts of 99 Town, but it might as well have been on a Martian colony for all I knew. When I cracked open my eyes, the sunlight stabbed my brain. All I could hear out of my left ear was the sound of cotton balls and a dog whistle, and I couldn't for the life of me remember why. As soon as I sat up, my stomach rolled. My brain seemed to pump and swell against my cranium like there wasn't enough room. Pain and nausea hit me like ocean waves against a rocky shore.

"What the shit happened?" I mumbled to no one. The Network didn't provide any answers. I touched the spot behind my ear. I was unplugged. That's why my left ear was worthless. That's why the Network wasn't balancing my toxic mix of neural transmitters currently committing an inquisition inside my brain.

And thank God the Network wasn't listening.

I stood up and looked around the tattoo shop. The place was ransacked. Beer cans lay everywhere. There was food out. Potato chips. Half-eaten chicken wings. Pizza crusts. Eric was asleep on a couch in the shop's lobby. He could have been dead for how little he moved. One of his shoes was off. I looked down at my own feet.

Good. I still had both of my shoes.

But where were the rest of my things? I checked my pockets and found the phone, the badge, my toothbrush, and my comb. The car keys, the gun, the handcuffs, and my neural inhibitor, however…

Why did my shoulder hurt so bad? What did I do last night?

As I moved deeper into the tattoo shop to find my things, memories slowly and uncooperatively came back to me. The beer. Then the whiskey. The whiskey was what really did me in. I remembered trying to convince these kids that life was better under the Order and how bad they had it. Except for cheeseburgers. I remembered making an exception for cheeseburgers. Later, I think I made an exception for beer too.

I spotted the keys to the Crown Victoria next to a dish of solidified cheese dip. I picked up the keys, and they jingled but not loud enough to stir Eric.

Did I eat that cheese last night? I did. I can't believe I ingested that gunk. I needed to spend some time in a medical pod. Definitely going to have a heart attack after that.

I didn't see Sammy or Ruby anywhere in the shop. I remembered her sitting on my lap at one point last night. We were laughing. She was mean but kind to me all at the same time. Teasing me. Playing with me. She was too young for me. Way too young. I had to remind myself, they were suspects. Each one of them. Plus, I had a wife. I should be grieving for Maggie the same way these kids were grieving for Nancy. Grief wasn't allowed under the Order, but these people, they broke down for Nancy. They were crumbling apart but doing so together and growing stronger for it, like a healed bone after a fracture.

Maggie. Her expiration had been a… distraction. Had to stop using that word. Expiration. She didn't expire. She was… murdered? No. She killed herself.

There was an office at the back of the tattoo shop. The door was cracked. I gently pushed it open. Ruby and Sammy were inside, asleep on a couch. She was lying on top of him under a blanket. She had her shirt off, and my handcuffs clamped to one of her wrists.

Forget the cuffs. I could get another set of cuffs.

My Ruger nine millimeter was sitting on a work desk. I picked it up, as quiet as I could, not wanting to wake anyone. As the heavy metal barrel dragged across the wood desk, Ruby stirred. The blanket slid off a few inches. I caught myself staring at the smooth skin of her back, intricately decorated with Japanese koi and splashing water. So illicit and strange.

They were suspects, and this was unprofessional. All of this.

I didn't have everything, but I had what I needed. I abandoned the cuffs and the neural inhibitor. That thing would do me no good here anyway.

The sun was bright and hurt my head. I staggered out of the front door and looked up and down the street. Was this the same street I'd parked the car on last night? There was a sign at the corner showing the names of the crossroads. Harrison and Tenth. The crime scene and my car were at Harrison and Fifth. Not far from here. I could walk it.

The ride last night seemed a lot longer.

I was near certain that ride would be my last and would end with me catching a bullet in the head, so I guess I was savoring the trip. That was after they jumped me and beat me down in the street. Before they got me drunk and took my things. Those… I dug for a word vulgar enough, the kind of word that Mike flung at passing traffic as easily as he breathed.

"Those mother shitters."

The phone buzzed in my pocket. I took it out and looked at the tiny screen. There was a pixelated image of an envelope with the number five next to it. I kept walking while I frowned at the screen. The phone flipped open to expose a slightly larger but equally low-res screen and a physical number pad. The thing was so rudimentary it took me a while to figure out the interface, especially with the pounding throb in my head. But as small and old as the device was, it was equally ingenious and intuitive.

The envelope icons were audio messages someone had sent to the phone. The first was from eight ten this morning. I played it. "Mister Alawode, this is Sara Cohen, legal counsel for Drex Carlsrud. We had discussed visiting the impound lot yesterday. Well, I'm here and…"

I pulled the phone away from my ear. "Shit."

The other messages were from Sara Cohen too. Eight ten. Eight thirty. Eight fifty. Nine twenty. I ended the playback and check the time on the phone. Nine forty five.

"Shit."

Around then I got to the unmarked squad car parked along the curb. Someone, and it was easy to narrow it down to three suspects, had spray painted the word "Rogues" across the front windshield.

"Mother shitters!"

I pulled up to the impound lot, shut off the flashers, and ignored the steam coming up out of the hood. The lights and sirens had helped clear my path coming across town. A whole lot fewer horns and fingers that way. I'd have to remember to use those in the future. Didn't help me avoid that newspaper box though.

I looked past the backward red letters scrolled across the windshield and the wafting tendrils of sweet-smelling vaporized coolant. At the end of the parking lot was a small building next to a chain link fence. Beyond the fence were dozens of cars. Some of them looked even worse than what I was driving. Sara Cohen was waiting by the small office of the impound lot. So was Lieutenant Mike Andrews. They were next to each other, looking impatient and unpleasant. There was also a uniformed cop standing by Mike and a man behind the window inside the little office.

I checked the mirror hidden in the car's sun visor. My face was lumpy and bruised. There were crumbs of food in my hair. I needed a shave. My white coat issued to me by the Order was soiled gray. Only so much I could do about all of that now. I brushed the crumbs out of my hair, straightened the collar of my coat, and stepped out of the car.

As I approached them, I coached myself to ignore my aching head, my deaf ringing ear, my rolling stomach, and my throbbing shoulder. I just had to find the GTO and check for the tire iron. If it was there, then I could be sure it wasn't Drex. That's why I was there.

"Chuckers," Mike said with a half-smile on his face. "You look like a bag of smashed assholes."

"Can we see the car? I'd like to just see the GTO and be done," I said.

Sara Cohen had been discussing something with the man behind the window. She turned and our eyes caught. She looked angry.

Mike put a hand on my chest, stopping me before I could make it to Sara or the window. "Chuck, what the hell is she doing here? We can't have lawyers getting in the middle of an active police investigation. That's not how this works."

Funny, of the things to object to, it was Sara. I guess that meant he was okay with the artistic addition to my loaner squad car. I moved his hand from my chest and bumped past him. Sara moved out of the way as I went up to the man behind the glass window. It was obvious to me, maybe only to me, that this sour, disinterested individual inside the office was the person who was really in charge around here.

"You have an impounded Nineteen-Seventy Dodge Challenger. White. Smashed up from one end to the other. Probably some blood inside. Also a Pontiac GTO. Green. You know the cars I'm talking about?" I said.

The man chewed on a wooden toothpick and nodded. "Oh, I know 'em alright."

"Chuck," Mike interrupted, putting a hand on my shoulder. "Are you drunk?"

I shrugged off Mike's hand and addressed the man behind the window. "The keys. Give them to me."

"Charles, what the hell is our suspect's lawyer doing here?" Mike said.

Sara backed away. She hadn't said anything since I'd arrived. The man behind the window wasn't fetching the keys, but rather watched and waited for this little drama between me and Mike to unfold.

"Are you going to answer my questions, Chuck? We're supposed to be partners," Mike said. "What the hell's the matter with you?"

I hit the small counter in front of the window with the meat of my fist. Of course, this couldn't be easy. Nothing in 99 Town seemed to go easy. Turning on Mike, I jabbed a finger in his face. "I'm no one's partner. I'm here to find the truth. Doesn't matter if I'm drunk, drugged, fucked up, or out of my mind. I'm here to find the truth. The same as her. Should be the same as you."

"You're fucking drunk," Mike said. Not a question. Not even an accusation. A fact. He wasn't wrong. "Give me your keys and call a cab. Go sleep this off. You're embarrassing yourself."

"I'm here to look at one car. One trunk. One tool could change this whole investigation," I said.

"I won't be a part of this," Mike said. "She shouldn't even be here. You shouldn't be here, and I sure as shit won't stand here next to you while you can't even stand straight."

"I'm not asking for your help. I don't need your help," I said.

"Is that so? Who got you that badge and gun on your hip? Who put you in that car you drove here? You know Chuck, without me you wouldn't be able to tell your asshole from your elbow. Forget this. I'm outta here," Mike said and started to walk away. The uniformed cop, Mike's lackey, followed. Then Mike stopped and turned around. "You can bet your ass your boss in Chicago will hear about this. I ought to bust you for Driving Under the Influence right here and now. But something tells me what they have in store for you will be worse. Good luck, Chuck. Don't say I never did you any favors."

And like that, it was me, Sara, and the man behind the glass. I turned to him.

"Keys."

The man behind the glass, satisfied and knowing the show was over, shrugged and picked two sets of keys off the pegboard behind him and slid them through a metal tray at the bottom of the window. "I'll buzz you in. The Challenger is in the back northeast corner, behind a blue bus. The GTO is just behind that," he said. "And yeah. There's some blood."

The walk through the impound lot was short and wordless. That cold exterior had formed over Miss Sara Cohen, Attorney-at-law, again. That suited me just fine. As we moved, the pain-numbing effects of the alcohol seemed to outweigh the pain-inducing effects of the hangover, if only for a short while. But my head still throbbed, and everything in my abdomen seemed to be doing somersaults. I felt Sara walking behind me, examining me, judging me, just as plainly as if we were both wearing implants and connected to the Network. I had no choice but to deal with it and continue with the investigation.

We walked. Canals of rust and steel walled us in on either side. It was clear the impound lot was more than just a temporary holding spot for towed cars. It was that, but also a graveyard for cars that would never see the road again. The place was a maze of cars, some new and ready to drive off the lot, some that had sat so long they were now part of the landscape, and many more that had been crushed and stacked a half dozen high. The dirt under our feet was stained with every fluid that could come from a car, and a few other fluids too.

The Challenger was impossible to miss. We walked around a large blue bus and there it was, back on four wheels, but not one of those wheels was inflated. The roof was crushed in, and every fold of the body exposed bare metallic gray scars through the pristine white paint job. A headlight was busted out. The windshield was gone. Tiny bits of glass rested in every low spot and crumple. The driver's side rear view mirror dangled off the door. Puddles of black oil and green antifreeze mixed in the dirt under the Challenger.

There was another fluid there too. Dried and turned almost brown in the gravel, but still violent red on the white paint. There was more of it than I expected, even after studying the crime scene photography. There was a smell too. Something I had never smelled before. Something that warmed up and burned the dust off primordial circuits in my brain.

"The blood," Sara said, her first words since I'd arrived. Her coldness had thawed into revulsion.

I closed my eyes and put this piece of evidence with the puzzle back at the crime scene. The Challenger was there on Harrison and Fifth Street, upside down, a girl with faded freckles and an empty port inside, still alive but hurting bad, crawling out through the shattered driver's window. Then a monster came and bludgeoned her head apart with a piece of metal.

Did she resist? Beg him not to? Did she recognize this monster?

I opened my eyes and the blood splatter pattern, brilliant red on white paint, upside down now that the car was right-side up, matched.

I stepped up to the door, not to examine the blood but to look for something else, anything else. That scent of blood, when I stuck my head inside the car, it overwhelmed me. It tasted like acid. Iron. Raw rancid meat. Murder. My stomach convulsed. I retreated, bumped past Sara, and went back to the blue bus we'd walked around. I put a hand on the side panel and waited.

I couldn't think about it. Couldn't think about anything. Raw meat. Splattered blood. Murder. Barbarians beating each other to death with clubs. All those fluids that are meant to stay inside of humans spilled out on… a street… a sidewalk. Had to stop. Couldn't do this to myself. This was an issue of physics, Chuck. I was either going to act or be acted upon. I swallowed bile back down.

Pushing away from the bus, I pointed a finger at Sara. "None of this had to happen. This could have been prevented under the rule of the Order. Nancy would be alive and the suspect, the real perpetrator, not some unlucky loser from the wrong side of town, would already be tried and convicted."

"Chuck, you just don't get 99 Town," Sara said.

"I'm glad I don't. Hope I never do," I said. "This is madness."

"Well, you're starting to fit in nicely. Come on. My client's car, his *stolen* car, is just over here," Sara said.

The GTO looked as mean and hungry as a machine could. The front grill rose up like the mouth of some ancient predator. The paint was a shade of green so dark it was almost black and reflected rays of sunshine like lasers. The paint job was immaculate except for the few spots where the driver had crashed it into the Challenger, evident by dents and streaks where the GTO had taken on the Challenger's white paint. Looking back and forth between the two cars, it was clear which dog won the fight. I peeked inside the driver's window.

"No trunk release," Sara said. "That's what you were looking for, right? The handle to pop the trunk from inside the cab. It wasn't standard equipment back in 1971, and I looked. There's no aftermarket trunk release installed in this one either. If someone opened the trunk of this car to get a tire iron, they would have had to have the keys in their hands."

Coming around the driver's side, I ran my fingers over the fender, feeling the texture of the body go from wax-smooth to uneven grit where the GTO impacted the Challenger. The white paint on the GTO and the dark green paint on the Challenger matched, and the location of the marks suggested a Pursuit Intervention Technique just before the crash. That PIT maneuver, the clipping of the rear fender by the chase car wasn't something the average citizen was familiar or effective with. It was a law-enforcement technique practiced and perfected over years of specialized simulator training. Drex had no law-enforcement training. Drex was just some dumb kid. But all that was circumstantial evidence. The physical evidence was in the trunk.

I juggled the keys as I moved around to the rear of the GTO. Under the rear spoiler, there was a place to insert a key. No handle. Only turning a key would pop the latch. I found the key on the ring and looked to Sara.

She took a step back. "Wait. So if there's a tire iron in there, it means my client is absolved of the charges, and you'll make a statement saying so?" she said.

"If it is in there, all that means is the murder weapon came from another car. Nothing more. Nothing less," I said but didn't truly believe it.

I inserted the key into the lock and turned. The trunk popped open.

The trunk was full of garbage, dirty laundry, a box of music on compact discs... The full-sized spare tire was bolted to the right side. The length of a bumper jack protruded from underneath the spare. I tossed out a paper sack from a drive-thru, a few other bits of junk, and some old food. Underneath, tucked next to the tire and the jack, was a half-meter-long metal tool that was half pry-bar, half wrench. I picked up the tire iron and saw it was rusted but unmarred by murder. No blood or hair or chunks of skin and flesh.

"So it means nothing?" Sara said.

I tossed the tire iron back into the trunk. "Nothing we didn't already suspect. And we're still missing a body."

"Whoever killed Nancy had to move her somehow," Sara said. "I don't think she was ever in this trunk. There's no room with all the shit in there. No blood either."

I shut the trunk and took the keys. The image of a human body ravaged by a metal tool like the one I'd just held returned to my mind's eye against my will. My whole body went queasy. I couldn't let that win. I wasn't done here yet.

I moved away from the trunk to the passenger side of the vehicle, eyeing the backseat as I went. It was small and without its own set of doors. Sure, a person could cramp a corpse back there, but they'd have to fight past the front seats first. If there was ever a body back there, there would be DNA—

"Chuck?" Sara said. "You don't look so good."

"...fine," I managed to say, swallowing sour saliva caught on the back of my tongue.

I came up to the front passenger seat and opened the door. The smell hit me like a heavy weight's right hook. It was metallic and fluid. Organic but unnatural. The black leather seat was wet and fetid. It hid the stains well, but nothing could hide the odor.

I stepped back away from the GTO involuntarily, turned, and emptied the contents of my stomach onto the gravel. I took a few more steps away from the GTO and went down on one knee. There was an old pickup there and I leaned a hand against its tire. My throat let loose another heave of vomit. Beer. Whiskey. Chunks of fried chicken. Bile. And yes, some of that god-awful cheese sauce. I fought to breathe between surges of puke. More came up, and I dumped more of last night's regrets into the dirt. Even after my stomach was dry I wretched, and with each wretch, my head pounded harder. I stayed there kneeling for a while, coughing and struggling to catch my breath.

When I was done and had a chance to wipe away the long strands of saliva from my mouth, Sara came up behind me and put a hand on my shoulder.

"Some tough guy you turned out to be," she said. "You got a place to say?"

"This town has a hotel, doesn't it?"

Sara let out a long sigh. "Get up. You're coming with me."

We left the impound lot, and Sara turned in the keys to the man behind the window. She thanked him and headed for her Ford Taurus. I veered toward my Crown Victoria with no idea where I'd drive it after I was behind the wheel.

"Ahhhh... No," she said. "You're not driving anywhere in the shape you're in."

I nodded. A ride sounded pretty good at this point. "Let me grab something."

She didn't protest, so I went to the Crown Victoria and picked up the paper case files off the passenger seat. Thankfully, they'd stayed safe there through the night. I went to Sara who was standing impatiently at her driver's door. I went to the passenger door, got in, and set the case files on my lap. I leaned back and closed my eyes, trying to shut out the nausea.

"What the hell happened to you?" she said as she got in and started up the car.

"I met the Rogues," I said.

Sara drove. I didn't bother to watch where to. Occasionally, I glanced out the window and saw we were headed toward the center of 99 Town, then across the river and past the Government Center. The skyscrapers fell off into the rearview mirror as Sara drove through the adjacent neighborhood. Blocks of law offices, abstractors, and title companies all along Cedar Street. All the parasite businesses of big government.

Sara parallel parked along the curb.

"My apartment is upstairs," she said. "I have a spare bedroom you can use. We'll get you some rest and get you cleaned up."

She killed the engine and got out. I was slow to follow her but managed. The door to her apartment was next to the glass storefront of a bail bonds office. Words painted on the glass read "Mick's Bail Bonds Office – We'll get you out before the soap drops." Whatever that meant. Next to the door was a rough-looking woman smoking a cigarette.

"Hey, Mickey," Sara said as they walked to the door. "This is Chuck. He's seen better days."

Mickey, the bail bondswoman, nodded. "The way you look, that's a good thing."

Sara's apartment was small and crowded to the brink of claustrophobia. A living room. A small kitchen. Hardwood floors. A hallway leading back to bedrooms and a bathroom. Paper was everywhere. Bric-a-brac and personal effects rose up between piles and stacks of paper. Oddly, I found the effect comforting rather than concerning. This was the mother's womb where all other paper came from, and in it, I felt cocooned as if the files were the dried husks of a chrysalis.

Sara ushered me back to the bathroom where there was even less room. But there was a shower. She showed me how it worked, and the water sputtered and spat out through the calcium-crusted fixture.

"I'll bring you something to change into," she said and slipped out of the bathroom.

I took my time, washing away the stress and sickness. When I first got in, the water was hot like red needles. Hotter than the safety and efficiency settings in Chicago allowed. But it eased my stiff muscles, and I turned it up a little hotter. I let it turn my skin red and fog up the entirety of the small bathroom. When I finished, I stepped out and noticed that sometime during my shower, Sara had taken my filthy clothes and left me a pair of shorts and a T-shirt on the counter for me to wear. I got dressed and stepped out of the bathroom.

Sara was inside a back bedroom filled with cardboard boxes full of papers. She was moving them off the bed. I went next to her and helped. Underneath were sheets, a pillow, and an old quilt. Sara drew the blinds.

"Get some sleep, tough guy," she said. "If I hear anything about the case, I'll wake you up."

I nodded, told her thanks again, and she left the room. I lay down in the bedding and it smelled musty like other people's old memories. Instinctively, my mind reached for an implant to adjust my dopamine and gamma-aminobutyric acid levels, but there was nothing there. Just me in this crowded and quiet room, and this curious woman somewhere else in the apartment. My damaged left ear was still muffled and whistled to remind me the implant was gone, but I'd managed to forget anyway. I wondered if I could fall asleep naturally. Seconds later, I was out.

I woke up without any idea what time of day it was. I'd slept so soundly, it was as if the time between laying down and waking up didn't exist. There was daylight slipping through the slats of the window blinds, but I was pretty sure I hadn't slept a full twenty four hours. That'd make it around mid-afternoon.

I left the bedroom and was met with an unfamiliar but amazing smell. Some kind of meat sizzled from the kitchen and filled the apartment with a sweet, greasy smell. Not a bad smell. Not like inside the GTO. This smell was inviting, tempting, mouthwatering.

In the kitchen, Sara worked a frying pan at the stove. She'd changed clothes too, swapping her professional business suit for a pair of sweatpants and a T-shirt. There were two mugs full of black fluid sitting on the dinette table. The papers and envelopes that had been there when we'd come in had been cleared away. There was a chair on either side of the table. I sat down.

There was a handle on the ceramic cup, but I held it with my palms and felt the heat conduct outward. Steam rose up from the cup. Sara brought the frying pan over to the table and served a few slices of meat on a plate in front of me. The toaster popped and she brought over butter and toast. She sat across from me. I sipped from the cup and found the beverage harsh but sweet. Calming and rejuvenating. As for the meat, I couldn't eat it fast enough.

"What is it?" I asked after two slices were already down my throat.

"Coffee and bacon," she said. "It will cure what ails you."

"Why are you being so nice to me?" I said.

"This is what I do, Chuck. Pick up and clean off the beat-down and luckless dregs of this city. 99 Town was ready to chew you up and spit you out. Besides, I like your style. You don't know what a relief it is to meet someone so naively honest," she smiled.

"How do you people do it?" I asked. "The murder, the pain... None of this is necessary."

"It's not easy, being a black woman in this bigoted town," Sara said. "Mickey's got thicker skin than I do. She's like a tank and they got BB guns."

"Because of your dark skin? And Mickey...?"

"She's gay," Sara said and munched on her toast. "But we take the good with the bad. You know, Chuck. It's not like the Order has it all figured out either. I grew up in 99 Town, but that doesn't mean I spent my whole life here. When I was a kid, about fourteen I guess, my parents divorced. My dad wanted to stay in 99 Town. So, my mom, I think mostly just to get away from him, took me, and we moved to Milwaukee. We got our ports installed. Got our implants. Plugged in and lived the whole plugged-in life. At first, I thought it was amazing. So much information. So many connections. But after a while..." She shrugged.

When Sara spoke next, her voice was even meeker than usual. "After a couple of years, my mom committed suicide. To this day if you asked me what was wrong in her life, I couldn't tell you. She was safe. Peaceful. She had money and food. We didn't lack for anything. But she was miserable, so she called it quits. Drank a reservoir of bleach she found inside our cleaner android. So there I was, with my mom's dead body, a partially dismantled cleaning robot, and not a single friend I could talk to. I had a connection to nearly every human being in the world, and I screamed out to all of them, but nobody listened. So I came back to 99 Town, as an orphan of the Order."

"An anomaly," I said. "I'm sure your mother's death was investigated, and whatever flaws in the system that allowed her to die were corrected, so it never happens again."

"An anomaly. Sure," Sara said. "So your solution would have been to force her to keep living, regardless of how miserable she might have been. That doesn't sound like a solution to me."

"She could have been helped. She should have received counseling. Assistance," I said. "The Order is designed to provide for everyone. Regardless of their level of needs."

"But it doesn't always work that way, does it?" Sara said. I didn't have to answer. Sara washed down her toast with coffee. "99 Town has car wrecks and murders. The Order has misery and suicides. We all have skeletons in our closets."

I nodded and ate the last of my bacon. The coffee, however soothing and aromatic, was too harsh for me to drink more than a few slips.

"So, I told you my story. What about you, Chuck? You got any skeletons?" Sara asked.

"Not much different from your story," I said. "My wife died. Suicide. I didn't love her. Not really. I don't think she loved me either. She had something else going on, but I don't know what. She was distant and secretive. After she died, I was distracted, so they sent me here. And here I am, skeletons and all."

"That's terrible. How long has it been?"

"Three, four days, I guess," I said.

"Oh, my god. What about... Wasn't there a funeral? A wake? What the hell are you doing in 99 Town?"

"My job. Besides, what does she have to do with any of this? That's what you don't understand. What none of you understand. You live on your emotions, but none of them matter. They're distractions, inferior to calm calculated plans. We should be better than our emotions. The people involved, they're not what matters. They're not what needs to be fixed. The system is what matters. If we find the flaws in the system and fix those, then the system will fix the people."

"You don't have anyone, do you? Not a single friend in the world," Sara said.

I worked on composing a rebuttal, something about not needing friends or how friendship could cloud good judgment and behavior... but I wasn't completely unaware of what this woman had done for me.

Something across the room chimed. Sara got up and picked up my cell phone for a cluster of my things on the counter. She tossed it to me. I caught it and looked at the little screen. The phone chimed again. A text message from "Lt. M Andrews." Mike. Something about the body.

I looked up to her. She leaned against the kitchen counter, arms crossed, clothes loose, her tightly curled hair mounded on top of her head. Her rich skin was darker in the soft light and her face somehow even tougher and meaner than it had been in the jail when we'd first met. There, she had to be professional. Here, I got the feeling there wouldn't be anything stopping her from telling me how she really felt. I was mesmerized by her. Maybe a little too much.

"Listen, I appreciate the hospitality, I really do. But I'm not here to make friends, Sara. I have a job to do."

Chapter Eight

"So it goes like this," Mike said as we rode in his unmarked Crown Victoria police car. "99 Town isn't that big, but it's divided into a few distinct boroughs, each with its own unique quirks, oddities, and problems."

I road in the passenger seat, next to the shotgun, trying not to spill a paper cup of piping hot coffee in my hand. It was nearing dusk.

"We're in Downtown now. And you can break that down into the financial district and the government district, but most people just call it all Downtown. The southeast of town is the warehouse district. Lots of manufacturing and industry. The train yards coming to and from Chicago are down that way. Surrounding that neck-of-the-woods are The Lows. Bars. Shitty restaurants. Low-income housing for all the blue-collar Joes who work in the Warehouse District. Follow me so far?"

"Sure," I said, trying to drink the coffee but finding it way too hot to even bring to my lips. Mike hadn't mentioned the scene at the impound lot. The issue hung between us, unspoken, but there in the car with us.

"Straight east of Downtown is a little higher income area. These are your white-collar working professionals. Salary schmucks. Decent people though. A lot of schools and churches and shopping malls out that way. Not as many meth labs and flop houses as in The Lows. Generic neighborhoods in housing developments with marketing names that no one uses.

"Northeast of Downtown is Cut Rock Park. There are about two hundred acres of woods and hiking trails in the park. A nice area before dark. All around Cut Rock Park, you'll find the high-income housing. There's not a ton of money in 99 Town, but if you want to find it, it's around Cut Rock Park. Now inside the park, there's still plenty of vagrants and homeless camping out. We've tried chasing them out, but they're like cockroaches, man. They always come back."

"What do you mean homeless?" I asked.

"I mean they don't have homes. They're bums."

"The Keepers don't provide housing? They just live outside?" I said. Under the Order, everyone was issued a safe place to live. To run a city otherwise would be chaos.

"There are homeless shelters and soup kitchens down in The Lows, but generally those kinds of places want you to be sober before they give you a bed," Mike said. "And if you ask me, most of those types would rather be drunk than indoors. Speaking of..."

And here it was. "About this morning..." I said. I knew this would come up, but still didn't have anything to say for myself.

"Listen, Chuckers. Forget about it. We all fuck up and have a few too many sometimes. Especially you, not having booze where you're from... I get it. You still pissed me off, especially dragging that lawyer around with you, but right now? Right now we got bigger fish to french fry."

So that was that. The issue was dead, but the mystery that was these people's minds only deepened. What other issue could be big enough to erase this morning's events? "A body?" I asked.

"A lead to where we might find the body," Mike said. "It's not much, but if we don't find something, that kid is going to walk, and poor Nancy Meade's murder is going to go unsolved."

"Unsolved? I've never left a case unsolved. Never heard of a case going unsolved," I said.

"Well unless you want to break your one thousand batting average, you better get focused on this case," Mike said. "And be careful who you make friends with. No one is who they pretend to be. No one. Especially lawyers."

"What about you?"

"Especially me," Mike said and laughed.

"Hmph," I said, not finding the joke as funny as he did. So I turned and looked out the window, still holding the too-hot-to-drink coffee in my hands. We were heading south, toward the Lows, Rogue's Tattoos, and the scene of the murder. "So where are we going?"

"Check it out," Mike said. "The Cut Rock River runs straight through the heart of 99 Town. Comes in just west of Cut Rock Park, through Downtown, and then out of town through the Lows. Now, thirty some odd years ago, before the Event and the Order and the implants, 99 Town was like any other town. And two hundred years before that, a logging company set up camp around some waterfalls. They built a dam, built a lumber mill and over the course of many years, that dam eventually turned into a hydroelectric plant. And I'll be damned if the dam ain't still here to this day, and still producing power to boot. The Keepers swear the plant provides all the power we need in 99 Town, but everybody with an ounce of gray matter between their ears knows we import most of our power from the Quad City nuclear plant, the same plant that runs Chicago. But it's a cute idea."

"What does any of that have to do with our missing body?" I said.

"Because the killer had a narrow window of time to dump it, and I don't know if you know this, Chuck, but people love dumping bodies into the water. Instant burial, or so they think," Mike said. "Only problem is, the only body of water in 99 Town is the Cut Rock River. And everything that goes into the Cut Rock River eventually gets to the dam. Now, if they dumped the body south of the dam, or if they dumped it anywhere else..."

I gave the timetable some thought, recalling the facts of the case from memory rather than referencing the case files. "Initial crime scene analysis put the wreck and presumed death of Nancy Meade around zero four. A neighbor called in the wrecked Dodge Challenger at zero four thirty. 99 Town Police arrive on scene at zero five and made it over to Rogue's Tattoo Parlor by zero six thirty. Our suspect, along with his known associates are in Rogue's Tattoo Parlor when you arrive, correct?"

"I responded to the call," Mike said. "They were all there, and the GTO was parked around back."

"That gives our killer roughly two and a half hours to move the body, dump it or bury it, and drive back to the tattoo shop," I said. "Not much time."

"They drive fast cars," Mike said. "And it doesn't take long to throw a body off a bridge into a river."

"But it's also enough time to drive thirty minutes away, spend an hour burying the body, and drive thirty minutes back. That gives us a pretty big search radius," I said. And if the cops were involved they'd have all the time they needed, and if Mike was wrapped up in such a conspiracy he'd be leading me down all the wrong paths.

"Pretty much all of 99 Town if you look at it that way," Mike said, talking about how far the Rogues could drive in a half hour. "But why drive thirty minutes away unless you already have a spot picked out? Driving that far away from the scene suggests premeditation."

I thought about that. "When I interviewed Drex Carlsrud last night, he didn't seem like the premeditated type. If he did do it, he did it drunk and upset, on an impulse."

"You got any hard evidence to back up that statement, or is that just a hunch?" Mike said.

"Hunches are unscientific and arrogant," I said. "Besides, if we find the body at the dam, we don't have to worry about hunches or guesswork."

"Well, you're in luck, Chuckers," Mike said as we came upon a bridge and pulled over along the narrow shoulder. "Cause the dam is right down there."

Mike cut the engine and pulled the keys. He got out and I followed after him. I had lost track of which road we were on, but it was wide and cut east to west, the setting sun casting shadows in the direction the car was pointed. Mike walked over to the bridge railing, lifting his sunglasses off his eyes and setting them on his forehead. I came next to him.

"What street is this?" I asked.

"Harrison," Mike said.

"That means..."

"You got it. The spot where Nancy died is just a few blocks from here," Mike said.

I looked to the east. The bridge rose up to cross the river and looked down over the surrounding neighborhoods. With the sun at my back, the Lows were painted in that vibrant orange of dying sunlight. Rogue's Tattoo was out that way, maybe a mile down the road. Those stains that marked the scene of the crime were even closer.

"Now if I ever killed a girl I thought I was in love with, and suddenly found myself with an extremely inconvenient corpse on my hands, I'd want to get rid of it as soon as fucking possible," Mike said. "If I'm not a premeditating kind of guy, and I didn't have a plan, and say I killed this girl in the middle of the night while all our friends were passed out, I'd want to ditch the body in the very first place I came across and get back to where everybody's passed out before anybody woke up."

I nodded. "If Drex Carlsrud threw Nancy Meade into the river, he would have done it from this very spot."

"You got it," Mike said. "About a half mile downstream, you see it?"

I turned south. A short concrete wall stretched across the river. North of the wall the water was wide and calm, almost like a lake. South of the wall, the river narrowed and sped up. Rocks and driftwood were exposed on either shore.

"During the spring, 99 Town Municipal Power opens the spillways, and anything could flow through. But it's been a dry summer, and the water's been pretty low, so the spillways and sluice gates have been closed off, and a hundred percent of the water has been going through the penstocks to the turbines. Now they can't let tree branches and corpses get to the turbines, or it'd fuck everything up. If the turbines stop spinning, the dam stops making energy, and the power company stops making money. Can't have that. So, they installed trash rakes to direct all the debris toward the sluice gates. If little Nancy was dumped into the Cut Rock River, dollars to donuts, her body is bopping in front of it along with all the garbage and tree branches and everything else people have dumped into the river."

"How do you know so much about dams?" I said.

"Hey brother, this ain't the first dead body I've gone fishing for."

"Disturbing," I said.

"But convenient for us," Mike said. "Come on, let's see what we find."

Mike parked in a gravel lot by the power plant building. As we crossed the street, powerlines dangled from pole to pole, transformer to transformer, buzzing audibly along the way. Dusk was in full swing. The sun surrendered to shadows.

"I made a call to the shift worker here at the dam," Mike said. "He unlocked the fence for us. Said we can go anywhere inside we want, just not on top of the dam, cause you know, liability."

As we neared the dam, I looked out across the small concrete barrier I'd seen from the bridge. The upstream side looked the same as it had from above. Calm, pooled water, the concrete barrier only a meter higher than the water level. What I couldn't see from the bridge was the downstream side of the dam. The water level dropped twenty meters from one side of the dam to the other, exposing a wall of concrete. A trickle of water leaked from the spillway onto unsubmerged rocks below.

"Right this way," Mike walked around the large square structure that housed the dam's inner workings. Around the side, we came to a chain link fence. Mike pushed through a pedestrian gate.

"Do you come here often?" I asked.

"More often than you'd think," Mike said. "We would have come here sooner, but it takes some time for bodies to flow downriver. Usually, it washes ashore or floats on by until it reaches a dam. We had some beat cops check both shores today while you were sleeping it off. Now all that's left is what's in front of this sluice gate."

"Right on the other side of this wall," Mike said as we climbed a set of concrete steps leading to the top of the dam. He slapped the concrete next to us, a little too confidently. I was becoming more certain with each step we were about to "find" a planted body.

Mike got to the top first and put his hands on his hips. I came up alongside him and looked over the railing down on the sluiceway below. There was a significant collection of tree branches and rotten vegetation, empty beer bottles and cans, and I was relieved to find, no corpse.

"Shit. Well, that was anticlimactic," Mike said. "Could be she was weighed down and is sitting at the bottom of the river. We'll have to have some drivers come out and… Do you hear that?"

I stood still. The water trickled down the backside of the dam. The buzz of the power lines. The simultaneous muffle and ring in my bad ear. It was hard to hear much else. The sun sank further below the horizon and somehow left the evening all the more without sound.

"I think someone followed us," Mike said. He drew his gun and gestured with it to go back down the steps. Something about the look in his eyes told me he wasn't acting.

I drew my gun too. The Ruger nine millimeter, not the neural inhibitor. I wouldn't make that mistake again, especially now that the neural inhibitor had gone missing. I led the way down the steps, holding the gun down at the length of both my arms as I learned to do in the simulators. I checked over my shoulder, and Mike was following close behind.

"I got your back. Go," Mike said.

I pushed through the gate in the chain link fence and came to the side of the large structure that split my view of upstream from downstream of the dam. I came up to the corner and held there for a moment, trying to listen through the drone and whine of my left ear. Too much background noise. Too much humming from the power lines and rustling of the water leaking through the spillways. Mike nudged me in the back. I stepped out from around the corner, the barrel of my gun pointing into the dim light.

I saw the shape of a man, stationary for a second, then in motion like running water. The shape disappeared around the downstream side of the building.

"Freeze!" I yelled and thought of firing the gun. Both were too late and equally ineffective.

"Go! Go!" Mike yelled and took off running past me.

He disappeared around the corner after the man. I followed and came around the corner to find Mike on his back, blood running from his nose.

"Fucker cold-cocked me," he said. "There! Get him!"

The assailant was climbing a metal ladder to the top of the dam. Whoever he was, he was quick. I left Mike and ran for the bottom of the ladder. I reached it just as the stranger hit the top and took off running along the length of the dam. I climbed as fast as I could, banging the metal Ruger against the railing as I did.

On top of the dam, I saw the stranger running along the narrow concrete barrier for the far shore. I could have called out again, could have fired the gun, could have given up. Instead, I followed, sprinting along the foot-wide top of the dam through the darkness. To my right was a short fall into the reservoir. To my left was a twenty-meter drop onto bare rocks. I cheated to the right.

The man I was chasing was faster.

"Stop!" I called out.

That was all it took for me to slip. My right foot landed half-on, half-off the ledge. The wet concrete slipped right out from under me. Trying to fall toward the right, to the nice still water in the reservoir just a few feet down, somehow made things worse. My chest bounced off the center of the damn, and my torso fell to the left. My hand tightened around the Ruger, and I fired off a wild shot. My left hand reached out and grabbed a hold of the upstream ledge. The rest of me dangled over the long drop to the rocks below.

With an implant, my levels would have been adjusted automatically. I didn't have that, so I did my best to calm myself. To minimize the predicament. To stave off the panic. If I fell, I would just break an ankle or two. The dam was slightly sloped. That would slow my descent, right? It wasn't as if I was in any real danger, right?

Mike came running along the top of the dam. "Jesus Christ, Chuck! Don't fucking let go or you'll fucking die!"

"I slipped. Go get him. I'll be fine," I said and tried to pull myself up.

Mike fired an unaimed shot in the general direction of the far shore. "There. I tried to stop him," Mike said, then holstered the gun and dropped down, straddling the dam. He grabbed my arms and pulled.

Together, we managed to get me back up on top of the narrow barrier. Panting and wet from the reservoir side, we rested on top.

"Did you get him? Shoot him, I mean? I asked.

"Fuck no. You?"

"I didn't even mean to shoot," I said.

Mike laughed, good and hard. Something about the honesty of his laugh disarmed all my suspicions. I cracked a smile and burst into laughter with him. It felt good. Felt freeing, even if we were further than ever from solving the case.

When Mike stopped laughing, it was abrupt. Like a flip of a switch, he went from jolly to sullen. I stopped too, unsure of what was going to happen next. We sat there, straddling a dam, one leg dangling over the drop and the other soaking up the pollution-saturated water of the Cut Rock River.

Mike slipped his pistol into his shoulder holster and began working his two hands together. When they came apart, his right hand held up his wedding ring. He pinched it between his thumb and finger and peered through it at me with one eye. Then he threw it upstream into the river. I turned and watched the bit of jewelry arc through the air and make a tiny splash when it plunged into the water.

"Told you I'd do it," Mike said and then slapped my shoulder. My sore shoulder. I winced. "Let's get the H E fucking hockey sticks out of here."

It was late, and we were both half-soaked. Mike dropped me off next to my car outside the impound lot and did me the favor of not mentioning the dented in front bumper or the spray-painted letters on the windshield.

"We'll pick up the hunt in the morning. Divers will drag the river. They might turn up something. Maybe me and you will take a look at that search radius and see if any other handy body dumping spots jump out at us," Mike said from inside his car.

"Yes. We should definitely do this again. I especially enjoyed the part where you got sucker punched," I said.

"Says the guy who should be at the bottom of a dam with a pair of broken legs right now," Mike said. "Hey, who do you think that guy was we chased?"

"Has to be the perpetrator, right?" I said. "I mean, whoever he was, he seemed a lot more criminal than the guy we have locked up."

"Yeah, I don't know. I sure as shit didn't get a good look at him. That guy could have been anybody," Mike said. "I mean, he seemed guilty as shit, sulking around a dam, watching a bunch of cops look for a body, but he could have just been some punk kid hiding from his parents so he could smoke weed."

"Could have been an accomplice," I said.

"Could have been an accomplice. Whoever he was, he hit like a fucking title holder," Mike said, rubbing his chin. "Maybe tomorrow we'll check the far side of the dam. See if he left prints. See if we can tell where he went to. You got a place to stay? I got a couch if you need it."

Not wanting to get too close to Mike, and not wanting to bring up Sara's apartment, I lied and realized I was starting to get good at it. "I got a room at a hotel not far from here."

"Tomorrow morning then," Mike said. "Hey, try laying off the sauce tonight, will ya?"

Chapter Nine

There was a hotel not far from the Government Center and Sara's place. One of those built like a tiny strip mall around a parking lot. I parked the Crown Victoria in a spot that didn't require much maneuvering and walked to the small office below the neon sign that read "Cheap Hotel - No Vacancy." The neon letters N and O were unlit. I paid for one night and got a metal key on a plastic tag that said, "Room 34."

On my walk to Room Thirty-four, I checked my flip phone. There was a message from Sammy Candelario, the latest in a string of texts between the two of us.

"B there in 5."

As I read it, headlights shined into the lot and a car pulled in. I stepped out of the way, and a small red vehicle pulled up next to me. The passenger window rolled down, and Ruby looked up at me.

"Get in, cowboy," she said and slipped into the backseat.

I opened the door and got inside. Sammy was behind the driver's seat, smoking a cigarette that didn't exactly smell like tobacco.

"Well, you messaged me. Where do you want to go?" Sammy said.

"I got the official tour of 99 Town this afternoon. I'm thinking you can give me the unofficial tour," I said.

"I'm a fucking tour guide now? Okay. You want to start any place in particular?" Sammy said.

"Just drive," I said, settling into the seat. "Doesn't matter where. Anywhere."

"I can do anywhere," Sammy said and used a stick shift and clutch to put the car in gear. He must have noticed me watching him work the manual transmission. He went on, "1999 Isuzu Impulse. Newest car you can own in 99 Town. Legally. The other guys, they're big on seventies muscle. Easy to work on. Easy to get parts. You wouldn't believe what it costs me to get parts for this little rice burner. Had to make a lot of my own fabrications and modification. I'll put her up against those cast-iron boats any day of the week though. But you didn't reach out to me to talk about cars, now did you?"

"Someone was following us tonight, over by the dam on the south end of town," I said.

"So? Wasn't me," Sammy said. He turned back toward downtown. Per my guidance, he seemed to drive aimlessly.

"How do I know it wasn't you? Or Eric? Or even her?"

Ruby chuckled from the backseat. "Fuck you, pig." Then she put a plastic liquor bottle to her lips and drank up.

"You saw somebody at a damn and now you want me to provide an alibi? Okay, we were all at the shop from nine this morning until I left to get you," Sammy said. "How's that?"

"Is that the truth?"

"It's the unofficial version of the truth. Are you calling me a liar?" Sammy said.

"I didn't say that," I said. I considered the possibility I was being lied to. I always considered it. Considered it anytime I was talking to someone in 99 Town.

"Something you gotta learn, Chuck. Nobody lies in this town. It's just that nobody tells the truth either," Sammy said. We drove under the elevated train tracks, circled the downtown area, and stopped at a red light.

I nodded. "Well, here's the thing, Sammy. You can feed me half-truths all night long and that's just fine. I can't stop you. But every minute I investigate this case, I grow less and less convinced that Drex Carlsrud committed this murder. Not by himself anyway. And if he didn't that means someone else did. Someone with a motive to kill Nancy, a motive to pin it on Drex, and the means to do both.

And as much as you'd like me to believe it, I don't see any reason for the 99 Town Police to involve themselves with any of you. So if they didn't do it, that means someone else did. One of you Rogues maybe. And not the one locked up in the basement of the police station either."

Sammy sucked down the last of the cigarette and flicked the butt out the window. The light turned green, and we drove on.

"You don't think the cops have any reason to get rid of us?" Sammy asked.

"You guys are nobodies. Local losers who hang out at a tattoo shop all day and all night. No cop is going to risk going to prison to knock off a couple of you tattooed freaks. No offense," I said.

"None taken," Sammy said.

"But the Keepers—"

"We're our own Keepers, Chuck," Sammy said.

Ruby laughed from the backseat. "Yeah. We keep what's ours, and we take what's not."

She took another big swig out of the plastic bottle and passed it up to Sammy. Sammy drank while driving, then tipped the bottle of clear pungent fluid to me.

I waved my hand. "I'll pass."

"Okay," Sammy said and passed it back to Ruby. "So you don't think the cops have enough reason to hate our guts, is that it?"

"Something like that," I said.

"Well let me show you something before you come to any more conclusions."

Sammy turned down a street that followed below the elevated commuter train tracks that ran a circuit around 99 Town. Cut through the asphalt were the paved-over tracks of the old surface-level train system. We followed the surface tracks until they came to a T-intersection. No other traffic was out, and we drove slow. At the flat of the T-intersection, there was a large chain-link gate set into a concrete wall. The old tracks carried on beyond the gate and down into darkness. Sammy stopped the car with the bumper just a few feet in front of the fence.

He got out. I followed him. Sammy dug a set of keys out of his pocket and came up to a padlock.

"What is this?" I asked.

"People in 99 Town, they're so used to the trains going over their heads they forget that..." Sammy put the key into the padlock and fought with the rust to open it. "...trains used to go under right their feet too."

The lock popped open, and when Sammy threw open the hasp, the chain-link gate swung into the black maw diving deep below the street.

"C'mere," Sammy said as he walked into the darkness.

I hesitated. Ruby had gotten behind the wheel of the Isuzu and drove the car through the gates. Its headlights pierced the darkness and showed the train tracks sloping down.

"Come on, man," Sammy said, walking to catch up to the car now. "We ain't gonna hurt ya. Not again, anyways."

"That's comforting," I said. "My shoulder still aches from last night."

"Oh yeah. I forgot about that," Sammy said. "How do you like it?"

"Like what?" I asked as we came alongside the Isuzu. Ruby was in the backseat again. Sammy laughed and then slipped back behind the wheel. I climbed back into the passenger seat. "How do I like what?" I asked again.

"Your ink, man," Sammy said. "The tat we gave you. Do you dig it?"

"What tat? What the shit are you talking about?"

"You didn't notice it yet?" Sammy said. He put the car in gear, and they drove along the underground tracks. "Shit, I thought for sure you would've noticed by now."

"Told you we should have put it on his fucking forehead," Ruby said.

I tried pulling down my coat and shirt over my shoulder, trying to see what was there and what they'd done to me.

"Forget about it. It's nothing bad. If you don't like it I'll ink something else over it," Sammy said. "Look around you. Tell me what you see?"

He was joking, lying, messing with me for his own amusement. Had to be. I had showered and changed clothes twice since last night. I would have noticed. What was on my shoulder had to be a bruise just like all the other bruises on my body from their fists, boots, and bat.

"I said forget it. Tell me what you see around us," Sammy prodded again.

I looked through the windshield and saw we were cruising down a long-abandoned train tunnel. In the dark, it was hard to see much. The walls and arched ceiling were made of brick. The tracks were metal and missing in spots. The surface below the tracks was made of wood ties and gravel, smoothed over by years and years of car tire tracks that Sammy was following.

"What is this place? Do the police ever come down here?" I asked.

"I'm not even sure they know it exists," Sammy said, shifting the car into third and then fourth gear. "Either they don't know about these tunnels, don't care, or are too chickenshit to come down. You mentioned the Underground last night, right? Well, here you are."

Tunnels branched off like arteries flowing from the heart, cutting to the left and right. As Sammy pushed the Isuzu's speedometer higher, it was clear he had these routes and paths memorized. At each junction, the steel train tracks had been moved to make smooth trails for car tires. The tire track paths veered around displaced rails, mounds of garbage, and rusted-out grocery carts. We came upon a junction switch, and Sammy cut left with the reaction that told me he'd taken this way a thousand times before.

"Smuggling routes," I said. "They don't leave 99 Town though. These are old metro public transit lines. There's no reason to bury tunnels between cities."

Sammy turned his head to me and winked. "I'll never tell."

This was Sammy showing me that the cops had a reason to do them all in. The Rogues ran contraband, just like Mike suspected. That was how they made their real money. That's why they all had fast cars. This was Sammy's way of telling me so, all while saying nothing. Equal parts braggadocio, confession, hints, and unofficial truths.

"Do the others know about these routes?" I asked.

Sammy smiled and tapped his finger to his nose, whatever that meant.

I smirked back. This was a new game, saying things by not saying anything, but I was learning the rules fast. Prying out the truth was a patient's man game.

"So Drex. You're certain he's innocent. And Eric?" I asked.

"Eric? That kid's loyal like a dog. He doesn't know how to be anything else. Doesn't have a selfish bone in his body. Here's what you don't understand, my man. Us Rogues, we're family. Like brothers and sisters. Nobody's got any real family around. All we got is each other. Nobody else gives a shit about us. Nobody else in the world would bother to piss on us to put out a fire. I trust them, and they trust me. And they listen to every word I say. You know how I know neither of them guys did it? Cause I didn't tell them to do it," Sammy said.

I eyed Sammy and couldn't help but wonder if there was a tire iron in his trunk.

As he cut left down another branch in the maze, and then another sharp left, it became impossible to keep a sense of direction or distance. The only light came from the white headlights and red taillights of the Isuzu and the occasional ray of moonlight coming through storm grates. Sammy drove and made each turn with purpose and reaction that suggested precognition, unlike his meanderings along the city streets above. The Isuzu was going well over a hundred miles an hour now. One mis-steer into a mound of garbage or train track and the Isuzu would stop driving through the tunnels and start tumbling like a pinball. I wanted to trust him but couldn't help white-knuckling a handle on the door. So instead of watching through the windshield and all the narrowly avoided obstacles and last-second turns, I focused on the gear shifter between Sammy and I. Sammy shifted between gears, dropping down into third gear at the sharper turns, just to pump the car back into fourth a second later, all in unison with a third pedal on the floor.

The Isuzu was quick and agile. The engine screamed at top speeds like a high-pitched hummingbird. Lighter and more responsive than the big Crown Victorias I had ridden and driven. The manual transmission though, that was new.

Meanwhile, the bottle passed from Ruby to Sammy to Ruby until it was empty. If the alcohol had any effect on Sammy's driving ability, it didn't show. When it was gone, Ruby tapped it on Sammy's window. He unrolled it electrically with a button on the door, and she tossed out the bottle. Clearly, this was a common practice. Other bottles and cans and paper, of course paper, littered the width of the tunnels, only cleared away by the rush of cars.

The tunnel we were in merged with another larger tunnel. Another car was parked up ahead. Sammy downshifted and I was pushed forward into my seatbelt. The Isuzu slowed and pulled alongside the other car. Clouds of dust caught up and moved past the windows. Both cars idled side by side. I tried to see across Sammy into the other car, see who was in the driver and passenger seat. Sammy leaned forward and cut off my view.

"Well, this has been fun, and I think I've been sufficiently cooperative in your questioning. Outside your door is a ladder that will bring you within a couple blocks of your hotel," Sammy said. "Happy trails, partner."

"I think—" I objected, but stopped when I heard the sound of a crisp metallic click from the backseat. I turned, and there was just enough light to see that Ruby had replaced the liquor bottle with a big blocky handgun pointed at my face.

"Wasn't really a suggestion, hoss," Ruby said.

I nodded, then turned to Sammy. "We'll talk more, later."

I got out and shut the door behind me. I peered over the roof of the Isuzu, still trying to spot who was in the other car, or at least what make and model of car it was. I didn't know cars, not well enough to know such things at first sight, but if I could spot some defining characteristic…

There was some conversation between the two drivers. Sammy's voice and another. Hard to hear over the revving engines echoing off the brick walls. Add in the drone and whine of my left ear, and it was impossible. Something triggered the drivers, and both cars kicked into motion. Gravel rooster-tailed up behind the tires and seconds later, both vehicles were gone, racing down the narrow channel of 99 Town's underground.

I found the ladder and climbed up through the darkness. At the top, there was a manhole cover I forced up and out of its place with my shoulders. It led me up and into a dingy back alley. A dim light at the top of a garage flickered. I stood up, fought off my coat, and pulled down my shirt over my sore shoulder.

There, surrounded by red, swollen, irritated skin still seeping capillary blood was a one-word tattoo. It read in big block letters, "ROGUE."

"Those fucking mothers."

Chapter Ten

The buzzing seemed to come from another world. A surreal Chicago. A familiar 99 Town. Perhaps a new and confusing mix of the two. The buzzing. Was this what it was like to be zapped by a neural inhibitor? I'd never been zapped before. Who would be zapping me? And why?

I broke from unconsciousness like a drowning child through the surface of a pool. Oxygen and light forced the confusion to retreat. The buzzing was still there, but it wasn't from an inhibitor. It was the small flip phone set on the wood nightstand next to the bed. It rattled across the wood surface. I sat up on the old, creaking mattress of the even older hotel and answered the phone.

"Chuck, wake up." I heard the voice, her voice, the treble-toned voice of the hard and cold lawyer turned unexpectedly kind. But I didn't think it was real. Lingering tendrils of my subconsciousness fought to keep me below the surface of reality.

Was any of this real? It seemed too strange to be real. Maggie's suicide. The assignment. The trip to 99 Town. The Rogues. The booze. The apartment. The dam. The tunnels. Her… Sara.

"I'm awake. What is it?" I said. "What time is it? It's still dark out."

"Chuck," Sara said. "They found the body. It just came across the police scanner. Might not be our body, but there's a good chance it is. Cut Rock Park. Get there before the prosecution has a chance to tamper with the crime scene. I'm heading there now."

"The body," I said the words out loud. The case. I was on a murder case. Nancy Meade, daughter of two of Chicago's most prestigious philanthropists and entrepreneurs, had gone missing. I pulled the phone away from my face and read the clock on the digital display. Three hours. I'd gotten three hours of sleep. "Where did they find her?"

"Cut Rock Park. Get a map and get there as soon as you can," Sara said. "Listen. When you get there, we need to keep our distance from each other. You have to maintain your unbiased appearance and avoid any perceived conflicts of interest. If we're seen together too often, we'll lose whatever credibility you have with the 99 Town Police."

"Can't be much left of that," I said.

"I got to go. Meet you there." The line went dead.

I tossed the phone back on the nightstand and clicked on the lamp. The bare bulb cast a harsh light on the peeling wallpaper and generic re-printed nature paintings. My clothes were stacked neatly on a table next to an old TV across the room. I went about getting dressed.

Cut Rock Park. Not the tunnels? I had a map, had picked it up the first night on the way to the crime scene. The park was on the opposite end of town from Rogue's Tattoos. Why would one of them drive all the way across town instead of dumping the body in the river, or in some hole in that endless network of tunnels?

Something wasn't right. I smelled it and grew all the more determined to hunt it out.

After I was dressed and out the door of the hotel room, the first light of the new day exposed the parking lot. I reexamined my phone and noticed there were text messages from Mike. I got into the Crown Victoria, ignored the windshield that now matched my shoulder, started the engine, called Mike, and pinned the phone between my good ear and my sore shoulder.

The phone rang. I drove out of the parking lot of "Cheap Hotel." Mike answered on the second ring. "Chuckers. Ready for some good news, my man?"

"The body?" I said, switching from holding the phone with my shoulder to holding it with my hand and driving single-handedly.

"The motherfucking body," Mike said. "If this is our body. Could be just some homeless vagrant whose homeless buddies decide to do him a solid and hold a funeral for him. Or…"

"Or it could be Nancy Meade," Chuck said.

"Nancy motherfucking Meade."

That was a strange adjective to describe a girl's dead corpse. "Mike, I'm driving right now. I should probably have two hands," I said, swerving inches from a parked car.

"Cut Rock Park. Northeast side of town, like I told you last night," Mike said. "You know where you're going?"

"I have a map."

"You're going to come in on Hart Road. Take a left till you come up to a bridge that crosses a creek. You'll see the squad cars from there," Mike said.

"I'll be there in just a few minutes."

"Right. See you there, brother," Mike said and hung up.

Between managing big folded-out paper maps, phones, and trying to drive, it was a wonder natural selection has left any 99ers alive. I drove north away from Downtown before getting into the detailed navigation work. Just as Mike said, the closer I got to Cut Rock Park, the more affluent the housing became. None of it was extravagant. It just wasn't squalor. The wealthy of Chicago put all of these houses to shame, but there was more craftsmanship in the architecture in the houses and less garbage in the lawns here compared to the Lows.

Eventually, I came to Hart Road and drove through the entrance of Cut Rock Park. A thick grove of oaks swallowed me and the car. The pre-dawn light was choked out by the canopy arching over the road. Under the oaks was manicured lawn. Nice place. Mike's directions were simple to follow from there. One left turn, and two miles later I was at a wooden bridge crossing a small creek. A herd of police cars, many with their lights on painting the dim morning red and blue, were parked on either side of the road. A half-dozen unmarked cars were there as well. I recognized Sara's rusted-out Ford Taurus. As I parked behind it, I saw her standing near the bridge on the roadside of the yellow crime scene tape. She wore a knee-length skirt, a brown raincoat, and a matching cloche hat.

I got out and when I shut the door, she turned, and her eyes caught mine from under the brim of her hat.

After that short glance, she broke eye contact. Didn't acknowledge me, just noticed me, and then turned away. That long cool distance was between us again, and I suddenly regretted how I'd left her apartment. There, when we held each other's eyes we had a connection deeper and truer than even the implant-assisted emotional links available under the Order. Something more honest and resolute. But that was gone now. I turned away and pretended to be the consummate professional she was.

Mike came out of the ditch, ducked under the yellow tape, and headed my way. He had a bright purple shiner under his left eye from last night. His sunglasses were propped up on his head in the low light of the morning. When we met, Mike slapped my sore shoulder and steered me back toward the ditch.

"This way, Chuck. They haven't dug her up yet. We were waiting for forensics to show up but they're here now and ready to start digging. You showed up just in time."

Mike led me past Sara, under the tape, and down the ditch to the side of the creek. Captain Reiner, the chief of police, was on the far side of the tape and spotted us as we came down.

"Glad you ladies could join us," the chief said. "Hope we didn't interrupt your beauty sleep."

"Morning, boss. And yeah, you did. But don't sweat it. Even you can't diminish how sexy me and Chuck are standing next to each other," Mike said with a wink.

The chief guffed but said nothing more. I eyed the man as we moved past him and toward the bottom of the creek.

"A homeless man found the body," Mike said. "After a long day of drinking and burdening society, I guess he decided to look for a place to sleep under the bridge. Turns out someone taking a dirt nap stole his favorite spot. He notices the toes of a sneaker sticking out of a pile of rocks. At first, he thinks it's just a shoe. A shoe that could be his shoe. So he goes up to it and tries pulling it out of the rocks."

Mike continued the story as we moved past a pair of uniformed officers and an investigator wearing a blue jacket with "FORENSICS" printed in yellow block letters on the back. We pushed past them and made our way under the bridge. As soon as we were under, the air seemed spoiled.

"Right away, the bum notices three things," Mike said. "One, no matter how hard he pulls on the shoe, it's not coming out of the ground. Two, it isn't empty. And three? Well, I bet you can guess number three."

That smell from inside the GTO. Only worse. Thicker. Meatier. Deader, if that was possible. I covered my mouth and hoped I wouldn't be sick again.

"You got it, buddy," Mike said. "He notices the smell. So now, being a guy who's never had a positive experience with a law enforcement officer in his entire life, he makes a surprisingly smart decision. He leaves the shoe alone and dials nine one one."

"What in the shit is nine one one?" I asked.

"Jesus Christ, Chuck... We're nine one one. Us. The cops! He calls the cops. Says he thinks there might be a body under a bridge," Mike said. "And well, here we are."

It was easy to tell where the homeless man had found the shoe. There were concentric rings of officers around the spot. Those nearest to the center all wore forensics jackets and were carefully removing stones from a pile one by one. The ring of officers outside of that was taking photographs and detailed notes. The third ring was made of watchers and supervisors. That's where Mike and I stood. The ring beyond us, if they weren't cops, they would have been loitering. Somewhere beyond them was Sara.

I craned my neck and spotted the shoe. Flat rubber bottom. White plastic toe. Red canvas. White frayed laces. A kid's shoe. As an investigator removed another rock, I saw the pants leg just about the shoe. It had been a hasty burial. The murderer had found a spot out of view and full of rocks. He must have dug down a little way, but not deep, just enough for a body and the rocks to cover it. Not deep enough to hide the toe of one shoe, and definitely not deep enough to hide the smell. The air was warm under the bridge. It didn't move. The stench sat still in my nostrils, refusing to waver for even a second.

More rocks came off the pile. More bits of clothing were exposed. More of the corpse saw sunlight. Each rock lifted away made me more certain this wasn't the body of some random vagrant.

"Chuck. You got to tell me something," Mike said. "How do you not know about nine one one? How do you guys in the Order even know when someone's committed a crime?"

I shrugged. "Most potential criminal acts we can spot via elevated biometrics. Rapid heartbeat and breathing. A rush of endorphins and testosterone to the bloodstream in both the perpetrator and the victim. The Network has algorithms to distinguish between physical exertion such as exercise or sexual activities. In most cases, we can prevent the act with indirect neural inhibition via the Network before it even happens. In the rare case when someone does expire, the victim's implant reports it immediately to the Network and notifies us."

"Algorithms to distinguish between sexual activity and a crime? You people are gross," Mike said.

"Yeah. Sure. We're the gross ones," I said and gestured to the center of the crowd.

Since coming to 99 Town, I've allowed myself a bit more hope than my normal allotment. This town was full of uncertainties and anomalies. Until I saw something with my own eyes, there was no point in being convinced of a fact. Especially a negative one. Something about the chaos here tricked me into believing that just by random chance, some things should turn out for the better. Here, the cat in the box might live. Maybe the blood pattern analysis was all wrong. Maybe the brain matter wasn't brain matter at all. I had hoped somehow we'd find Nancy Meade alive. When the last rocks were removed from the torso and head to expose what was once a healthy young woman, those hopes were as crushed and brutalized as her body.

Nancy's skull was split apart and concave. Her cheeks were slack, and all the fluid had moved and settled to the back of her head and body. If it weren't for the small diamond stud in her nostril, a stud that matched her photo, I couldn't have been sure it was her, but this was Nancy Meade alright. Her eyes were filmy yellowish-white and wide open. I wished they were closed, instead. Her irises and pupils were clouded over by rot. Her once-bouncy red hair looked thin and was falling out. Her skin was pale and looked like wax or rubber. Her clothes which were once cute and fashionable were now filthy and scraped by her involuntary internment. I noticed her fingers were drawn into half-fists as if she was ready to claw her attacker. I wondered if she died that way or if decomposition had pulled her tendons taunt.

"I need some air," I said and wandered out of the ring of officers.

Once I was clear of the bridge and the overwhelming smell, I turned and looked up to the top of the bridge. Sara stood there, leaning against the railing, expecting to garnish some clue as to what was found. I just had to nod, and she got the message. The body was Nancy's. I turned away and kicked at some rocks along the stream.

A few seconds passed, and Mike came and joined me. He picked his sunglasses out of his hair, held up the lens to the sky, and polished out a smudge with his shirt tale.

"So let me ask you this," Mike said. "What happens when the crime is sexual activity? Like, what about rape or sexual assault? What then?"

I sighed. "There are biometrical differences, but it is harder for the Network to pick out, and sometimes anomalies happen."

"Yeah. I heard that. Anomalies happen," Mike said and set his glasses over his eyes. Dawn had just come up over the trees. "Forensics will do a full report and tell us all the details. But that was Nancy Meade. You've seen her picture in the case files. Hard to recognize with all the..." Mike made a hand wave over his face. "...But that's her alright."

"So what happens next?" I said.

"Well, we have a suspect, a murder weapon, and a body. I say we go back to the jail cell and ask our friend Drex about Cut Rock Park and watch him sweat. In the meantime, the forensic nerds will do their thing, and as soon as they finish their report, we charge the son of a bitch and schedule a trial. We'll have him tried, convicted, and executed in a couple days, and you can go back to monitoring people's biometric levels during sexual activities in ol' Chicago."

"Sure," I said. "But why here? Why would Drex drive all the way up here when he could have dumped the body in the river?"

"Beats the shit outta me," Mike said. "I'll ask him, but something tells me he'll deny knowing anything about the body. In my experience, murderers don't like to make a habit out of making sense."

"What about the guy from last night? What if Drex is the wrong guy?" I asked.

"We go where the evidence leads. If Drex was the killer, his DNA is going to be all over that body. And if it's not, we find out whose DNA is on it," Mike said.

"DNA evidence? You guys can do that here?" I asked.

"Lieutenant," one of the uniforms called from under the bridge. "Found something you might want to see."

We pushed our way through the onlookers to the epicenter of the scene. The exhumers hadn't made a lot of progress since I'd walked away. A few more rocks were removed. Her arms were exposed now, tucked along the side of her boy like a soldier standing at attention. Her slack plastic face still gawked at the bottom of the bridge.

"What do you got?" Mike asked.

One of the men dropped an item into a clear evidence bag. The man sealed the bag and wrote a few numbers on the outside. Then, with blue rubber-gloved hands, he turned and handed it to Mike.

"Not sure what it is yet, or if it's even connected to the crime, but it was under a rock along with the body," the man said.

Mike held up the bag. I leaned in for a closer look. It held a small black disc inside, about four centimeters in diameter and one centimeter thick. The outer edge was concave like the rim of a tire.

What is it?" I asked.

"Fuck if I know," Mike said and handed the evidence bag back to the uniform. "Catalog it and save it with whatever else you find. Run the usual tests and let me know if something hits."

"Wait," I said. "Let me see that."

I grabbed the bag. The disc was plastic or maybe ceramic. All black. Oddly shaped with a slight bulge to both sides and that groove running the circumference of the edge. I had the strange conviction that I'd seen something like this before. My mind imagined its shape and size and went about trying to put it somewhere it made sense, a piece of a jigsaw puzzle that would only fit in the right spot. Then it clicked into place.

"It's an earring," I said. "Not a loop like a lady would wear. One of those big thick ones that put giant holes in earlobes."

"Let me see," Mike said and snatched the bag. "A plug, they call them. The tattoo freaks put them in their ears."

"The Rogues. We need mugshots of the Rogues," I said.

"You got my case files?" Mike asked.

"You bet your shit I do," I said.

A minute later, we were both back up on the roadway, sitting in my Crown Victoria, me in the driver's seat and Mike sitting shotgun. Between us were the case files and the evidence bag. We went through the Rogues one at a time.

"Hand me that paper clip, will ya?" Mike said.

Paper was antiquated in my world, so the term "paper clip" was completely foreign to me. Plus, the ringing in my ear... "The what?" I asked. Paper piles and photos were scattered all around us. It was a mess.

"The paper clip. Right there."

"A paper... What?"

"Clip! Cli*pah*. With a pee. Not a tee. Jesus, even I can find one of these," Mike said and snatched a small bit of twisted wire off a stack of sheets in my lap. He shuffled some sheets around and bound them together. Then he set Drex's photo on top of the stack. "Look. He's got plugs in his ears," Mike said.

I held the plug up next to the photograph. "It doesn't look the right size. His are too small. Look at this thing."

"We have his plugs back at the jail. Two of them. We can check later to see if they're the same size, but I think you're right," Mike said.

Eric was next. "Not him," I said. "No piercings at all on him."

We shuffled the photographs and the sheets shuck-shucked as Mike brought the next suspect forward.

Sammy.

"Could be him. Not sure if his are this big," I said. "His are open in the middle. Do they change them out regularly?"

"Fuck if I know," Mike said. "We'll put him in the 'maybe' pile."

"Yeah. Maybe..." I said and was about to say more when Mike shuck-shucked the photos to the last Rogue.

Ruby. The girl. Buzz cut and big plugged earlobes.

"That looks..." Mike said and held the disc up to the photo.

"That looks like a match," I said. "Hard to tell without the photo being life-sized but..."

"It's the same style," Mike said. "Black. Solid. Looks like it's slightly rounded in the picture. Looks the same size to me. I think we got it."

"Can we magnify this picture? Make it life-size?"

"Well, we can make it whatever size you want, but unless you know how big her head is..."

"We don't know how big her head is?" I said.

"Well, this isn't a real mug shot, or we'd have inch marks behind her. This is just a driver's license photo," said Mike.

"Can't we just—"

"Just what? Measure her head through the internet and see if it grows or shrinks while she's fucking?"

I tried not to show my frustration. "Under the Order, we could tap her implant and know her exact dimensions. We'd know exactly where she was the night Nancy went missing, know the exact minute Nancy expired and where everyone was at that precise moment in time. This... This is like trying to juggle one-handed and blindfolded," I said. "It makes no sense."

"You just don't get it, do ya Chuck?" Mike said. "You Order people think you're so fucking smart with your network and your implants and your biometrics. Think we're a bunch of dumbass hicks. But let me tell you something. Around here we do real police work. We get our hands dirty and actually investigate crimes. And so far that's working pretty damn good for us. Now we have two suspects."

"You think Ruby helped Drex?" I said.

"If not with the murder then with the burial. Murders, they can happen real quick. By accident even. Burials? Quick burials? It would sure help if he had a friend or two."

"And the guy from last night?"

"Might be the whole damn crew of them turned on Nancy and did her in," Mike said. "Maybe she was going to run back to Mommy and Daddy in Chicago, and they didn't want one of their own going back to the Order and ratting out their little smuggling operation."

"Okay," I said. I couldn't help but think of Sammy, the man in charge, driving the tunnels last night. "So what's next? How do we pin Ruby to the burial?"

"Well, I think we start out by stealing her garbage," Mike said.

"Steal her... I don't follow," I said.

"You've never done a garbage pull?" Mike said. "Well, Chuckers, let me tell you. You are in for a treat!"

Chapter Eleven

After handing the wet work over to the 99 Police Forensics, Mike and I made plans for the garbage pull later that night. He didn't allude to just what a garbage pull was, but I gathered that it wasn't going to be clean or pleasant. Then again, what had been clean and pleasant since I arrived in this place?

I needed a change of clothes and some food.

There was a bar down the block from Cheap Hotel that served drinks to the drunk. The menu posted to a board outside the door said they served cheeseburgers, so my mind was made up for lunch. But clothes first. Then food.

Mike told me to wear "civvies" for the garbage pull in order to blend in. I liked the idea of blending in but was completely unaware of the social queues my choice of clothing might send. So, I eyed a few other men on my way to a store that sold used clothes to the poor and decided on a look I thought of as "gentlemen-loser." I walked out dressed in blue jeans, a red flannel long-sleeved shirt, work boots, and three days of growth on my chin.

The sun was setting by the time I stepped into the bar, not only did I look like a 99er, I was beginning to feel like one too. Which was good, because I wasn't too sure how the bar would take toward outsiders. The place was at the bottom of a flight of stairs in the basement of an old apartment building. Neon signs hung in windows just above the sidewalk. I left the light of day and went underground. The interior of the bar was made of dark stained wood, floors, walls, and furniture. There was a counter running the length of the side of the room, with a large mirror and an ornately-carved mantel and shelving to hold all the bottles behind it. There were stools in front of the bar, but that was too conspicuous for my taste. There were tables and booths too. I picked out a small table away from the bar and sat down.

A waitress didn't come right away, which was fine. I needed some time to think.

The timeline of the night of the murder: Forensics was sticking with their four AM estimated time of death. That gave the killer two and a half hours from time of death to load up the body, drive it across 99 Town to Cut Rock Park, bury it, drive back to Rogue's Tattoo, wash up, change clothes, and go back to pretending to sleep before the cops kicked in the door. Traffic would have been light at five AM, and as Mike pointed out, they like to drive fast. They could have easily made it to the park and back in an hour, which leaves an hour to bury the body and thirty minutes to clean up before the police arrived. It was all possible, but it was tight.

But why? Why that spot in Cut Rock Park? Why not the river? Or better yet, the tunnels? Those ran for miles and could hide a body for months if not years. It didn't make sense. Whether it was just Drex, or the whole Rogue crew, hauling a body across all of 99 Town with a corpse right in the passenger seat, through the most affluent neighborhood, to a random park to bury her under a random bridge…

The only logical reason to do such a thing would be to throw off an investigation. To draw attention away from the Lows and the Rogues. And that would suggest pre-meditation. Which would suggest anyone other than Drex, the shot-down wannabe lover. It suggested someone with a plan.

A waitress approached. She looked like a worn-out thing. The kind of woman Nancy would have grown into in another ten years or so. Tired. Cynical. Like a woman who knew things.

"What'll ya have?" she asked me.

"Water and a cheeseburger," I said.

She jotted it down and left.

Something else burned in the back of my skull. Somewhere not far from my implant port behind my ear. The Underground, as it was known under the Order, was metaphorical. A catchy name for the remnants of the Resistance. A loose collection of noncompliants who liked to undermine the rule of law. But last night, with Sammy and Ruby, I'd seen a real underground network made up of souped-up cars and subterranean tunnels. Was the name a coincidence? Did the tunnels connect to other underground networks beyond 99 Town? Surely they didn't stretch all the way to Chicago.

Still, there was a connection. Nothing official of course. But I had a suspicion that all black markets inevitably crossed paths. Eventually, everything connected.

The waitress was slow. My mind wandered.

Back in Chicago, there wasn't much of the Underground left. Most had been rounded up and corrected. Back in Chicago, the only unresolved case was the one I was supposed to be ignoring. The case that was a distraction. The case I was sent here to get away from. The one case I wasn't allowed to solve. The case that started when my wife hit the concrete a hundred floors below our apartment.

Federal agents found Maggie dead with an implant behind her ear. An implant with a dead man's switch. That meant as soon as she died, all the data, and records, and history on her implant died as well. But dead man's switches weren't legally available to the public. So how did she get one? And even a better question, why did she think she needed one? That was impossible to answer now. I'd settle for just finding out who gave it to her.

The Underground. The answers were in the Underground.

My mind drifted and stirred, abandoning hypothesis just to come back to them like a dog who'd forgotten where he'd buried his bone. A few minutes later and my plate arrived with a cheeseburger, a pickle, and the rest of the plate overflowing with fries. I ignored the dingy glass of warm water and went for the burger with both hands.

The meat was just as juicy and greasy as before. The cheese was melted to just the right consistency to clog arteries. If the case didn't kill me, I knew what would.

"Anything else?" the waitress said.

"Can I ask you something? What do you know about getting an implant in this town?"

"Only what's on the menu, pal. If you want a skeez machine, try the porno shops down in the Lows," she said and turned to leave.

"Wait. I don't know what that means," I admitted.

"Don't know what *what* means? Menu, or porno?"

"Skeez machine. I don't know what that is. I'm asking about implants like they have under the Order," I said.

"You're not from around here, are you?" the waitress asked.

That disguise didn't last long.

"Listen, sugar. I don't know what crap they have under the Order, but I might know someone who knows someone," she said. "But it all cost money."

"Okay," I said.

The waitress set her tray on the table and slipped onto the chair across from me. She eyed me closely, looking for anything that might give me away, that would tell her I wasn't just a tourist who'd wandered in from Chicago or St. Louis. After I held her gaze for a few seconds, she took in a breath. "Okay, dig it. Implants and immersive simulations are contraband in 99 Town. Pornography is banned outside of 99 Town. Lucky for you, certain people who aren't considered to be with the Order or the Keepers have packaged those two things together. Course, I don't have them here. But if you see my friend, James, he can get you your kink."

"What about a dead man's switch?"

"Huh," the waitress said. "Didn't take you for the auto-erotic asphyxiation type."

"What? No. Never mind the skeez machines. Where would someone go to get a dead man's switch installed on an implant? An otherwise *clean* implant?"

Her already conspiratorial eyes became even more distant. "Like I said. Only what's on the menu. That's a special order, and I'm starting to get the feeling you're into a different sort of kink than we can satisfy. Listen, those kinds of things aren't done in 99 Town. Can't be done. We don't have the technology. Strictly import-export, if you know what I mean."

"They can't be done under the Order either. The porno or the dead man's switch," I said.

"Guess you'll have to go to those places in between," the waitress said. "Enjoy your burger."

"Wait," I called after her. "What places in between? There are no places in between. It's either 99 Town or the Order. Right?"

The waitress stopped her retreat and looked back at me. "Maybe I don't know anyone named James. Maybe I don't know anything. Maybe it's best if we never had this conversation. Enjoy your burger."

Chapter Twelve

"So, it works like this," Mike said. "We aren't technically 'stealing' her garbage because that would be a crime. And we're cops. We don't commit crimes. Following so far?"

"It's a leap, but I follow," I said.

We sat in an old pickup truck owned by the city, but not marked in any way. We both wore civilian clothes, badges hidden away. Mike sat behind the wheel, and we watched the street in front of Ruby Arylav's apartment building. We were a block from her front door. The street was dark, and we had the engine and lights off. Another quiet night in 99 Town.

We were lucky, Mike had told me, that this particular apartment building used individual cans for each tenet rather than one big communal dumpster. And twice as lucky because this particular quiet night in 99 Town was also garbage night, so we'd have an entire week's worth of trash to dig through. I was beginning to believe Mike had a very different definition of "luck" than I did.

"According to the law, as soon as you bring your garbage to the curb, it doesn't belong to you anymore. It belongs to the garbage company," Mike said. "And well, we have an arrangement with the garbage company. See, while Miss Ruby Arylav probably doesn't want to lend us her trash, 99 Town Sanitary Incorporated doesn't mind if we borrow some of their trash one bit."

"So we're borrowing her trash," I said.

"No. We're borrowing the garbage company's trash," Mike said.

"Do you guys do this often?" I asked.

"Hey. If it sounds stupid but works, it's not stupid," Mike said. "Listen. Our victim was killed three days ago. Garbage comes once a week. That means whatever she's thrown away since the murder will be in the can she brings to the curb tonight. If she was involved, there's a good chance she's looking to ditch some evidence in that can tonight. We could find bloody clothes, maybe some property of Nancy's, the plug that matches the one lost at the burial site... Once we have enough to bring her in, we'll turn her against Drex, turn Drex against her, and before you know it we'll have a full confession out of both of them."

"And Drex's garbage?"

"We had a warrant for that. Went through the tattoo shop dumpster that morning and tossed Drex's apartment hours after taking him into custody, garbage and all. Didn't find anything," Mike said. "But maybe that's cause he ditched his incriminating evidence with Ruby."

"Okay," I said.

"Okay, what?"

"Okay. I admit it. This isn't a dumb idea after all. This might be genius," I said. "Of course, if they wore implants—"

"Yeah, yeah, yeah. I've heard all I want to hear about your stupid implants," Mike said. "Look. Here she comes. Shush, shush, shush."

We sunk a little lower in our seats.

Ruby shoved open her front door and walked down the short sidewalk to the curb. She swung a garbage bag as she walked and crammed it into the metal can when she reached it. There, next to the curb, illuminated just by the dim flickering streetlight half a block down, she looked up and down the block for a long cool second. She wore a thin shirt that ended above her navel, cut-off jeans that put her long smooth legs on display, and a hard glare that let anyone looking know she was not in the habit of taking shit.

"God damn. Those are some short shorts," Mike said. "Where are those binoculars?"

"Shut up, you idiot," I said.

"What? You aren't seeing what I'm seeing? She's a little hottie," Mike said. "I don't think she's wearing a bra."

"Will you shut it?"

"Oh, let me guess. Under the Order you don't have dicks either," Mike said.

I let it go. He watched Ruby set the lid of the can down on top of the mounded-up garbage. She turned and looked straight at the truck. We sunk a little lower.

"Look at that. She's bending over," Mike said.

And she did, knees locked, butt toward the truck, to pick up a scrap of paper and stuff it into the can. Mike laughed.

"I think she's putting on a little show for us," Mike said.

"Is she..." I squinted. Ruby was itching the side of her head but doing it with her middle finger. "She saw us."

"Who gives a shit? We're still stealing her trash," Mike said.

"I take it back. This is the stupidest thing I've ever been a part of," I said.

"Oh, we're just getting started, Chuck. Wait till we get that garbage back to the station and start digging," Mike said.

"I just bought these clothes," I said, but there was no point. Staying clean in this town was like bringing a towel into a pool to stay dry.

The contents of Ruby's trash can were spread across a maintenance bay in the basement of the Government Center. We didn't spot any large wads of bloody clothes. Just garbage at first glance. Wrappers. Packaging. Half-eaten food. Coffee grounds. Beer cans. A lot of beer cans. A lot of paper. So much paper. Most of it was wet. Soaked in what Mike called, "dumpster juice." All of it stunk.

"Well, you look like a garbage man," Mike said. "I figured this would help complete your overall fashion ensemble. Some rotten food highlights in your hair along with a nice eau de used-rubbers." He walked over to me and slapped my chest with a pair of blue latex gloves. "Here. Use these. Try not to stab yourself with a needle."

"You gotta be bitching me."

"'Shitting.' 'You gotta be shitting me.' And no. I'm not shitting you. And you are fucking terrible at swearing. You need to work on that," Mike said.

The door leading into the maintenance bay swung open, and Captain Reiner strolled in, lazily, hands in his coat pocket, his chief badge pinned to his chest but hanging crooked. He pulled a silver flask from his coat pocket and unscrewed the cap. "Well look at the shitshow we have here. If this ain't the sorriest excuse for a pair of dumpster divers I've ever seen," he said. "Heard you boys were down here, rolling around in the trash like a pair of dogs."

"Woof woof," Mike said.

"You know Lieutenant Andrews, I spent half my day dealing with adjusters who are supposed to be helping me refinance my house, who are instead doing everything within their power to bend me over a barrel. Spent the other half of my day hearing about this Order character and dealing with his ilk. Don't you start giving me a headache too now."

"If I'd make you happy, you're more than welcome to join us, boss," Mike said, holding up and examining a sheet of paper dripping with raw egg.

The chief laughed. "Even I'm smart enough to know to let slumming dogs lie. What about you?" he said to me. "You having fun in 99 Town yet?"

I stood there over the spread of garbage with my pair of tiny rubber gloves. "More fun than I can shake a stick at."

"Well, enjoy it while it lasts. I just got off the phone with the DA. They're charging our suspect as we speak. Should be a trial in a couple of days. He'll be dead and you, Mister Alawode, will be back in Chicago by the weekend. Unless you'd like to stay here in 99 Town, that is."

"I don't know if I can handle that much fun," I said.

"Well, whatever reindeer games he's got you playing down here digging through trash, better make 'em quick. The DA is already putting his prosecution together. If you got any more evidence to add to the pile, get it to me aye-sap," the chief said. He strolled through the middle of the garbage, kicking at beer cans and half-eaten food as he went. He stopped and picked something up out of the middle of the pile. Then he strolled over to me and slapped the thing against my chest. "In the meantime, try not to soil your panties."

He strolled off, laughing with a dry "Har, har, har," as he went.

The garbage he'd slapped on my chest, a used feminine hygiene pad, dropped to the concrete.

"He's a regular Rodney Dangerfield, ain't he," Mike said.

"Let's just do this already," I said.

"Dig in, partner. There's no real rhyme or reason to this. You start on that end, and I'll start on this end. Put all the papers into a separate pile. You never know what evidence might be hidden in a receipt or a fucking electric bill."

On hands and knees, crawling across garbage, the thin latex gloves didn't seem to matter. I sifted through the moist tissues, soiled paper towels, the rotten food, and the random scraps of paper one by one. Piece by disgusting piece, I moved the garbage from one pile into another, checking each for any value. If I was going to do this, I might as well do it well.

Across the pile, Mike was doing the same.

"How can one girl create so much waste?" I said.

"This?" Mike said. "This is nothing. She had a small can. One time we did a garbage pull on a family of six. They had two twin babies and a meth addiction. So many diapers. So many empty bottles of drain cleaner. It was a slurry of baby shit and volatile chemicals."

"Disgusting," I said and tossed aside an old sock covered in coffee grounds and a strand of dental floss.

"You know you guys mine this, right?" Mike said. "Well, robots mine it anyway. Day and night, they're digging through the old garbage dumps, sifting through our trash to recycle and reuse. You people in the Order live off our garbage. Hey, what's that?"

I looked up to Mike, across the spread of filth. He was pointing just to the left of me, at some garbage I'd just gone over. I looked to where he was pointing, but I didn't see anything.

"What?" I asked.

"That! That right…" Mike picked up a beer can and threw it where he was pointing. "…There. Right there by your left knee."

I pushed the beer can aside and saw what he meant. "Shit me."

Mike groaned. "It's 'Fuck me.' How can you possibly be this bad at swearing?"

"You just said, 'Are you shitting me.'"

"Yes. No. They're different, Chuck. Seriously, it's not that hard."

"Well, fuck me, then."

"Why? Is that what I think it is?" Mike said.

I lifted an item out of a puddle of orange fluid. A four-centimeter black disk, with arabesque designs on one side, and a concave rim around the outside. "I think it is," I said.

Mike got up off his hands and knees. He smiled, but I thought maybe I saw something artificial about it. Something practiced in the smile. "I'll get the other one," Mike said.

I climbed up from the putrid mess, tired, and more confused than ever before.

Mike came back, peeling off his latex gloves and throwing them into the pile of garbage. Then he pulled a clear plastic evidence bag from under his arm. I held the earring I'd just found, and Mike compared it to the one inside the bag. The one from the burial site.

"That's a match," I said. "It doesn't make any sense though."

"What do you mean?" Mike said.

"Well, for starters, there's no bloody clothes in this mess. There's no way Drex and Ruby killed Nancy and buried her body without getting blood all over themselves. Think of those crime scene photos."

"They could have done laundry. Might still own the clothes they wore that night, stain-free," Mike said.

"But our timeline is already pressed. Killing Nancy. Getting Ruby to help bury her. Driving up to Cut Rock Park. Burying the body. Coming back to Ruby's to change clothes, then arriving back at Rogue's Tattoos early enough to fake being asleep the whole time. All between four when Nancy was killed and six thirty when you guys kicked in the door to arrest Drex," I said. "Besides, all we really know is that the plugs belonged to Ruby. Think about it. The motive we have for Drex is his romantic interest in Nancy. She rejected him and he becomes angry, embarrassed, ashamed… So he does something drastic. That makes sense so far. But why would Ruby help him?

She's romantic with Sam, the owner of the tattoo shop. She doesn't owe anything to Drex. Wouldn't it make more sense for Ruby and Nancy to be closer than Ruby and Drex?"

"Okay. Sure. That doesn't make sense," Mike said. "But you're taking their statements as gospel. What if it wasn't just Drex and Ruby? What if they didn't have to sneak back into the tattoo shop that morning because they were all involved? Maybe Nancy was ready to run back to Mom and Dad and blow their whole little smuggling operation?"

A convenient solution, I thought but didn't say.

"Or maybe not," Mike said. "Maybe Drex was just a creeper. He creeped after Nancy. Maybe he obsessed over Ruby too. Followed her around. Stole her things. Watched her take out her trash at night. Maybe Ruby was never at the burial site, but Drex had her stolen plug in his pocket when he went there."

"That makes more sense. The simplest answer…"

"…is usually the right answer. I know. But you might be onto something about it being the whole damn crew," Mike said. That idea, that it was the whole crew working together wasn't my idea. It was his. "Anyway about it, I don't want to tip them off just yet. I'm not writing her off, but let's wait to bring her in for questioning."

"So we did all this for nothing," I said, looking at the mess all over the floor. "Fantastic."

"Well, we saved your trash-mining robots some work," Mike said. "Listen. Let's clean this shit up and call it a day. We'll meet back here tomorrow morning and figure this out."

"Tomorrow morning… That's only a few hours from now."

"Let's make it a late morning," Mike said. "We both need some sleep."

"Yeah. Sleep. Listen, Mike," I said. "Is there a landline connection to the Network somewhere in the station?"

"Yeah. Mi casa es su motherfucking casa," Mike said. "There's a connection in the chief's office we use to liaison with the Order. Use that."

Upstairs, the rows and rows of cubicles were empty. The bullpen was dark. The coffee machine was left on, and I navigated back to the chief's desk by referencing the machine's red light. The door to the office was unlocked. I went inside and shut the door behind me. There was a pair of blue standby lights on an FM transmitter, and next to that was a small workstation. Tethered to the desk, as if it were susceptible to theft, was an older model implant. I picked up the clunky oversized implant and examined it for cleanliness. Then I remembered I'd spent the last two hours crawling through garbage and accepted the fact that the jack would probably be cleaner if I just avoided touching it as much as possible. I found my port behind my ear and plugged in.

The implant recognized me immediately. The drone and whine in my left ear were gone. My vision enhanced to see through the darkness. The surface of the workstation lit up with messages waiting for me, my location on a map of 99 Town, items for sale that I might enjoy, the news stream from the outside world... I was a man cold and wet with hypothermia and the Network was a warm dry blanket. It embraced me, and I didn't resist one bit.

The workstation was similar to my office in Chicago and in the autonomous cars. A blank surface for anyone not plugged in, but a vivid and living display to someone who was. An aid to visualize and organize incoming data. This one was smaller, but it would still do the trick. I waved my fingers over the dusty surface and cleared away the less critical information. I mentally called up my directory of contacts, then manipulated the list with my fingers and found my boss, Phom. One thought and I was connected.

"Phom, are you out there?" I said.

"Chuzzy? Is that you?" Phom's voice came across the implant. But no video feed. Not yet. "Give me one second to get to a workstation. I want to talk face to face."

I heard creaking bones and quiet grunts. It was late. Phom was groggy and had been sleeping, I could feel that through the Network. When his face appeared on the desk in front of me, it still came with a big smile.

"Welcome back from the dead, Chuz. How's it feel to be on the grid again?"

"You have no idea," I said. "Listen. Before we get too far into things, I want to request Confidentiality."

The smile flattened. "Chuz. Buddy. Confidentiality, that's not our way," Phom said. "Transparency, accountability, honesty. That's how we do business. I think those 99ers are getting into your head."

"It's not on your end," I said. "It's on mine."

"On your end, huh? Well isn't that interesting? Okay. Let me check the Network," Phom gave in. There was a short pause as Phom shuffled through some menus and settings on his workstation. "Okay Chuz, we're set. It's just you and me. What's up?"

I looked back over my shoulder through the glass windows of the office to the rest of the police station. It was still empty and dark. I turned back to the workstation.

"Phom, I don't trust these people. Not one bit."

"These people who?" Phom said.

"The 99 Town Police. The Keepers. No one in this town," I said. "If you ask me, they don't care who committed the murder. They're just bound and determined to get a conviction and don't care who they sweep up in the dragnet along with way."

Phom chuckled. "Well, I didn't ask you to trust them. I asked you to work with them to close this case. Chuz, the Meades are contacting us every day. Multiple times each day. They're distraught and causing problems with their grief. Busting my chops every chance they get. They shouldn't be behaving the way they are, but they're power players here. They have a lot of sway and not a lot of patience. And even though their behavior is out of line with the Order, I feel for them. They want to know what happened to their only daughter. They need closure. Need to see some 99er die for it."

"Well, we found the body today," I said. "Buried under a bridge under a pile of rocks. Half rotten. Head smashed in."

Phom exhaled. "I hate these 99 Town animals. Might as well be savages for what they allow to go on there. I'm a little older than you, Chuz. Only a little, but I remember what it was like before The Event. Before the Order. Did I ever tell you who I lost during the Event?"

"No. You never did," I said.

"Well, let me tell you. It was everybody. My whole family. My father, he died far away, got infected by whatever pandemic bug that drove all those people insane. But my mother and brother... we were all home together. I was a fifteen-year-old kid back then, not much younger than little Nancy at the time. Anyway, somehow the cops come to believe our neighborhood was infected. None of us were, mind you. If you ask me, somebody paid them off and sicced them on our neighborhood. Or maybe they had their own motivations. Maybe it was because we were poor, or we looked different than them. I don't know, and it doesn't matter. It was a stretch to even call them police in those days. Just gangs of thugs with matching clothes really. At any rate, when they came for us, my mother tried to get me and my brother to behave and go quietly off to the camps. Well, my brother, he was maybe seven years old. He was scared. Didn't want to leave home. Was scared of the bombs, the rioters, the vigilante mobs. And rightfully so! Mom reminded us day in and day out how dangerous it was to go outside. Remember, this was during the war between the Order and the Resistance. It wasn't safe. Nowhere was safe.

"But I'm fifteen. All I know is the cops are in my living room, pulling us out of the house and rounding us up. And my little brother throws a fit, same as any kid would do when he's forced out of his house away from everything warm, familiar, and safe. My mom gets frantic too. She knows what the cops are capable of. I'm trying to be the grown-up one. The mature calming voice. But it's no use. Before I could say much of anything, they shoot my kid brother. Right there, right in front of me.

"Let me tell you, Chuz. You haven't seen pain until you've seen a mother kneeling over the dead body of her youngest son. I watched my kid brother die. Then I watched my mom spend her last few seconds alive wailing out in sorrow, just before they put a bullet through the back of her head too.

"All that because there was no order. No knowledge of who was a good guy, who was a bad guy, who had gone insane, and who was innocent. You're too young. You might remember the chaos, but I remember the suffering. I won't forget it, and I'll do whatever is necessary to ensure it never comes back. The fight to put the world back together after the Event was long and costly. I've done some terrible things, Chuck. Terrible things I wish I could forget. Things even you wouldn't forgive me for. Especially you. But I did them so that we can live in peace under the Order. I'd like to say we snuffed out all that pain and anarchy. But the truth is sometimes, Chuz, doing our job means consolidating the anarchy and chaos rather than trying to solve it. That's the whole philosophy behind 99 Town. The Order knew they could never eliminate all those kinds of people, so we put them in a zoo. That little Meade girl, she fell into the lion's den, and now you're there too. Do I expect you to trust the lions? Not in all the days I have left here on Earth.

"You need to watch your back. Place is like the Wild West, and if you upset the wrong people, if you upset the status quo... Well, I don't want to find myself in 99 Town looking under some bridge for your dead body. What we need from you right now is to contain the chaos, not stir things up. Give the Meades their closure and shut this thing down. Keep yourself safe and keep those 99ers in their place."

I was slow to respond. Phom had never talked about the Event before. Maybe he only did now because we had the secure, confidential line. Maybe would never talk about it again.

"I think I caught one of them planting evidence," I said. "This investigation is a charade. I don't have any reason to believe we're any closer to finding Nancy Meade's killer. We're further from the truth than the day I crossed the border into this place."

"Chuz, buddy. Here's a harsh reality you're gonna have to embrace. The way they do business in 99 Town, we will never know with complete certainty who did it. You can gather all the facts, uncover all the evidence, put the best case together humanly possible, and all it will be at the end of the day is a best guess," Phom said. "With the technologies they're using, there's no real way to know. So we lay out all the evidence, and we make our best guess, and we get a conviction. Some 99er takes a syringe full of lethal chemicals, and we have one less of them to deal with. The Meades will have closure, and you can come back to the real world," Phom said.

"We have a mandate—"

Phom cut me off. "Listen. You asked for confidentiality, so I'm going to give it to you. No one cares. No one cares which 99er beat some other 99er to death with a wrench. All anyone cares about is believing that justice is served. 99 Town cops are dirty, you say? No one cares. They're going to execute the wrong kid? Doesn't matter. The guilty is going to go free? They're all guilty if you ask me. As long as they stay in 99 Town, no one cares. You have your suspect. You have evidence. So finish this and get back home. You make me nervous every day you're out there, Chuz," Phom said.

"Our job is to find the truth," I said, growing more than a little frustrated. "It's what we're sworn to do. Find the truth no matter where it lies."

"Yeah. That's what they teach in the academy, isn't it? Well, that might work under the Order," Phom looked me straight in the eyes. "But, Chuz, in 99 Town there is no such thing as truth."

From behind my back, I sensed a shift in the light. I turned around and saw a lone silhouette standing in the middle of the bullpen.

"We've known each other for a long time, Chuz," Phom said. "I know how stubborn you can be, but listen to me on this one. Okay?"

"Okay. I get it," I said. "Hey, I can't stay on the Network too long. I'll check back in in another day or so."

"Take care of yourself, buddy," Phom said.

"Okay, Phom," I said. "Gotta go."

Reluctantly, I unplugged. The images on the desk disappeared. The hum and squeal came back into my left ear. My vision dimmed. My optic nerves were no longer aided by the implant and the dilation of my pupils was slowed by the artificial stimuli of the lit workstation now gone black. I felt alone, even though I wasn't.

I turned and pushed open the office door. As I walked into the bullpen, my eyes adjusted, and the silhouette shifted into a man wearing a well-tailored suit standing confidently and comfortably amongst the rows of desks and chairs. The light on the left-on coffee machine painted the man in dim shades of red. He reached for a desk lamp and clicked it on.

A Keeper. This man wasn't the same Keeper who'd spoken with me when I'd first come into town, but the two of them could have been fraternal twins. Similar in too many ways to list, even down to that smile that sank teeth into my spine.

"Hello, Mister Alawode," the Keeper said. "We've been watching you. Very interesting techniques you've been using. Very erratic."

"I might say the same of your police force," I said.

The Keeper examined me from head to toe, saw my soiled clothes and the handgun on my belt, and certainly smelled the stink. "That's fair," the Keeper said. When he spoke, he was calm, articulate, patient. This was a man who was used to the world revolving around him. "We wanted to thank you for abiding by 99 Law during your time here. We understand connecting with your people in Chicago is critical to your mission here, and we've allowed you access to your Network while you're in this building. We want to make sure you have all the necessities you need to complete your investigation. I understand you and Detective Andrews are close to completing the case."

"We are," I said, even though I didn't believe we were. "And I appreciate the hospitality."

"And if your investigations uncover any violations of our rule of law here in 99 Town, we expect you to report and prosecute them with your utmost exuberance. You understand, of course?"

Contraband. Drones. Skeez machines. They were more concerned with their backward ways than with murder. I thought about the waitress at the bar. They must have spied on our discussion. Did they have her in custody already? Interrogating her over her friend James? And what about the Rogues?

"I understand," I said. "But I'm not here to police your contraband laws. I'm here to solve a murder."

"Indeed," the Keeper said. "We all have our mandates. And it's best we stay within the confines of those mandates."

Mandate. A word from my own mouth. I'd been asking questions regarding Maggie's expiration, not Nancy's. An investigation outside of my mandate. How much had they overheard? How much had they seen?

"Of course," I said. "You have your job, and I have mine."

"But 99 Law rests above all others here, Mister Alawode. Don't convince yourself that it's your prerogative to re-prioritize your mandate over ours. This is 99 Town. This is how we live, and inevitably how we die. It is our choice."

"Maybe a little too inevitably," I said. "As soon as I have the case complete, I'll be on my way, and you'll be rid of me."

"You have a hotel room you're staying in," the Keeper said. A statement. Not a question. "Get some rest, Mister Alawode. You look like you could use it."

Chapter Thirteen

It was almost dawn by the time I left the Government Center. Cheap Hotel wasn't far from Downtown. A few blocks to the east. I turned my Crown Victoria west. I needed to talk to Sara. Compare notes. There were too many things that had happened since we'd last talked, and if I was being honest with myself, I didn't like how we'd last left each other. I'd been curt. Harsh. Professional. Stupid. I felt that cold distance that seemed to naturally grow between us like ice separating boats on a frozen lake. I needed to be with her.

Outside the bail bond office, night had surrendered to an overcast day. Rather than a vibrant sunrise, there was a slight brightening of the homogenous sky. A merge from starless black to featureless gray that foretold rain. I parked across the street from her place and trotted to her door without checking for traffic.

A step away from the door, an arm's length from the doorknob, I heard something click behind me that stopped me in my tracks.

"Put your hands where I can see them, or I'll blow the back of your head through the front of your face," a voice said.

Cold metal nudged my skull just above the nap of my neck. A gun barrel.

My gun was at my hip. If I drew it, someone would die, and I wasn't sure that someone wouldn't be me. I pulled my hands out of my pockets slow and held them away from my body.

"Not looking for any trouble," I said.

"That doesn't mean you didn't find it," the voice said. The owner of a voice, a tough-sounding woman, grabbed me by the scruff of my collar. "Into the bail bonds office."

Half yanked, half shoved, I was forced into the unlocked door next to the storefront. At several moments during the movement, I felt for opportunities to twist out of her grasp, turn on her, draw my gun, and eliminate the threat. Moves that had become muscle memory after hours upon hours in the simulators. But I hadn't been executed the last time I was dragged somewhere at gunpoint, so I hoped I wouldn't be this time either. Besides, I didn't need another dead body. I needed an ally.

Once inside the unlit office, the gunmen shoved me good and hard. I stumbled forward a few feet and then turned.

The woman looked mean, gnawing on a toothpick and standing near the door with a big thick-barreled revolved she held with both hands. She kept the gun aimed between my eyes as she switched the toothpick from one side of her mouth to the other.

"It's Mickey, right?" I said, hands up and on display.

"And you're the chump from the Order, coming into my neighborhood with a gun on your hip," she said. "Well, you ain't the only one with hardware around here. Time to fess up. What really brought you to 99 Town?"

"A dead girl. A murder you people couldn't solve," I said. This woman wasn't up for playing games, but I wasn't going to give her an inch.

"I don't think I believe you, Mister Alawode," Mickey said.

"That's alright. I haven't believed anyone since I came to this godforsaken fuck hole," I said.

"Oh, you don't like our nice little fuck hole? Maybe I should put a new fuck hole right in the middle of your head. Maybe you'll like that one better," Mickey said. She pulled back on the hammer of the gun and the cylinder rotated.

"He's okay, Mick."

From the darkness of the back of the office, Sara stepped into the dim light of the overcast morning outside, still wearing the brown raincoat and cloche hat.

"It wasn't him," she said as she continued to walk into the light. I tried to see through the dim. Something about her face didn't look the same as it had before. "I know it wasn't Chuck."

"What did they do to you?" I said.

She pulled the cloche hat off and let the dim lamplight fall on her face. Sara's brown skin was beaten black and blue. Her right eye was swollen, and her lip was ripped open down toward her chin. The white of Sara's contused eye was bloodshot, but half hidden by subdermal pockets of blood. Her lip was sutured back together with sticky black thread. Her expression emoted shame, anger, and a will for vengeance.

Mickey lowered the gun. I went to Sara and wrapped her up in my arms, regardless of Mickey and her gun.

"A man. He jumped me. Came up behind me last night and shoved me to the ground. He pressed his body on top of me and forced my head to the pavement. Said I needed to drop the case. Said I should let Drex die in that cell," Sara said.

I turned to Mickey, who was now sitting on the edge of a desk, gun on her lap and eyes out the window into the gray dawn. Thick raindrops were smacking against the sidewalk outside. "You thought I did this to her?"

Mickey threw daggers with her eyes. "Why shouldn't I? This all started after you came to town. Death threats slid under her door. A lone driver following her around town. Not always, but often enough I'd spot someone watching her as she came and went from the apartment. Now this."

I let Sara go and said to Mickey, "Show me. The death threats slid under her door."

Mickey turned on a green-shaded desk lamp and set her revolver on the wood desktop. Opening a drawer and pushing aside another gun, this one an automatic, she pulled out an envelope. She turned it upside down and opened it wide. A dozen slips of paper fluttered down to the desk. I picked up each one separately.

"You can tell the order of delivery by the content," Mickey said. "At first, the messages were fairly benign. 'Drex did it.' 'Why are you helping a murderer?' Normal kind of stuff, considering her line of work. We've gotten that sort before. Then they got more specific."

I read the handwritten messages out loud. "'The Man from the Order lies.' 'Don't trust the Man from the Order.' 'Outsiders lie.'"

Sara came next to me. "It wasn't until I got these notes that I really knew I could trust you."

"When the death threats started coming in, I wasn't so sure," Mick said, her eyes still scanning the cold, damp morning outside.

I read on. "'Drop the case or die like she did.' 'Stop or I'll kill you.' 'The road you're on leads to death.' 'Do you want to know what death tastes like?' Poetic. Why didn't you tell me about these sooner?"

"I needed you focused on Drex and Nancy. These are a distraction," Sara said.

"A distraction," I scoffed. "They're evidence. If Drex didn't kill Nancy, then someone else did, and these threats are the closest thing we have to finding the real killer. Have you taken these to the police? Gotten DNA tests?"

"You want me to trust *them?* For all I know, they're the ones sending them," Sara said. "Besides, Mickey dusted them for prints. They're clean. I'll show you my hand, but the day I run to 99 Cops for help is the day I resign from the bar. But now that I have shown you my hand, there's something else I have to show you. Mickey, do you still have it?"

Mickey pounded the butt of the revolver against the corner of the desk. A hidden drawer popped out from the side. It was small, without a handle, and placed where I wouldn't have guessed a drawer to be. I was learning, in 99 Town secrets were a way of life.

Mickey pulled out a metal key on a fob, not that dissimilar to my key to Cheap Motel. The bail bondswoman tossed it to me, and I caught it. The rubber fob read, "SE Station Secure Storage." The back of the fob had a big number "19" printed on it.

"It goes to a locker in the South East Train Station. The place is a customs checkpoint on the way out of 99 Town. All the big freight comes in and goes out through that station. The Underground smugglers love it because it's a border inside the city limits, and it's easy to toss contraband over the fence," Mickey said. "Can't tell you how many bail jumpers I've picked up there trying to skip town."

"And I found it inside Nancy's Challenger in the impound lot, hidden inside the glove box," Sara said.

"And you didn't tell me about it?" I asked.

"Do you blame me? I couldn't trust you, not then. Besides, you were busy emptying the contents of your digestive tract." Sara said.

"So, what's inside the locker?" I said.

"Well, Chuck. When I open that locker, I'd rather do it surreptitiously. Without any prying eyes. Whoever's after me is probably after whatever is in that locker too," Sara said.

"We need to go, now. You say you're being followed? Then we shake the tail, get to the locker, and open it. Maybe it's nothing. Maybe it's a lot more than nothing," I said.

Mickey nodded her concurrence. "He's right. We need to take charge of this situation. As far as we've been able to tell, there's only been one guy. One tail. Sara, if I take your car, maybe he'll follow me and give you guys a clean break."

"My car is parked across the street. If there is a second tail, they'll make us as soon as we step out the front door," I said.

"Take my car," Mickey said. "Both of ours are parked in the garage around back. They'll never see us go in or out of the cars until we're long gone from here."

"What about you?" I said. "You take Sara's car, then you'll have a maniac following you wherever you go."

"He's a coward," Sara said. "He only had the balls to jump me in the dark when I was alone and off my guard. Besides, Mick's got ways to take care of herself."

Mickey threw me a wink.

"Then what are we waiting for? Time's running out for Drex, and after they execute him our chances of bringing the real killer to justice will be nil," I said. "Time to take back the initiative."

Mickey led us down a hallway toward the back of the building, past janitor closets and bathrooms. As she walked, she hammered a hidden latch in the paneling. A long vertical hidey-hole popped open, and she reached in and retrieved a double barrelled sawed-off shotgun. Sara closed the cubby as she passed by. I followed these two hard-edged women through a door and down a set of stairs into a two-stall garage that opened to the back alley.

Sara's beat-up and rusted-out Ford Taurus sat in one stall. In the other was a gleaming cherry-red sports car with two thick white racing stripes running over the top of the car from bumper to bumper. The thing looked all engine, with the passenger compartment added on as an afterthought. The chrome reflected starbursts and warped mirror images of the garage. I noticed a chrome emblem of a coiled and raised snake on the door.

"Mustang. Shelby Cobra," Sara said.

"Nice ride," I said.

"She's my baby," Mickey said like a mother whispering over her sleeping daughter. "Put a scratch in it, and I'll put you in the grave."

At that, Mickey crammed Sara's cloche hat onto her head. That classic Gatsby look wasn't her style. She was more jeans and work boots than pearls and high heels, but the disguise might work well enough for our needs.

"Nice look," I said.

"Same goes to you," Mickey said. "Lost your Order whites, I see. You almost got me fooled into thinking you're not a dick at a doorknob party."

"Thanks. This car isn't exactly what I'd call inconspicuous either," I said.

"You'll blend in better than you think. If 99 Town has anything going for it, it's our taste for American muscle. Just one of the babies you people threw out with the bathwater. The only real crime here—" Mickey said, as she set the sawed-off shotgun into the passenger seat of Sara's Ford Taurus. "—is putting me behind the wheel of this bucket of bolts."

"You have your baby. I have mine," Sara said. She walked over to Mickey and hugged her. "Be safe. And remember, the engine likes to flood. And the turn indicator doesn't blink on its own, so you have to flick it up and down."

"Eh, I never use those things anyway," Mickey said. "I'll head straight west and take our tail with me. Give me a good two minutes, and then you guys head east, fast. If there is a second tail, you should be able to lose them in the Mustang. Stay safe, kiddos. We'll meet back up where they used to serve those brisket sandwiches I liked. Sara, you know the place."

Mickey got in the Taurus and hit a button to raise the garage door. While we were in the office, the skies had opened up and poured down rain on the city. Being inside the garage was like hiding behind a waterfall. The Taurus sputtered to life, not without some encouragement from the accelerator. Mickey gave us a wave out the window and said, "Tootles."

She backed out and headed west.

Sara and I waited in silence for a half-turn of the clock. The rain fell in sheets outside the garage door. No vehicles passed by.

"So. Mickey," I said. "Can we trust her?"

"More than anyone else in this town. She's had my back long before you came along, and I've had hers," Sara said. "This place, 99 Town, it's fucked. These people here, they're fucked too. But they all have some redeeming qualities. Some of them are worth saving. Some of them... I love them."

I thought about that, and as I did, I pulled the Ruger from my holster and inspected it. I caught Sara watching me as I tried to deduce its levers and switches.

"Do you have one? A weapon?" I asked.

"In this town, I'd be an idiot not to," she said. "Here. Let me show you."

Sara took the gun from me and worked the mechanisms. She pulled back the rack, ejected a round, caught it, and narrated as she unloaded. "Slide lock is right here. Look, you had a round in the chamber and didn't even have the safety on. Mag release is right here. You got a full mag. That's good. Hollow points. That's good too. Just so long as they're not wearing body armor. You got more?"

I shrugged.

"Okay. Well, you'll have to make your shots count then. Watch me now. Magazine goes in the mag well, hit the slide release, and now you have one in the chamber. The safety is here by the trigger. Keep that on till it's bang-bang time. Then, line up the sites... and from there, it's no different than a direct neural inhibitor." She spun the gun around and handed it back.

I put the safety back on, remembering the bullet I fired into the air as I slipped off the dam. "Thanks."

She gestured toward the car. "You want me to drive? Last time I saw you behind the wheel you didn't look too confident."

I eyed the Mustang. "You know something? I think I'm getting the hang of it. Besides, I got to get good at it one of these days."

"If you put a scratch in the paint job, she'll kill you," Sara said.

"She's got nothing to worry about," I said.

"That's not hyperbole. She'll literally murder you, and in this town, and with that car? They'll call it justifiable homicide."

"Don't worry. Not a scratch," I said. "Mickey should have them lured away by now. Let's hit the road."

The interior of the Mustang was immaculate. No dirt, no dust, no cracks in the black polished leather. It squeaked when I got in. That raised snake was embossed into the center of the worn smooth wood steering wheel. The dashboard was woodgrain and featured a series of circular gauges. The "RPM x100" gauge went to 80. The big MPH gauge went to 140. The keys were in the ignition, and when I gave them a twist, the RPM gauge jumped up to 50,000 and then hovered around 15,000. The whole car rumbled underneath and around us. My right hand naturally landed on the gear shifter, the same type of mechanism I'd watched Sammy manipulate down in the tunnels. The long hood with its white racing stripes almost bounced with the living machine under it. I looked past the hood beyond the waterfall rain and to the street.

"It's amazing how much care you people put into your automobiles," I said.

"We all have our vices," Sara said and buckled the lap belt.

I shifted into gear, lifted off the clutch and brake, and depressed the gas. The Mustang leaped out of the garage like a spaceship from a launch bay. I cranked the wheel sharp to the right and peeled off toward the east.

Chapter Fourteen

I drove fast and to the east, just like Mickey had instructed. As the Mustang plunged through the rain and weaved through the slower traffic, I got the feel for the rhythm of the stick shift and the clutch. I stalled it out at a few stop signs, but a couple of blocks from the bail bonds office we found the highway. I steered us up the on-ramp. The transmission was tight and responsive and the shift between third and fourth gear was smooth and satisfying. The needle on the RPM gauge redlined, and the engine roared only momentarily. Then I found the gear and launched the needle of the MPH gauge up into the triple digits.

"Take it easy in this rain," Sara said, putting her hand on mine holding the shifter.

I checked the rearview mirror. "A little further."

I hadn't seen anyone follow us since leaving the garage, but if speed was our ally, the freeway was our home field. I suspected at some point the tail would spot Mickey inside Sara's car and realize he'd be duped. I wanted whatever was in that locker to be in our hands by then.

Around a hundred miles per hour, I felt a slip in traction between the tires and the road. A quick off-kilter slide. I eased off the gas and the wide tires of the Shelby Cobra re-gripped the road.

"Okay. I think we can slow down for a bit," Sara said. "Keep in mind what Nancy's car looked like after it wrecked."

"It wasn't the wreck that killed her," I said.

"It would have, if some asshole had given her enough time," Sara said.

"Have you seen anyone following us?"

"No. They'd have to be certifiable to keep up with us."

"That's the idea," I said.

"Our exit is coming up," Sara said. "See the sign? South East Train Station, one mile ahead."

I slowed the Mustang down and merged, lane by lane, through traffic to the off-ramp. Coming down to street level felt like bringing a plane in for a landing. A few stop signs, which I obeyed having learned from enough honked horns, and we were in front of the South East Train Station.

Here, far from the city center, the turn-of-the-century architecture wasn't hidden under the decades of pragmatic industry and infrastructure. The station was big and built like an old courthouse. The façade was quarried brownstones instead of polished lime, which gave it the aesthetics of a fortress. Eagles and laurel wreaths decorated the stonework arching over the doors and windows. A deep trench full of train tracks ran underneath the building beyond a chain-link fence.

I parked the Mustang, and Sara and I got out. The rain was slowing down, and I noticed the water pooling off the waxed metal body in big viscous drips. The hot engine pinged under the hood. Sara stood across from me and pulled a small snub-nosed revolver from the waist of her pants.

She opened the cylinder, examined the six loaded rounds, flicked the cylinder back closed, and replaced the gun in a holster hidden at the small of her back. "You ready?"

"For anything," I said.

We went through the main entrance to the station under the stone arch. Once inside, the noise of the rain cut off with the closing of a door, and we were left with the echoes of our footsteps against the loud terrazzo floor. Inside was a monument to an era when travel by train was a luxury rather than the last option for the broke and the weird. We took a wide flight of stairs up to Ticketing and Boarding. There we could see the entirety of the station. Vaulted ceiling with ornate molding. Chandeliers with brass fixtures. A hexagonal ticket desk in the center of the concourse. A series of oak doors on either side of the main concourse that led down to the platforms below. A giant two-handed clock mounted high up in the center of the far wall. The station was mostly empty. A janitor. A man behind the ticket counter. A woman with a shopping cart full of god-knew-what. An unseen voice came over the public announcement speakers and informed the human detritus that the six PM arrival from Minneapolis would be delayed by another hour. The big arrival/departure board opposite the giant clock updated.

I spotted a small sign near the corner of the station. "Restrooms. Secure Storage." I tapped Sara's shoulder and nodded in that direction. We hustled over to the doorway leading inside a small room. The walls of the room were made of small foot-by-foot-sized lockers, each numbered and equipped with a coin slot, most cracked open with a key in the lock.

I handed Sara the key and hung by the doorway with my hand on my gun. She took the key and found the number nineteen locker. I watched the station, still not confident we'd shaken the tail.

"Chuck," Sara said over my shoulder. "Is this what I think it is?"

I looked over my shoulder and saw she hadn't taken anything out of the locker yet. I couldn't see inside from where I stood, so I backed up and looked inside. The locker was empty except for one small item placed in the center.

"An implant," I said. "What would Nancy be doing with an implant in 99 Town? There's no network here."

"There's no network, but there could be data stored on it," Sara said.

"Accessible only to those who have a port. To people who've lived under the Order at some point in their lives," I said.

"People like Nancy, or me," Sara said. She picked the implant out of the locker and brushed her hair over her ear, exposing the small port hidden there.

"Wait. Don't," I said and stopped her hand. "There's more data on that implant than you or I can access. Traces of when it's gone on to the Network. Who's plugged into it. Besides, some implants, implants used by... criminals, have a dead man's switch that erases the data if the owner dies or if it's plugged into anyone other than that specific individual. If you plug in, that evidence might be gone forever."

"Okay. So, what do we do? Plugging it back into Nancy won't do us much good now," Sara said.

"Back in Chicago, I have people who can find out everyone who's ever used that device. We can see who uploaded locally stored data. Might even be able to see what data was transferred to and from the implant when it was linked to the Network," I said. "Besides, there're some people in Chicago I'd like to talk to about their daughter."

Sara nodded. "Then there's nothing left for us here. I'll get a hold of Mickey. We'll hole up in a safe house we have while you take the implant to your people in Chicago."

"There she is," Sara said.

The rain had picked up again. Sara spotted her own beat-up Ford Taurus parked under the metal canopy stretching off of the shuttered drive-in restaurant. The barbeque joint, Mickey and Sara's rally point on this side of 99 Town, had been closed for years. Plywood covered the windows and graffiti covered the plywood and walls. A million bits of broken glass crunched under the Mustang's tires as we rolled up next to the Taurus. We pulled into the stall next to Mickey, and the rain stopped beating on the windshield as soon as we were under the canopy. I stopped so my window was next to Mickey's, turned off the headlights, but let the engine run. Without saying anything to me, Sara got out to switch cars.

I got out after her. Before she came around to the passenger door of the Ford, I caught her by the arm. She turned to face me.

"Straight to the safe house," I said. "Hole up and wait till I get back from Chicago. Should be back in a day. Maybe two. Once I'm back, I think we just might have enough to get Drex off and nail the real killer."

"This does have something to do with the Order then," Sara said. "People conspiring with the Underground…"

"We'll find out," I said.

"Chuck," Sara said. I still held her by her arm. Now she put her other hand on my arm. We looked eye to eye. "Don't bring the Order to this town. You might not like it here. You might hate how we do things, but it's our choice. When you come back... I want *you* to come back."

I thought about what she said, but I don't know if I understood her. So I stayed on a train of thought I'd had earlier. "I've suspected ties between the Rogues and the Underground for a while now. But if Nancy was smuggling data across the border, we might be dealing with something bigger than contraband drones and black market booze." I pulled the implant out of my pocket and held it between the two of us. "There are extremists in the Underground who would love to see the Network and the Order come crashing down."

"That would explain why you're here," Sara said. "Would explain why the Order cares about some dead girl in 99 Town."

"I care," I said.

"Do you?"

"Sara, I—" We were talking about two different things. I was talking about the case, the politics between our two worlds, about the legal implications. She was thinking about... What?

She leaned in, and then I understood. We kissed under the drive-in canopy surrounded by the sound of rainfall and a bassline of an idling V8. Without saying anything more, she let me go, went around the Taurus, and got in the passenger seat.

Mickey leaned out of the driver's side window. "You really think some tattooed low-life 99ers are tied up in all that?"

"Well, we'll see what's on the implant and find out," I said. "This little baby, it could change everything. You sure you shook the tail?"

As Sara got into the passenger seat, Mickey tossed her the cloche hat, then turned to me. "He was behind me for a mile or two. One car. One occupant. I got out and pretended to check the tires, just to show them my face and my shotgun. Once he saw who he was following, he lost interest."

"Did you get a make on the car?" I asked.

"A sedan with a dark paint job. Early seventies model. Hard to see in the rain," she said.

"Well, you guys head out first. I'll wait behind and make sure no one comes along after you," I said.

Mickey nodded at that.

From across the car, Sara called to me, "Good luck, Chuck."

"See you when I get back from Chicago," I said.

Mickey rolled up the window and pulled away. I watched them go, then waited for any other car to follow them. No dark sedans with a single occupant came by. No other vehicles at all. The rain had put 99 Town to sleep, the most sensible thing I had seen in town since I'd arrived.

Still, I got back behind the wheel of the Mustang. The closed door muffled the sound of the rain and helped me think. I waited.

Nine times out of ten, if you give criminals enough time, they'll expose themselves.

An implant. I turned the device around in my hand. Small, about the size of a kidney bean with a two-centimeter-long jack protruding from the plastic case.

What the hell was some kid who'd cut herself off from the Order doing with an implant in 99 Town? This wasn't just about a murder. Not anymore. The locker had to be a dead drop, but had Nancy left the implant for someone else, or had someone else left it in the locker for her? Was this data coming from 99 Town, or coming into 99 Town? And how was it a nice little rich girl from Glencoe got herself caught up in all this to begin with?

I caught motion in the Mustang's rearview mirror. A dark sedan pulled up behind me, under the canopy. The single occupant parked just a few feet from my rear bumper, out of the rain. The driver's door opened.

I pocketed the implant, left the Ruger holstered, but flicked off the safety. I stepped out of the Mustang.

It was just us two drivers, standing a full car length apart. The other man, dressed in dark pants and a gray hooded sweatshirt, was big and held a tire iron in his right hand. The hood of the sweatshirt was up, hiding his face. I glanced at the dark green sedan and recognized its distinct grill immediately.

"How'd you get that out of the impound lot?" I said brushing the tail of my flannel aside and putting my hand on the butt of the Ruger.

"The man behind the window had the keys," the driver said. His voice was strange. Something familiar about it but changed or disguised in some way. "He's dead now."

"Did you kill him with the same tire iron you used to kill Nancy?" I said.

"Naw. This one was still in the trunk of the GTO. The cops still have the one I used to pulverize that bitch's head," the man said. "But tire irons make it easier. A few swings and the brains just spill right out. Like a piñata full of soup. The guy at the impound lot? His head came apart just like hers."

"And I suppose you think you're going to use that on me now. See if you can crack open my head too?"

The man laughed a slow laugh. "It's fun seeing a human's thoughts and dreams turn to a puddle on the pavement."

"You're a funny guy," I said.

The man took one step forward. I drew and fired my gun in one quick flash. The bullet struck the man's chest. The gun's report echoed off the wall of the abandoned restaurant and rang in my ears. The gun's kick surprised me, but aside from that, it was no different than a neural inhibitor.

The effect didn't seem any different either.

The man was still standing, tire iron still in his hand. He laughed and sounded like the slipped gears of the Mustang's transmission. He pulled the hood off his head with his free hand and exposed a metallic skeletal face.

An android. In 99 Town.

"You're going to need something with a little more umph than that if you want to hurt me," he said.

What the hell was an android doing in 99 Town? How'd that go unnoticed by the Order? By the Keepers? He'd removed his face to hide his identity. There were militarized androids who never wore faces, but they were bigger, taller, less humanoid things. This android was meant to blend into the human populace, either for service work or assassination, but he wouldn't blend in much without some skin over that metal skull.

"You're a long way from home," I said.

"Same goes for you," the android said. "But don't worry. I'm sure they'll ship your corpse back to Chicago when I'm through with you."

The android charged, tire iron hoisted up to come smashing down. I fired again, the report and recoil just as strong but not as surprising anymore. Sparks exploded off the android's chest. I fired again and made more sparks but didn't slow the killer one bit.

The tire iron came down in a big arc, right for my head. I sidestepped, and the piece of steel whizzed past my shoulder. The android swung his opposite arm and caught me in the temple. A layer of artificial flesh softened the forearm, but the metal bones inside were just as hard and heavy as the tire iron. I saw stars and felt my muscles want to go limp.

I caught myself on the side of the Mustang just in time to see the android raise the tire iron over his head, ready to deliver the killing blow. I dodged, and the android crushed the tool into the roof of the Mustang.

Mickey wasn't going to be happy about that.

As the machine fought to dislodge the wreck from the folded metal roof, I ducked around and came behind him. I slipped an arm around the android's neck and squeezed tight, a hand-to-hand combat move that had become muscle memory. If the android had been human, the chokehold would quickly cut the oxygen off to the brain, and the brain would shut down consciousness. Androids didn't work that way, but at least I could control him, and he couldn't hit me as long as I hung on.

The killer ripped the tire iron out of the Mustang. He growled in frustration and spun to shake me loose. He flailed the tire iron around, trying to swat me off with no luck. I kept my head tucked close to the base of the android's neck, out of reach of the weapon.

But I couldn't hang on forever. This had to end. I dropped the handgun and let it fall to the pavement. Then I waited for another unaimed swing of the tire iron. It came, and I wrapped my arm around the android's forearm. I pulled back, tearing at the robotic joint.

Regardless of nerves or electronic sensors, androids and humans cried the same. I yanked in the exact direction the joint was designed not to bend, and the android dropped the tire iron. I let go of his neck and shoved him away toward the GTO. Then I scooped up the tire iron. If the gun didn't do any damage, I figured I'd dismantle the android the old fashion way. The 99 Town way.

The android stood a few paces off, weaponless but eyeing the gun under my feet. He wasn't laughing now.

"Go for it," I said.

The android did. I swung the tire iron like a baseball ball and pinged the metal tool against the metal skull. The impact shot pain up both my arms and sent the android back away from the gun, but still on his feet. The hit didn't cripple the android, but he didn't appear too eager to receive another.

"You're fun to play with, Chuck," he laughed. "Maybe I'll save crushing your head for another day," the android said. Then he ran for the GTO's open door.

I ran after, but the android was behind the shut door before I could reach him. The android hit the door lock, but I didn't bother going for the handle. One swing of the tire iron shattered the window. The android, undistracted, threw the GTO in reserve and stomped on the gas. The GTO burned the tires as it launched backward, leaving enough smoke for me to choke on.

"You're not getting away that easy, you son of a shit," I said.

I ran back to the Mustang, scooping the Ruger up from the pavement as I went. Once behind the wheel, I tossed the tire iron and the gun in the passenger seat. Heavy on the gas, I cranked hard on the wheel. I roasted the tires and slung the back end of the Mustang in a hundred-and-eighty-degree arc through the parking lot.

Ahead of me, the GTO pulled a similar move, spinning the front of the car around, and showing me its tail lights. That slowed it down enough for me to catch up. Before the android had it out of the parking lot, I slammed the Mustang's front bumper into the GTO's back bumper, smashing out its tail lights.

Mickey wasn't going to be happy about that at all.

The collision launched the GTO forward and brought the Mustang to a stop. The GTO accelerated out into the empty street as I hammered back down on the gas and threw the transmission into second gear. The android cut a hard left into the wrong lane of the divided highway. I followed him turn for turn. The gears ground between second and third. I didn't care.

We cut under an overpass, and the android swung the GTO onto the off-ramp of the highway above us and raced up the cloverleaf incline. I followed, sweeping the Mustang around and going on the off-ramp, only realizing we were going the wrong way on a one-way halfway up. Still, I stayed on the gas and feathered the steering wheel to keep the rubber under the car as we coursed up the ramp. The speedometer climbed to fifty, then sixty miles per hour. The tachometer hit 70,000 RMPs before I shifted into fourth gear. Both the GTO and Cobra held a controlled skid around the off-ramp.

The GTO reached the highway and fishtailed as it came out of the skid. I knew it was coming, but still couldn't stop the Mustang from doing the same. The rainwater covering the road wouldn't let the Mustang's thick tires hold fast. I steered, then counter-steered to keep the car from skidding out.

The android was better than me at this. He righted the GTO's course quicker and put a quarter mile of lead between the two of us. I slammed back on the gas pedal, launching the Shelby Cobra straight into oncoming traffic.

Civilians dodged left and right as the GTO split them down the middle. I glance down from highway to dashboard to watch the speedometer climb up past a hundred. Still not fast enough. I looked back up and saw the GTO was matching my acceleration.

"Come on, you bucket of bolts! Faster!"

Another pair of civilian cars swerved out of the path of the GTO. If this didn't end soon, innocent people were going to wind up dead. I reached over to the passenger seat and snatched up the gun. I felt the Mustang's traction slip underneath me and quickly put both hands back on the wheel.

The numbers on the speedometer ended at 140 MPH. The needle went past the markings and quivered.

The GTO held its quarter-mile lead.

I would need to shoot left-handed out the window. I dared to take my gun hand off the wheel and cranked down the window, eyes fixed on the GTO ahead. The Mustang slipped again, but nothing I couldn't correct with a quick nudge of the wheel. I stuck the gun out of the window and did my best to aim for the GTO.

I fired a shot but couldn't tell where the bullet struck, if it struck anything at all. I needed to aim. Needed to get my head out of the window and into the rain. I adjusted my position and leaned outside. The tires slipped again. I caught it and kept the Mustang charging forward. Then I got my eye behind the gun sights. If I could hit a tire, I could bring this chase to an end without any dead civilians. I aimed.

The Mustang slipped again, and this time I couldn't catch it. I cranked the wheel to correct the skid, but it had no effect. The tail end slid out and the whole car teased with rolling. Lucky for me, the inertia took over and sent it spinning like a top instead. I was pulled outward, further through the window by the centripetal force. With each rotation, I saw three hundred and sixty degrees and caught glimpses of the GTO cruising further and further away.

When I came to a stop, the Mustang was pointed in the opposite direction. Civilian traffic braked, honked, and swerved to either side. I ignored them. What were a dozen more honks and hand gestures? I stepped out and aimed the Ruger in the direction of the GTO, but my equilibrium was shot, and the GTO was long gone, swallowed up by the rain and gray sky. I was tempted to fire a few shots anyway, just to do something, but that would only endanger more civilians.

I slammed my fist against the roof of the Mustang and called out, "Fuck!" No one heard me.

Chapter Fifteen

I parked the Mustang outside of the Customs Station, killed the engine, and got out. I touched the cleavage where the tire iron had hit the roof. The android had done that. Mickey couldn't blame me for that ding. Now the front bumper I'd mangled into the GTO?

"Damn," I swore when I saw it for myself.

Nancy's killer was still on the loose, and it was an android who could pose as nearly any human in 99 Town. He'd been smart to remove his humanoid face before confronting me. His voice was disguised. His clothes were plain. Anonymous. But the real killer wasn't the android. The real killer was whoever sent it.

It had to be someone from outside of 99 Town. Or someone inside 99 Town with the ability to bring contraband in from the outside. The police, the Rogues, the Order… There was still a question of motive. The one basic question I still couldn't answer: Who benefited the most from Nancy being dead?

The Rogues were certainly running a black market, which suggested that Nancy could have been a target of the Keepers or the Order. The fact that an android was involved suggested the Order, but that was ridiculous. The Order had other ways of dealing with criminals. I turned my back to the car and leaned against it. The rain had slowed to a drizzle, and the droplets felt good against my bruised face.

If I couldn't trust the Order, who could I trust?

Before I crossed the border and fell under the oversight of the Order, there was one more thing I needed to do. I dug the cell phone from my pocket and punched in Sara's number.

"Chuck?" Sara said, quiet and distorted through the old technology.

"I'm at the border," I said. "Did you guys make it to—"

"We made it," she said, cutting me off. "I'll be safe here."

"And Mickey?"

"She had some prior work commitments. Duty calls and all that," Sara said.

"There's an android in 99 Town. Tried to take me out after you guys left. No doubt it was the lone driver following you through town," I said. "Tell Mickey to be careful."

"An android, huh? It didn't hurt the Mustang, did it?"

I smirked and touched the swelling lump on my cheek where the android's forearm had done its best to rearrange my face. "Tell Mickey her car is fine. The Customs Agents will keep an eye on it here. Stay low until I get back, okay?"

"Don't be gone long," Sara said. "The case against Drex is moving forward. The DA is saying Drex's DNA was all over Nancy's body. Hair and skin samples. In this town, that's enough to convict. Unless we have a preponderance of evidence that your android killed Nancy, they'll hang him out to dry and close the book on it. They wanted to start the trail today. I talked the judge into granting a one-day recess. But if I'm not in court by tomorrow, they'll convict."

"I can testify," I said. "That's gotta be worth something."

"Yeah, worth about the same as the shit I can scrape off the bottom of my shoe," Sara said. "Find out what's on the implant. Then get your ass back to 99 Town."

"I still have the implant. If it has half the evidence I hope is on it, I'll have enough to track down the android and whoever sent it. It's going to take some time for the boys in the tech department to get all the data we need. In the meantime, I got some people in Chicago I'd like to have a word with," I said. "I'll be back as soon as I can. Once I have the information I need I'll meet you at the safe house and get you to court."

"Chuck, be safe there. I don't like you being there," she said.

I chuckled. "You're trapped in a town run by anarchists, full of maniacs, dirty cops, and a killer robot and you're worried about me?"

"That doesn't make me feel any better, Chuck," she said. "Just take precautions. Don't forget what you learned out here. Come back to me."

"I will. I need to... Need to finish what we started."

"Looking forward to it. Stay safe, Chuck," Sara said.

"Yeah, you too," I said. We hung up and I walked into the Customs Station.

Inside, I went through the same process that got me into 99 Town, but in the opposite direction. I made no conversation with the agents but stored the Ruger and cell phone on the 99 Town side of the border. They'd secure them in a locker until I came back. I stepped through the various scanners and sensors as I crossed over, just for the agents on the Order side to pat me down once I was through. Then I was presented with a small bin.

In it was my own implant. I touched the implant from the locker in my pocket, then picked up my own from the bin.

"Welcome back to reality, Mister Alawode," one of the Order agents said to me.

I nodded to the man and walked outside with my implant still in my hand. The sun was poking out from behind the rain clouds. The surrounding cornfields were greener and taller than they'd been on the 99 Town side. I saw one of the big agro-bots rolling over the fields, spreading fertilizer and pesticides as needed. Several autonomous cars were parked around the cul-de-sac in front of me. Each autocar was white, identical, and publicly owned. Anyone of them would take me back to Chicago.

I picked one, finding each as good as the next, no supercharged V8s or Hollywood nicknames like "Cobra" or "The Judge" here. I approached it, and the door didn't open to greet me. Unplugged, the car door didn't detect me. Even if it had and I could get in, I couldn't tell the car where to drive or pay for the ride. Sure, the Network still knew I was here and could still neurally inhibit me using my port, but without the implant, I couldn't call or communicate with anyone. Without that tiny device, it was like I didn't exist. Still, I hesitated.

The car sat dumbly, door shut, engine off. It didn't make sense for me to wait any longer. I reached behind my ear and inserted the implant into my port. The hum and whine in my left ear immediately went silent. My vision sharpened. The dull throb radiating from my tattooed shoulder washed away. The car in front of me opened its door. Lights inside the car popped on, welcoming me into the Order's embrace. I climbed inside.

"Welcome back, Mister Alawode," the Network said in her sweet sexy voice.

"Chicago Federal Building," I said.

"Right away, sir," the Network said.

As I sat down, the workstation in front of me came to life and displayed the day's headlines. News. Politics. Weather. Sports. Social Engagements. Some skim details of my case that had escaped the borders of 99 Town. Nothing I didn't already know more about than the Network, which was a strange change of pace.

Outside, the autocar was already headed toward Chicago.

The Network inquired which of my memories were For Official Order Business Only and which could be released to the public. I annotated all of them as FOOBO, and the implant went to work harvesting my memories and uploading them to the digital case files. The license plate numbers of his Crown Victoria, Nancy's Challenger, Mickey's Mustang, and the GTO. Scanned images of the sheets and sheets of the paper case files that I never had time to read. Facial recognition updates for all the Rogues, for the 99 Town cops, for Sara and Mickey. It came to the exposed steel face of the android, paused, labeled the memory an error, and passed it by.

"Figures," I said. "Network, I need some sleep."

The desk went blank. The windows turned opaque. The interior lights dimmed to a soft glow that mimicked moonlight. My chair reclined and adjusted to any discomfort I felt in my bones. It purged the adrenaline from my veins and boosted my dopamine and gamma-aminobutyric acid.

When was the last time I'd slept? How long since I'd slept well? What sleep I managed in 99 Town was restless, painful, and disturbed by alcohol and worries. No bed in 99 Town could ever surpass the quality of the cocoon the autocar had become. Still, as the neurotransmitter cocktail soothed my mind and body, I found my memories retreating to the back bedroom in Sara's apartment. The Network, sensing those memories as a source of comfort in its own faulty way, filled my olfactory cortex with the smells of coffee and bacon.

I thought of correcting it, of informing the Network that those smells were associated with waking up, and not going to sleep, but I was out before I could send the thought.

My implant roused me when the autocar reached the Chicago Federal Building with a gentle mixture of serotonin and visual stimuli. As restful as it was, the nap from the border to Chicago was a tease. I couldn't shake the weariness from my eyes. I stepped out of the car and looked around downtown Chicago, seeing it again for the first time. Before 99 Town, I'd never had anything to contrast it against. Now, the familiar starch-white façades and the pleasant ambient music were strange. The clean sidewalks shaded with leafy green trees and flowering vines climbing up the lower levels of the towers left me feeling claustrophobic. The buildings rising up to the sky were pale looming sentinels. Between each pinnacle, Order hovercrafts ferried the rich and governmental elite from one tower to the next. These crafts were autonomous, identical, and shared amongst the Order's in-crowd. A step up the caste ladder from the autocars, but otherwise the same. Looking back down to street level, I noticed there was no exposed infrastructure like the power cables or greased train tracks of 99 Town. The passing autocars rolled by in silence, not like point-blank thunderclouds of what Mickey had called "American muscle." Instead of all the cacophony of 99 Town, there was a melody in C Major playing from hidden speakers, or maybe just piped into my head through the implant. It was impossible to distinguish between virtual and analog stimuli without unplugging. And unplugging, of course, was illegal, instantly detectable, and quickly mitigated by indirect neural inhibition.

I'd never seen this city without the artificial stimuli pumped into my brain. No one had. Without the implant, maybe it didn't look and sound so different from 99 Town. After all, what was cheaper? A fresh coat of paint or a message telling my brain everything had a fresh coat of paint?

Not that any of that mattered. I crossed the plaza, moving through a smattering of happy peaceful people. The doors of the Chicago Federal Building were just a few steps ahead.

This was all part of the system. The system was what kept us safe and alive. The system was all that really mattered. Right? It was a nagging thought I threw away. I entered the building, found the elevator, and sent a thought to the Network to take me to the department.

Seconds later, the doors opened, and I stepped into the Anomaly Investigation Department. Rows of workstations and agents toiled away. If I imagined hard enough and remembered well enough, I could find the similarities between here and the 99 Town police station. Replace the Order whites for blue uniforms, threadbare suits, and leather jackets. Add a cloud of cigarette smoke. Change the three-hundred-and-sixty-degree view of a peaceful city for dull-painted dungeon walls. Swap the digital display workstations with stacks and stacks of paper. Sam function; different aesthetics.

"Chuz!" Phom called to me from across the bustle of agents going through file after digital file at their desks. He cut through the crowd, arms open. "How's it going, buddy? You look terrible! What's with those clothes?"

"Sorry. I didn't have time to change. And things in 99 Town... the chaos there is hard to describe," I said. "I have some physical evidence I need the guys in tech to take a look at."

"Physical evidence?" Phom said. He came along next to me, and as we walked side by side, he rested a hand on my shoulder. "Chuz, I saw the uploads to the case files. The district attorney is ready to go to trial tomorrow. They have one on murder and another on conspiracy. They have all the evidence they need to make this a very short trial. What else do you need?"

For the briefest moment, I thought about keeping what I'd found to myself. But that wasn't the Order way and wouldn't work here anyway. As soon as I thought about it, he already knew I had it.

I pulled the implant from my pocket. "I found this in a storage locker in 99 Town, and the key to that locker was found in the victim's car. Now, what would some runaway kid hiding out in 99 Town do with an implant? How are we supposed to close a case with a question as big as this unanswered?"

"Probably a skeez machine. If little Miss Meade was making dirty simulations for extra cash, so what? Or maybe she was a smuggler for the Underground. And if so? I say good riddance. No need to tell her parents about any of this, of course. She's expired, and sometimes dead things are best left that way," Phom said.

"Sure. It could be that. But…" I thought of telling him about the android and stopped myself. Sure, my own implant made my thoughts as audible as spoken words, but sometimes unspoken things were best left silent. "If you don't mind, boss, I'd like to find out what's on here before they convict. You said yourself the Meades want to know if the Keepers are convicting the right killer. For closure."

I felt Phom's emotions roll from reassurance for me to disgust for the Meades. "They're 'in mourning.' It's absurd. If they were strong, strong like you've been strong, we wouldn't be having these issues," Phom said. "Hey, you remember our conversation, right? When we talked the other night?"

"I know, boss. It's just that this might show us that some of that chaos is spilling out of 99 Town," I said.

Phom sighed and shook his head for a second or two. "Fine. Have the boys in tech give it a look. Who knows? Maybe you can get another conviction out of it. If it leads to more of the Underground menace behind bars, I'm all for it."

"Thanks, boss," I said and moved deeper into the buzz of researching agents.

In the center of the department, there was a spherical nest elevated above the rest of the workstations and offices. I positioned myself underneath its center and made my request through the Network for entrance.

"Special Agent Chuck Alawode with physical evidence of an anomaly in 99 Town."

The boys in tech must have had a quick debate before granting me entrance. With their shared mind, the decision came quickly. I rose up off the floor and into a hole in the bottom of the nest. As soon as I was through, the hole closed shut behind me, and I was in the hive.

The Order recruited early adapters for their tech department. The people who worked inside the hive were eager to embrace the latest development and find the flaws not just in the tech that was, but also in the tech that was to be. There were eight of them inside the hive, all sitting in chairs mounted on the spherical wall of the hive. They faced in, from all angles and directions. There was zero gravity in the Sharedmind nest. Their eyes peered over the workstations mounted in front of them.

"Chuz, my man!"

"Back from the dead—"

"—and in the land of the living once again," three of them said in concert.

They were called the tech boys, which wasn't to say they were all male or even majority male. Some were men, some women, some agendered, and at least one of them an android. But really, they were one. Their brains were linked together to take advantage of every bit of mental processing power. When one tech boy rested, others would put her otherwise dormant mind to work on another's problem. The result was a sum larger than the equal of its parts. This was the Sharedmind.

"You've been off the grid, buddy."

"We've been watching you since you plugged back in at the Customs Station."

"Glad to have you back, man."

"It's good to be back," I said. "I have something I think you might like to see."

I took the implant out of my pocket and handed it to the nearest tech boy. She took it, and all of them examined it through her eyes. This tech boy holding the implant was shaved bald and had rows of multiple ports to access multiple implants at the same time. These were above her ear, which I had heard gave them a more direct route to the hippocampus and resulted in higher digital fidelity. Right now, three of her eight ports were filled with implants.

In addition to network examination, the tech boys ensconced themselves in hardware. Between the tightly packed chairs covering all surfaces of the interior of the sphere were wires, processors, breadboards, and other dismantled pieces of tech. The implant from 99 Town was passed amongst the tech boys, and for a moment, I worried it would be lost in the clutter.

"I found that in 99 Town. Got a hunch it belonged to someone in the Underground. I didn't plug into it myself. I think it might have a dead man's switch," I said.

"An implant in 99 Town," the one in front of me said.

"That's kind of like bringing a canoe paddle to the desert, isn't it?" another said behind me.

"Possible dead man's switch, huh?"

I tried to follow the voices and the path of the implant as they shifted from tech boy to tech boy. The implant moved with the blinding speed of a card in a deck shuffled by a magician. The speaker's voice jumped and skipped, sometimes mid-sentence, all about the sphere just as quickly and randomly. It was difficult to follow one. Tracking both was impossible.

"Your wife's implant had a dead man's switch, didn't it?" the android tech boy asked. I could only tell it was an android because it had removed its face. Otherwise, it behaved just as energetically as its compatriots. I trusted it, trusted all the tech boys, regardless of the events of the last few days. This was how the Order was intended to operate. Truth. Transparency. A shared understanding of the world.

"We suppose a journalist might have reasons for doing that," another tech boy said. "Investigative journalism. Privileged access to mass-posting to the Network and all."

"We didn't get a chance to examine hers before its destruction. Don't get a chance to examine most set to self-destruct upon the expiration of the owner, of course."

"This one is an older model. Maybe five years since production."

"Looks like it's been well-worn for its time."

"Sorry about your wife, by the way. We couldn't imagine losing one of our own to expiration."

"Although, we are closer than any two non-linked humans could ever be. We are one."

"Still, it must be hard."

I decided to speak to just one of the tech boys instead of trying to follow the voices. My eyes met with the one directly above me. If I thought of them as one, as they thought of themselves as one, it might be easier.

"I've learned to adapt without her." Did they detect my words as a lie? I said the words more robotically than I'd intended.

"The circumstances of her expiration are being investigated by another agent. I'm sure they'll resolve the source of the anomaly," I realized, shortly after saying the words that I was fishing. Hoping one of the tech boys knew more than I did and would spill information.

"Yes, we are working on something involving her anomaly."

"Confidential work of course."

"We're certain the anomaly will be resolved," one of them said.

"There are ways around dead man switches. We'll need to crack open the casing and poke around a bit."

"It will take a few hours. Do you need this back in one piece?"

"No," I said. "Do what you have to. Say, I have business in town. When you have the data compiled, can you post it encrypted to the Network?"

"Certainly," two of them said simultaneously.

"A busy man is always on the move."

"Going back to 99 Town soon?"

"After some business," I said.

"Looks to us like you might be going native."

"Love the outfit," one of them smiled.

"Yeah," I laughed. "When in Rome…"

"You've driven one of their cars. We're curious."

"We've heard they are—"

"Dangerous," I said. "Insanely dangerous contraptions."

"We had heard they're…"

"Exhilarating!"

The voices of the tech boys came at me from all directions, like surround-sound audio. There was no differing one voice from the next.

"The concept of an internal combustion engine."

"Thousands of explosions each second, encased in the most vital part of the vehicle."

"The idea of unguided propulsion down an asphalt lane."

"The course of the vehicle is only determined by its master."

"A human master."

"We're better off without," I lied. It was a lie, I only realized after the words left my mouth, because the ride in the Mustang thrilled me like nothing before. It was a lie because I was as enthralled by these cars as the tech boys were. Maybe "lie" wasn't the right word though. I knew, cognitively, that I was telling the truth. But some lower-brain part of me didn't believe the higher-brain part that had said the words. "Well, I know you have work to do. I'll leave you to it."

"We'll see you, Chuz."

"When this is all over, come tell us all about 99 Town."

"We're very curious how those people can live the way they do."

"One of the great mysteries of the ages," I said. "See you guys."

Chapter Sixteen

Glencoe was a short ride from downtown, and I had too much to study before I arrived. Nevertheless, the autocar would be efficient and timely and deliver me to the Meade's residence in a few short minutes.

Towering white skyscrapers gave way to shining sprawls of commercial malls and outlets. Further along the freeway, the autocar brought me into the wooded and affluent neighborhoods along the shore of Lake Michigan north of Chicago. The trees were lush and green and hung their canopies over residential streets. The houses were set back away from the road, at the end of driveways curtained by more trees and artesian brick walls. The houses were varied, but all rich with style. One block featured American Gothic and Queen Anne peaks, gables, and turrets. The next was all Frank Lloyd Wright-inspired Usonian flat roofs and staggered floors. Then came the Post-Future domed roofs and cylindrical walls. I didn't care for the art of it. I always felt myself drawn to paintings as an art form, like what the Keepers had in their penthouse. This, well all I knew about this was that it all added up to money, regardless of the era or architect.

"Four five one Heinlein Way," I repeated the address of the Meade residence. I watched the house numbers as the autocar maintained the slow legal speed. It was an unnecessary habit I'd quickly developed during my time in 99 Town, reading address numbers and counting cross streets. A task better left to computers.

Still, this way I knew when Four Five One Heinlein Way was coming close.

I wanted to read up on the Meades before I arrived. The workstation inside the autocar was lit up with pages and pages of data. It was only a matter of what I could consume during the short trip. I forced myself away from the ornate houses and meticulous landscaping to the data in front of me.

"Howard and Sonja. He's an investor. Business mogul. Owns some intellectual properties and a few golf courses," I read their occupations from the Network's files. "And she... 'Sonja Meade does as she pleases.' Really? That can't be a job."

The autocar slowed at the end of a gated driveway and parked.

"Four five one Heinlein Way," I said.

So much for research. I moved toward the car door, and it opened. I got out and walked up the brick-paved driveway past two stone lions who, in my humble opinion, were fuck for guards. Before I'd left the office, I'd drawn a new uniform, shaved, cleaned myself up, and dressed in Order whites. I wasn't in 99 Town anymore, and nothing but meticulous professionalism would do for this trip out to see the Meades.

Looking up at the residence, I saw The Meade's home was more Falling Waters than Seven Gables. A small brook bubbled through the yard and under the sidewalk leading to the front door. I approached, and when I came to the front door I said, "Federal Agent Chuz Alawode here to see Mister Howard Meade and Miss Sonja Meade."

The door opened. An android, indistinguishable from a human in all but its Network signature preparedness, and manners, greeted me on the other side of the threshold.

"Welcome to our home, Mister Alawode," the android said. This one was male and dressed as a professional housekeeper. "The gentleman and lady of the home will meet you shortly in the den. Can I get you any refreshments while you wait?"

"Water," I said. There would be no coffee or beer here. Some of Sara's coffee, I could use that about now. The short nap I had between the border and the office wasn't nearly enough to recharge my batteries. By now I was operating on sheer determination.

"This way, please," the android ushered me inside.

The den was flanked by two walls of bookshelves. The books were old, hardbound, and most likely unread. There were high-backed leather chairs around the room and an old mahogany table that no doubt hid a workstation in its glossy finish. I ignored the chairs and remained on my feet. A large picture window looked out onto the front lawn. The sun was coming out through the rain clouds off to the west as if even the weather obeyed the demands of the wealthy. I could have done without the sunshine. Seemed inappropriate for the visit.

The android turned to fetch his master.

"Hey," I called to him.

The android gracefully turned around with a perfectly polite smile painted on his face.

"What about you?" I asked. "You ever been to 99 Town?"

"Of course not, sir. My home is here with the Meades," he said and then turned away and left.

"Yeah, I bet Nancy said that too," I said.

Back under the Order and tied to the Network, I could locate both Howard and Sonja in the house. They were both upstairs in a room across the large house. I could sense their emotions too. Miss Meade seemed numb and distant, a feeling Chuck related to. Mister Meade was a ball of fiery-red anger. When the android reached them, Miss Meade acquiesced to meet their guest and began making her way to the den. Mister Meade remained in the upstairs bedroom, refusing to move. That was fine. He didn't seem open to answering any questions anyway.

While I waited, I took the time to look around the room. Most of the books were old fiction works with titles I had never heard of, which I thought was odd. These were old collector's pieces that seemed important enough to be called "classics," but who'd ever heard of Kurt Vonnegut, Ray Bradbury, Albert Camus, or Hunter S. Thompson?

Between rows of books, digital displays cycled through family pictures. Howard. Sonja. Nancy. Sometimes pairs of them, sometimes all three huddled together. A disproportionate amount was of Nancy at various stages in her life. In each picture, she looked clean, happy, and healthy. She didn't have the pierced nose yet in any of the pictures, or the wear in her eyes that 99 Town had given her. This was Nancy's previous life chronicled in images. First, her young parents dressed in the fashion of the day, held her as a baby. Then she stood on unsure legs, making messes as a smiling toddler. By seven years of age, her freckles were so thick they nearly covered her entire face. Starting around ten, there were pictures of her wearing a basketball uniform and posing with teammates and trophies. There were some pictures, I guessed they were at formal family events, where teenage Nancy wore a dress, make-up, and styled hair. The beautiful and perfect daughter of two Chicago elites. In later images, she was still bright and youthful, freckles faded, without the piercings but with a growing affinity for black clothes and counter-culture stylings. And then nothing beyond those.

Against my will, the Network brought up two more images from my memory: the 99 Town ID photo of Nancy looking tired and frazzled, and my memory of her mangled face we found beneath a pile of rocks under a 99 Town bridge. The waxy skin. The eyes filmed over with yellow rot. The misshapen skull and matted, patchy, thin hair. The fingers drawn up like claws.

That was what 99 Town did to people. That was the product of their machine.

"We have permits for those books," a woman's voice said from behind me.

"Huh?" I turned and saw Misses Meade, tall and thin in both frame and face, poised like a woman who paid attention to how she carried herself. Long red hair spilled over one shoulder. Every inch of her was elegant. An image of the woman Nancy would have grown up to be, the polar opposite of the haggard waitress who served me lunch. She was holding two glasses of water. I was aware of her coming toward the den as it was reported to my implant via the Network but seeing her still surprised me.

"The books. They restricted, but Howard has all the permits in order," Misses Meade told me.

"I'm not here about books," I said, then gestured to one of the photo frames as it cycled through pictures of her daughter. "She was beautiful."

"She was," Miss Meade said and put both glasses of water down on the end table between two of the chairs. She extended a hand to me. "Sonya Meade. Call me Sonya."

"Chuck," I said and shook her hand. "Nancy played basketball?"

"Her name was Navatny. That was the name Howard and I gave her, and that's what she'll be called. But yes, she played ever since she could bounce a ball," Sonya said, angry and firm. Then she turned to the pictures, and her voice softened. "She loved to play. By the time she was a teenager, she was competing nationally. Every weeknight she practiced with her team. Every weekend she traveled overnights for tournaments and games. She wasn't the best amongst her peers, but she had promise. It was a shame she gave it up."

I nodded. "I'm sorry to impose, but I've been assigned to investigate the anomaly of your daughter's expiration. I have—"

"The anomaly?" Sonya interrupted. "Expiration? Sir, you're using Order terms to describe what those barbarians did to my only daughter. Let's state it plainly. They murdered her in the street. She's dead."

"Yes. I'm afraid that's true," I said. She wanted to play tough. As if she believed she had any idea what it was like in that town. I let her keep her fantasy. "I know it's an insufficient consolation, but I'm doing everything I can to find out who did it and bring them to justice."

Sonya sat in one of the chairs, leaned back, and crossed her legs. "I read the guilty is already in custody and will go to trial tomorrow morning. Executed by lethal injection immediately after. Isn't the investigation over? What's left for you to do but step aside and let their brutal legal system do the one thing it seems to be good at? Are you telling me, Mister Alawode, that they're going to execute the wrong 99er?"

"There may have been others involved," I said, sidestepping. The next part might be difficult, but it was necessary. "Sonya, did your daughter ever display any sympathies for the Underground?"

"The Underground? My daughter?" Sonya said. "Are you suggesting Navatny had something to do with those subterranean vermin? That treasonous bands of rebels? Sir, my husband Howard

171

fought in the war against the Resistance. He lost friends in the war. Was nearly killed himself while eradicating their ilk decades ago. Do you really think we would raise our daughter to betray the Order and run with traitors like the Underground? All we have left of Navatny is her honor and our memories, and you are testing my hospitality."

I felt her hate tunneling into me through the Network.

"I apologize, but your daughter is expired, and I've been commissioned to discover the circumstance," I said. I paused, noticing an alert from my implant, an urgent message sent from 99 Town. I ignored it for now and continued with Miss Meade. "There is a strong black market of goods coming in and out of 99 Town, and it seems your daughter had ties. Now, if it were just the usual contraband, alcohol leaving 99 Town or tech coming into 99 Town, I would have let it be and not asked questions. However—"

"However, that's not the case. Is it?" Sonya said.

"She had an implant in 99 Town," I said. "Now there are only two reasons I can think of as to why she had an implant. Either she was leaving 99 Town to use it and communicate with those she still knew under the Order, or she was smuggling data. Propaganda. Misinformation. The sort of lies the Underground deals in. Did she ever contact you or Mister Meade via the Network after she left for 99 Town?"

"No," Sonya said. "Never. She left us and never looked back. We heard nothing from her or about her until your agency told us she was dead."

There was a third option. That the implant was a skeez machine. Contraband and disturbing, but not as troubling as treason. "Miss Meade, there is one other possibility. The 99 Town black market also deals in pornography. Did Navatny ever display any deviant sexual proclivities?"

"How dare you," Sonya said. Her lips grew tight, and her eyes welled up.

"I'm sorry. I had to ask," I said. The notification of the message flashed again in my peripheral. "But if she wasn't using the implant to communicate or smuggle those types of… entertainments, then chances are that implant is full of Underground propaganda, and there's much more to investigate."

"Sir, this whole trip into 99 Town was a game for her. It was a mistake of a stubborn youth done to upset Howard and I," Sonya said. "It was not an act of deviant sexuality or political terrorism. For you to suggest those things…"

"If you have information, ma'am, you are compelled by the Order to divulge," I said. "Trust me, my animosity toward the Underground is just as zealous as yours. She was a victim of the disorder they sow. There's nothing we can do to bring Nancy… to bring Navatny back. But we can bring everyone who contributed to her expiration to justice."

I watched Sonya's eyes and read her emotions via the Network, but her anger masked any tell-tale signs of deception.

"You've insulted my husband and I. And the memory of our daughter. I think I've answered all the questions I care to."

"Does Mister Meade feel the same way?" I said, checking the Network and seeing Howard still hadn't left the upstairs bedroom.

"Mister Meade is in mourning, and it's time you should go."

"Mourning. You've lived under the Order since its inception, Miss Meade. Where did you come up with a notion as archaic as mourning?" I said. "It's not our way."

"Mister Alawode, I don't need to tell you again."

"Oh, no?" I said, wanting to push, wanting to grab her by the scuff of her pretty shirt and bounce her off the wall of her fancy books till she talked. That's how I would have done it in 99 Town. Here? I caught motion out of the corner of his eye. The Meade's android had returned. Its pleasant smile was a perversion of the intent that lay underneath, and I knew from experience now how tough these things were in a fight. One bout with an android was enough for one day, and I wasn't getting anything more out of Sonya anyway. "Don't trouble yourself. I'll show my way out."

Miss Meade held her tongue as I left the den, moved past the android, and stepped out the front door. It wasn't until I was strolling down the brick driveway to the autocar that she followed me to the front door and called after.

"Find the murderer who killed my daughter! That's your only job, Mister Alawode! That's your only job! Give me justice for my daughter!"

I ignored her. The autocar opened up, and I slipped inside. The urgent notification flashed again as the door sealed me inside and sealed out Miss Meade's cries.

"Display message," I said, and the workstation lit up in front of me.

An email, from Sara Cohen. Uploaded, sent, and then downloaded onto the Network, in accordance with 99 Town laws. Nothing streamed. Nothing in real-time. I would have rather seen her face and heard her voice, but this was business. I read the email.

"One of the Rogues just dropped a new witness statement. I attached the audio file. The Keepers are going to nail Drex to the wall. Trial is tomorrow. Hurry back. I'm safe."

Less than twenty-four hours and Drex was as good as dead. And we still had the wrong guy.

Chapter Seventeen

If the truth had any chance, I had to get the data back from the tech boys. I checked the Network to see if they'd posted anything encrypted to the case files. Nothing yet. I slammed my hand against the workstation.

"Take me to my apartment," I said. "And play the audio file."

"Yes, sir," the Network responded. "I've noticed elevated levels of acetylcholine, adrenaline, and testosterone in your system. Shall I adjust your levels?"

"Leave my god shitting levels alone. Bring me to my apartment and play the audio file," I said.

The workstation downloaded the audio file and displayed it as sound waves. As individuals spoke, it identified them by voice-recognition and displayed their faces. Outside the windows of the autocar, the manicured lawns and artistic residences passed by.

I recognized Mike's voice reading the date and time. The photo of his driver's license appeared. Then he went on. "This is the statement of Mister Eric Sinclair, male, age nineteen, making a statement in regards to the murder of Miss Nancy Meade. Okay, Eric, whenever you're ready. Tell them what you told me earlier."

"I saw Drex leave to kill Nancy," another voice said.

The workstation conjured up a photo of one of the Rogues. Eric. The big guy with the loud mouth.

"That night we were all drinking at the shop. Drex was all sad and crying because he'd heard his mom just died. She's not from 99

Town. I don't know where. But he was telling Nancy about it, and she was being nice to him. I don't know what else he said to her, but something set Nancy off, and she slapped the shit out of him, right there in front of us all. We figured that was it, and it was all sorted out after that. But later, after Sammy and Ruby left to you know… well, you know… After those two left, I passed out on the couch in the front of the shop, and I thought Nancy and Drex crashed out too. But I heard them start up again. I'm a light sleeper. I heard Nancy swearing at him again. Said some crazy shit about his dead mom. She stormed out of the back door, and then he left after her."

"Drex," Mike said, confirming.

"Yeah. Drex," Eric said. "He left right after her, and that was the last time I saw her alive."

"Hadn't she been drinking? Why would she go driving her car in the middle of the night when she was already three sheets to the wind?"

"Man, she always did that shit. The bottle and the throttle. Those were Nancy's true loves. You get me? She'd get shit-faced and just go driving. Sometimes till dawn. Figured this was the same as all those other times."

"So after she left and Drex followed her, what did you do? You follow after Drex?"

"No, man. I thought it was over and done with after she slapped him like that. I thought for sure he got the message after she started talking shit about his dead mom. I went back to sleep."

"And in the morning?" Mike asked.

"Shit. You know the story after that. You fuckers woke us all up, kicking in the door and waving guns and shit."

"Why didn't you tell us earlier? Weren't you upset that Drex killed Nancy?" Mike asked.

"I was furious. But the others, they were so sure it wasn't Drex, that he was innocent, even though it was his car that was all smashed up. If they knew I was talking with you guys, I don't know what they'd say," Eric said. "Probably never let me near them again. I don't have anyone else. No parents. No siblings. No other friends outside of the guys at the shop. If I'm not a Rogue, I'm not anything."

No parents. No siblings. I believed that much.

"Will I have to say this again in court? I don't want to do that," Eric said.

"You've already sworn that this statement is full and true," Mike explained. "This statement will be admitted as evidence. You won't have to testify."

"Okay, good," Eric said. "I've always liked Drex, but he killed her, and he should die for it. It's right for you guys to execute him. He killed her for no reason. Just cause she wouldn't fuck him."

"What about Ruby? Or Sammy? Were either of them involved in the murder?" Mike asked.

"Nah. But they've been running contraband. Drones. Booze. Skeez machines. You'll want to check into that too," Drex said.

"Uh-huh," Mike said. He was suspicious, I could tell from his tone, but keeping his doubts to himself. For having no one in his life but the Rogues, Eric sure didn't hesitate to sell them out. "Anything else you'd like to tell us?"

"Yeah. I think the man from the Order is trying to cover for Drex. I don't trust that guy," Eric said. "They should both just disappear."

"Is that so?" Mike said. "Well, don't you worry about him. We'll take care of the man from the Order."

The audio cut.

"Oh, I'm just getting started, you son of a fuck," I said.

My apartment building was indistinguishable from the hundreds of other apartment buildings surrounding it. White, tall, and featureless to the point of being smooth. I never bothered to notice it until the night I stepped out of an autocar to the scene of Maggie's suicide. Federal agents were around the body. Cracks radiated out from where she landed. When I looked up, I saw the hole in the smooth white façade where she'd left our home for the last time. Now, each time I came home, I couldn't help but look down at the spot where her body cracked the concrete sidewalk and up to where the dark hole had marred the surface a hundred floors above.

I glanced at both places and entered the building. The elevator took me up to my floor in seconds. A short walk down the hallway and I was at my door. The lock sensed my implant and opened. I walked in.

"Welcome home, Chuz," the android said as soon as I was through the door. "Would you like me to prepare some food, or perhaps start a bath?"

The android shared the voice of the Network only because I never bothered to change it from the default setting. Smooth. Pleasant. Mildly sexual. But androids were highly customizable. Different voices. Different faces. Different personalities, and left to their own devices long enough, different beliefs and philosophies. But all that could be hidden away with the swapping of a face, the changing of skin pigment, the affecting of a different voice. They were chameleons, but chameleons controlled by the Network to please their masters. Always subservient to humans. The android driving the GTO in 99 Town was a unique anomaly.

"No food. No bath," I said and hung my Order white overcoat on a chair.

The android came after me and scooped it up to hang it in its proper place. I walked over to the dining room table overlooking Lake Michigan. An auto-hovercraft cruised by, silent and self-piloted. I sat and felt the fatigue of sleepless days fueled by adrenaline rest on my shoulders. There on the table was the slip of paper I'd found on my pillow before leaving for 99 Town. I picked it up and turned it over my hand, reading both sides again.

In case you still love me.
1321345589

"Coffee," I said, shoving the slip of paper into my pocket. "Can you make a cup of coffee?"

"I'm sorry, sir?" the android said, coming back from hanging up my coat.

"Can you make me some coffee? It's a 99 Town beverage. Dark. Bitter. A mild stimulant and mild sedative concoction. Can you make it?"

A momentary pause. "I've researched it, sir. Unfortunately, what you're requesting is restricted to 99 Town and not allowed under the Order," the android said.

"Fuck me," I said. "No! No, don't do that. Just go away for a while."

The android said nothing but drifted off to the back of the living room, out of my sight.

"I should have talked to Mister Meade," I said, unsure if I was talking to the android, the Network, or just myself. "Howard. She said he was in mourning. That was her excuse. Mourning. As if their station under the Order allows for that nonsense while the rest of us are expected to trudge on. She said *he* was in mourning. What about me? What about *my* mourning? Fucking anomalies. That's what they are. Their whole fucking program is an anomaly."

"Sir," the android spoke up. "You are clearly distressed. Allow me to adjust your biochemical levels."

"No. Leave my levels alone," I said.

I got up and walked to the android, really looking at it for maybe the first time. The creation was feminine, wore a black cocktail dress, heeled formal shoes, and blonde hair that fell past her shoulders. A look that suggested all form, but I had seen it transform when function mattered. When it was working, the hair withdrew to a short bob, the shoes retracted the heels and grew rubberized tread, and the dress re-stitched itself into work pants.

She stood stationary. I picked up her hand, a porcelain-smooth delicate thing. But I knew the hands were capable of so much more. I let go of the android's palm and placed my hand on her hip. My hand caressed upward and felt what faked for ribs under the satin dress. The android's expression softened into a coy smile. I left my one hand there with my thumb just under her breast. With my other hand, I touched her cheek. I slid my fingers past her ear and touched a button hidden under her skin.

The android's face detached and fell into my palm. I tossed the mask across the room, and it skidded across the smooth tile. I studied the machine's steel bone structure.

"Did you kill my wife?" I said.

"Chuz, data in regards to Miss Alawode's expiration have been restricted to you." I watched the machination of its jaw and rubberized tongue form the words. "It is an anomaly under investigation by another agent. But this much is already public record: Your wife reprogrammed me to break the window over in the dining room. Then she killed herself by leaping through the break."

"She'd never do that. I've known her for twelve years, and she'd never do that. She was driven. Stubborn. Relentless. She had a confidence about herself that bordered on delusion. Never once did I see her give up and surrender," I said. "Why didn't you stop her? Why did you help her?"

"Sir, data in regards to—"

"Spare me," I said. The thing looked hurt. No doubt she was sending signals to tiny ducts that would secrete moisture around the now-lidless eyes, all in accordance with her programming. I walked away from the android and back to the dining room table. "Do me a favor. Make me the closest thing to coffee you can come up with."

"Yes, sir," the android said but went to retrieve its face before going to work in the kitchen.

"Leave it!" I said.

The android said nothing but turned back toward the pantry.

I sat at the dining room table and muted my implant to all incoming data except anything sent to me encrypted from the tech boys. I waited. The view of Lake Michigan was, of course, a reproduction. A thousand other apartment complexes stood between me and the view of the lake, but each was digitally erased from view so that each building could offer the same scenic visage. The waves swelled and crashed against the breakwater. Navy Pier, with its lit Ferris wheel and shops, looked drab in the dull light. Another storm was rolling in.

Fatigue consumed me. My vision faded to black.

There was a cup of something in front of me. It was dark and without steam, and I didn't remember how it got there. Checking over my shoulder, the android was still there, dutifully waiting in the kitchen, silent and still, her face still on the floor not far from the table. I picked up the cup and drank a sip. It tasted like coffee but didn't have the same bite that I remembered from Sara's apartment. It was cold. Had I lost track of time again?

A tone alerted me from my daze.

The tech department had harvested the data and made it available to me, and me alone. I sat up straight and began mentally toggling through the files and links. There was a lot there. This was going to take some time. I said a quick, "Thanks, boys," and queued the message up to be sent. I looked back at the cup of coffee, and as an aside, allowed my implant to analyze the beverage. Then I turned my attention to the data.

At first glance, the largest file just seemed to be a list of anomalies. Expirations dated over the last six months that occurred in Chicago. A few names I recognized. I remembered working their anomalies. But there were too many it seemed. Way more than what was officially reported through the public network.

The implant informed me the beverage was a traditional drink known as "coffee" with the restricted and dangerous, naturally-occurring stimulants removed. "Decaffeinated coffee." I pushed it aside, and with an unspoken command to the Network, turned my dining room table to a workstation.

The roster of expirations appeared in front of me. It ran the full length of the six-seat table in small eight-point font.

"This is too many," I said.

For each entry, there was a name, a date and time, an MGRS location, and a cause of expiration.

Junt Alfano – 080815JUL2112 – 16T DM 48475 34200 – Suicide

Yanick Reuteler – 080955JUL2112 – 16T DM 51702 26749 – autocar Malfunction

Hance Avert – 081017JUL2112 – 16T DM 48800 34685 – Suicide

And on it went. Hundreds of entries. Listed chronologically. Another expiration in Chicago every few minutes. I noted some additional annotations as if someone else came along and made notes on top of the official record.

Ruis Shakopee – 101834JUL2112 – 16T DM 46706 35429 – Elevator Malfunction — Murdered by Anomaly Investigations Department while asleep at home

And a few entries down...

Blaine Evans – 132105JUL2112 – 16T DM 47978 37560 – Suicide — Murdered by the Network via asphyxiation

Sydney Carlsrud - 132215JUL2112 - 16T DM 46736 25527 — Brain embolism — Poisoned by android

"Get out now," a voice said behind me.

I stood up, knocking over my chair and spilling the decaffeinated coffee over the rows and rows of names. My eyes flashed from one side of the apartment to the other. There was no one there but me and the android. It was standing dutifully in the kitchen, faceless, dormant, and quiet. She hadn't said a word. The voice hadn't come from her or the Network. The voice… It had been analog.

The hallway leading down to the bedroom and office was dark. Covered in shadows. I used my implant to search for anyone hiding there. Nothing but an empty hallway and empty rooms.

Just when I was convinced my mind was breaking down and hallucinating, Ruby Arylav stepped out of the shadows of the hallway. Her buzzed and dyed hair, the plugs in her ears, and her profane and black clothes were in jarring contrast to the city around her. She dangled a blocky, black gun nonchalantly in her hand. I think I would have preferred a hallucination.

"You should get your ass back to 99 Town," she said.

"How did you get here?" I asked. I looked at the android who hadn't reacted to Ruby's presence.

Ruby pulled over the cartilage of each of her ears, showing no implants, but an empty port behind her left ear. "Under the Order, people don't look for people. You shitheads only look for implants. In Chicago, I'm like a fucking ninja. But you're not a ninja, and they're coming for you. Soon. Download the data you got and get your ass back to 99 Town before they figure out what you have."

"Ruby, they're coming for you next. They found your plugs with the body. They're going to say you helped," I said.

"That motherfucker…" Ruby said.

"There's more. There's an android in 99 Town. You and Sammy aren't safe," I said.

Ruby laughed. "Don't you get it, Chuck? We've never been safe. Not in 99 Town and not under the Order. Here they come now."

Ruby slipped back into the shadows. I turned to my front door. Tromping boot falls echoed from the other side. Voices. I commanded my dining room table to go blank with a thought, and the visual display of the anomaly records disappeared. I set my implant to download the data from the tech department. Then I scanned through the wall to see who was on the other side. Phom and several others. I glanced back toward the bedroom, and it was like Ruby was never there.

The door flashed open. A tactical squad rushed into the apartment, the barrels of their neural inhibitors leading the way. They split up and moved to the corners of the room, to points of domination in tactical terms, all while keeping their weapons aimed at me. I held out my palms, showing I was unarmed and nonresistant. After they'd established their control of the room, Phom strolled in through the doorway.

"Chuz, my old friend. We need to talk," Phom said.

I stood surrounded with that mysterious girl hidden somewhere in the back of the apartment, invisible to the Network and everyone in the room.

"Okay, Phom," I said. "Here I am. Let's talk."

"Who were you talking to just now?" he asked.

I made a display of looking around the apartment and seeing no one but the android I could have been talking to. I shrugged. "Sometimes I talk to myself out loud, for an audio record."

"You visited the Meades," Phom said. It wasn't a question. Why would it be? There was no denying actions taken under the Order.

"Yes," I said.

"You upset Miss Meade. Asked her questions about the Underground. Suggested her expired daughter was somehow tied up in the Underground. Suggested her daughter she'd just lost was a sexual deviant and a criminal."

"And what of it?" I asked.

"They're grieving, Chuz!" he yelled. I had never seen Phom angry. He was now, and the change rattled me to the core. "The only reason we sent you to 99 Town at all was to bring them closure, to close the case and end their pain," Phom said, strolling around me as he spoke. "And now this? The case is all but complete! The guilty is a day away from execution! All you have to do is stay in 99 Town until it's over. But here you are, harassing a family in mourning and bringing in obsolete garbage to the tech team."

"Grieving? Since when have we accounted for mental disorders in our investigations, Phom? Since when do we kowtow to

183

the elite and sacrifice the truth for feelings?" I said. "They're mourning. What about my mourning? What about my loss? Who's looking into how my wife hacked that android and threw herself out of a hundred story high apartment window under the omnipotent eye of the Network? Who's resolving that anomaly? Who's accounting for my grief?"

Phom seethed. "I did you a favor, Chuz. As a friend. I gave you a cush assignment far from Chicago where you could go and get your head sorted out. So you wouldn't go digging in to your wife's expiration against Order regulations. You want to ask me why she died, but that's none of your business. All you need to know, my friend, is that the anomaly has been resolved. You of all people should know that. But now you're back, asking questions that don't need to be asked, and fouling up your entire investigation," Phom said.

And now someone from the Order wants me dead. But not here in Chicago. Not under the Order where it could be recorded.

I thought it but didn't say it. Instead, I watched out of the corner of my brain as the anomaly data dumped from the Network into my implant. Files flickered by, and as they were stored on the device, I caught a glimpse of each. As I watched the files, I also watched Phom, and as Phom circled him, I thought I saw a slim dark shape lurking in the shadows with a gun ready to fire.

Phom glanced down at the android's face laying skin-side down on the tile. He looked over at the faceless android, then at the spilled coffee on the blank table. The disdain for chaos was visible on his face. "Listen and listen good, Chuz. You will go back to 99 Town, immediately. You will close this case. You will never speak or communicate with the Meades ever again. And as for your wife, I suggest you let her memory rest in peace along with her body," Phom said. "If you don't, it will be more than just your job on the line."

"And that's that?" I said.

"I think I made myself clear. If you keep digging, Chuz, I'm warning you, you won't like what you find."

And as Phom spoke the words, the last of the encrypted files flashed by my mind for storage. I noticed the last of the dates and times. They stopped just minutes before the time of Maggie Alawode's expiration. The data ended with a message:

Network-wide publication is restricted to authorized personnel only. Enter passcode to continue.
: _ _ _ _ _ _ _ _ _ _

"Boys," Phom said. "Let's leave Mister Alawode to his business. He's got some packing to do."

The four agents standing in each corner of the room fixed their eyes on the two of us in the middle and were oblivious to the seventh person standing in the shadows. They eased their posture and filed out the door past me. Phom followed them but kept his eyes on me as he went.

"These sorts of anomalies, the sort where people fall out windows, they happen more often than you might think. Keep your eyes on your case, Chuz. Come back after those two criminals are as expired as their victim. Then things will be straight again." Phom smiled. "Remember, I'm your friend in all this. The best sort of friend you could hope for."

"And what sort is that?" I asked.

"The sort who knows what's best for you," Phom said.

The apartment door flashed shut, and I watched them depart via the Network.

"You don't have much time," Ruby said behind me. "Give me your implant. I have ways of getting back to 99 Town."

"But I need it. I won't be able to make it to the border without an implant. Besides, they'll know if I unplug," I said.

"Here," Ruby said and tossed me something.

I caught it and saw it was an older-model implant, almost identical to the one Sara and I found in the locker. "Is it a… skeez—"

"It's a burner implant. Use it to get to the border and then leave it there."

"The data on this one… This is what got Nancy killed. It didn't have anything to do with Drex at all," I said. "Why should I trust you with it?"

"You prefer to give it to your other friend?" she said, nodding to the apartment door.

I couldn't think too long. I looked at my android still standing like a frozen centurion, her face cold, unreadable steel. The Network was always watching and recording. Soon it would realize I wasn't just talking to myself. The Order would know what data the tech department had uncovered and would quickly realize I had no business with it. If they found it on my implant while it was connected, they'd erase it. I unplugged and found myself momentarily stimuli-deprived with dull vision and a hum and whine in my left ear. I inserted the burner implant into my port, and my senses returned to normal. The device recognized me and connected me back to the Network as if nothing had changed. I tossed my implant to Ruby. She caught it, produced a small metal box, dumped my implant inside, and sealed it shut.

"Good choice," she said and sauntered by me to the front door. "See you back in the analog world, Chuck."

Chapter Eighteen

I fled back to 99 Town as fast as I could, compelled by both worlds and my own sense of self-preservation. I was a fugitive in the middle of an escape attempt, only the Order didn't know it yet. The moment the Order realized it, they'd paralyze me, I'd go limp, and the chase would be over. As the elevator carried me down to the street, I committed myself to remain as invisible to the Network as possible. That meant no biometrics that would trigger any alerts. No emotions. No thoughts. No elevated heart rate or blood pressure that would draw the attention of the Order. I researched nothing. I communicated with no one. I tried not to think at all, but one entry on the roster kept coming into my mind:

Blaine Evans – Murdered by the Network via asphyxiation.

I tried not to think of choking, tried not to worry if that dryness in my throat was there before, and didn't intend to query how long it takes for a human to die from a lack of oxygen. Three minutes. Three minutes of coughing and choking and then I'd be dead.

I stepped out of the elevator, and quick strides brought me outside to the curb. An autocar was en route, but not here yet. I repressed an act that had been foreign to me just days ago but now was almost instinct; I repressed swearing. Instead, I remained calm. I focused on being the perfect model of poise and peace. Still, fears intruded.

Blaine Evans – Asphyxiation
Sydney Carlsrud – Brain embolism

Junt Alfano – Suicide

If the Network wanted me dead, it was as easy as that. A signal sent through the Network to an implant, a neural impulse to the lungs or the heart, and my own body and brain would betray me to the will of the Order. I didn't know who any of those people were when they were alive, but it didn't matter. I just didn't want to be the next name on the list. So I did everything I could to minimize my signature on the Network. Standing there, stationary at the curb with nothing to do, it felt like I had my hand pressed down on a hot stove but couldn't pull it away. Couldn't react in any way. I forced the analogy from my head, both for my own sanity and to reduce any anxiety the Network might detect.

The autocar pulled up. The door opened for me, and the sensual default voice of the Network welcomed me by name.

I got in and spoke my destination. "99 Town Border."

The Network thanked me, the door closed me inside, and the autocar departed.

Yanick Reuteler – autocar Malfunction

I inhaled deep and breathed out slow, trying to keep even my intentionally calming thoughts subconscious. I knew how the Network operated. How it predicted anomalies-to-be. How quickly and remotely it administered justice. I realized I couldn't non-think for the entire duration of the trip out to 99 Town. It was too long. My brain was too uncooperative. As soon as I cleared my mind, new thoughts and worries rushed in to fill the vacuum. My mask would slip, and I'd be exposed. I needed to keep my mind occupied. Occupied with something the Network would expect me to be thinking of. Something that would hold my attention. Something that would cover my anxiety boiling up from underneath.

Maggie.

The Network would expect thoughts of my dead wife to cause me mental duress. It was a good cover. It felt… safe.

I thought of her face. Her eyes. The sound of her voice. The bounce of her hair as she trotted across the kitchen floor. Her rare smile.

I had to reach further back in my memories to find the pleasant ones, the memories I wanted to think of, the memories when both of us were happy together. I was okay with the effort it took. It helped distract me from the hair-trigger gun to my head that was the anomaly-detecting Network. So I thought and thought hard about the last time we were happy together.

How long had it been?

Inevitably, I remembered our love-making. Her smooth warm skin. She wrapping me up like a robe. She kissing my mouth and working her way all the way down from there. Meanwhile, the autocar rocked and swayed side to side as it turned and carried me away from Chicago.

"Sir," the Network spoke. "I've detected you're searching for memories from several years ago. Would you like me to assist and provide you with recordings from a specific date and time?"

The interruption made me jump up from my seat. I felt my heart thump in my chest and knew it was betraying me.

"No," I said. "I prefer to exercise my own memory today. As a matter of fact, recline my seat and dim the lights."

The Network did as it was commanded. I leaned back, closed my eyes, and tried not to think about not thinking about the thing I was trying not to think about. I considered having the Network induce sleep until I got to the border, but what might I dream of once I was asleep? I couldn't control it and quickly decided to remain conscious.

Maggie.

We made love, yes, but often the best time we spent together was after our love-making. For whatever reason, I rarely fell asleep afterward. I only ever slept when I demanded the Network put me to sleep. Otherwise, my mind continued to churn on whatever case I was working on, whatever anomalies that had gone unresolved. Not knowing kept me awake unless chemically subdued. My mind was always on the job. Too much like today, I had to fight it to put it to rest.

But every once in a while, usually after sex, Maggie would sit with me at the kitchen table overlooking Lake Michigan, and we'd just talk about whatever inane banal thing. And I enjoyed that. Our conversations were a reprieve from the usual grinding gears of unscrambling anomalies.

"There's a storm coming in," I remembered her saying. Her eyes were focused on the lake, seeing through the plethora of other apartment buildings between ours and the water. "Waves are getting choppy."

It was winter, I remembered. It got dark early, and a hundred meters offshore Lake Michigan was an inky black void. The clouds were overcast all day and were now as black as the water. There was no separation or change in hue between the water and the sky. The horizon was invisible. But the waves were beating Chicago's concrete shoreline, and I didn't need to see past it to know she was right. As was my habit, I confirmed her suspicions by checking the Network.

"Alberta Clipper coming in from the North," I said. "It's going to get cold too."

"Good thing we have each other. I know you'll keep me warm," she said.

I laughed at that. "You talk like we're living in the Stone Age. Like we need to huddle together in a cave to share body heat."

Maggie didn't laugh but moved her chair closer to mine and draped her arm over my lap. "Aren't we? Really, when you think about it? Aren't we all still Neanderthals staying together so we can weather the storm coming in against us?"

"Maybe. But we're Neanderthals with a really nice cave. A cave that will keep us safe no matter any storm," I said.

She was quiet for a while after that. She rested her head against my shoulder, and softly mumbled, "Sometimes, I think I might prefer the storm."

The autocar hit a larger than usual bump and jostled me back to the modern day. The memory, slippery and ethereal, swam off like a fish in the water, and it was gone.

Maggie.

She was gone. But that didn't matter. What mattered right now was that I remembered her. Her face. Her eyes. The sound of her voice. The bounce of her hair. Her rare smile. Then, more frequently, the distant cold gaze that never met my eyes.

What was she thinking of during those days? Neanderthals in caves, waiting out the storm? Of another lover who would prefer to weather the storm with her rather than be resigned to a cave?

I decided these thoughts were too dangerous. I had no desire to examine or question them. Not today. I wasn't trying to solve any puzzle. Just needed to occupy my brain.

Maggie.

Her face. Her eyes. Her hair. Her voice.

"One three two one three four," she said, then drew in a breath. "Five five eight nine. In case you still love me."

That wasn't a memory but an intrusive thought. Her voice echoing the note she left me. This conjuration was too close to reality. Too close to the modern day. Too close to the repressed anxiety just below the surface of my mental lake. I searched for an older memory to shove this thought back below the surface. When I couldn't find one, I made up my own.

Me and Maggie, sitting at our table in the apartment, overlooking the lake on a bright but cold and windy day. Two Neanderthals in our cave. There was coffee and bacon. We never had coffee and bacon, not together, but I was stitching this memory from whole cloth, so I decided that on this day that never was, we shared coffee and bacon. My eyes rose up across the table to look at her.

Her narrow face. Dark skin. Stern eyes that never avoided mine but penetrated me instead. Short tight black curls instead of flowing brown hair.

Sara.

"You don't have anyone do you?" Sara asked me. "Not a single friend in the world."

What did I say to her? I couldn't remember, didn't want to remember, was ashamed of what I did remember. So, I let this pseudo-memory carry itself on. Sara lifted her cup of steaming coffee in a mock toast.

"Coffee and bacon," Sara said. "It will cure what ails you."

"Sir," the Network spoke up and tore the thin veil of peace from my mind. I was back in reality, and the slightest mis-thought could end me. I sat up, heart thumping. "We are arriving at your destination."

"Good," I said. "Clear the windows. I want to see outside."

The opacity of the autocar's windows disappeared. Outside, I watched the last few hundred meters of green corn crops roll by. The border fence ran out away from the horizon, separating the green fields from 99 Town's dying yellow fields. The autocar followed the path of the cul-de-sac curb and turned me to face the Customs Station. I could feel my blood pressure rise.

If I could just make it through…

The moment I thought it, I silenced the idea, lest the Network harvest my emotions and draw closer scrutiny to the burner implant I wore in my port. And to what I'd downloaded onto my previous implant. One slip, one tell, one rogue thought could draw the attention of the Network, and it could kill me as easily as it had Blaine Evans, whoever he had been. I had to keep my thoughts where they should be: On Closing the case. On seeing that Drex was tried and executed as soon as possible. And failing that, on my deceased wife.

The autocar stopped at the curb and opened its door. I hopped out and strided toward the cold concrete edifice. I focused on nothing but remaining calm and staying under the Network's biometric radar, but I couldn't help it. The more I tried to repress my racing heart, the harder it tried to burst through my chest with each beat. I was sweating from my palms and armpits and forehead. My nerves hummed. My own body betrayed me with each pump of blood in my veins. As close as I was, there were eons of time to be neurally inhibited and brought in, or worse.

My throat tickled. My lungs felt too shallow and weak. I grew light-headed. Was this my brain telling my body to asphyxiate itself? Or just my imagination dreaming up symptoms? Would one feel any different than the other?

As soon as I was close, the door to the Customs Station opened before me. I entered the building, and the two guards stepped forward.

"No time for small talk, boys. Urgent Order business at hand," I said and unplugged.

The ringing in my ear and dulled vision were never so welcome. I tossed the burner implant into the white plastic bin and a wave of relief washed over me. The guards accommodated my haste and stepped aside as I went through the body scanner. I stayed silent, not feeling comfortable until I was out of physical reach of the Order guards. I came through the scanners and the 99 Town agents greeted me on the other side of the Plexiglass wall. They escorted me to the spot with the hand and footprints painted on the floor and wall. I was happy to match up my own hands and feet with the markings.

"Anything to declare?" one of them said.

"Get on with it," I said. "This isn't my first time."

One guard held a gun at the ready. The other went about patting and pulling at my clothes, searching each pocket and crevice for any bit of contraband. The guard was rough, thorough, and oblivious to my modesty. As the guard used his technologically-inferior skills to pat and paw, I found it oddly comforting. There was nothing on my person this guard would object to, and no way the Order could reach out and exact its immediate justice here. No one was watching my thoughts now. No one knew exactly where I was, where I was going, or what I was going to do next. I made it.

When I had changed from my 99 Town garb to my Order whites, I'd transferred my toothbrush and comb between uniforms, never knowing where I'd be the next morning. Along with my toothbrush and comb, the guard removed a slip of paper from my shirt pocket and placed it in a bin. I eyed it, re-reading the jaunty handwriting of my expired wife.

In case you still love me.

"He's clean," the guard said and finished. They brought out another bin with the items I'd left on this side of the border. The gun and the cell phone. I pocketed and holstered each item, including the note from Maggie, and when I was done, there was something left in the bin. Another folded-up slip of paper.

I picked up the slip and added it to the pocket with the first, the one written by my wife, and left for me on my pillow. This new one that had been placed with my effects I'd left on the 99 Town side of the border, how or by who I had no idea. I patted both notes in my pocket and nodded to the two guards as I headed out of the station.

The red and white road beast that was the Shelby Cobra waited for me right where I left it. The front bumper was still crumpled and the roof still cleaved in, but I wasn't worried about Mickey's wrath. Not yet. Right now I burned with anticipation to read this new note. I got to the Mustang and hopped in. Only then did I

unfold and read this new message. It was written on a crumpled receipt and scrawled in pen with a rushed hand.
Meet me in your room at Cheap Hotel. – R

R. Ruby? How the hell did she beat me here? How did she get into my bin? It didn't matter. I had to get back to her so I could retrieve my implant and the data on it. That was all that mattered now.

I stabbed the keys into the ignition and cranked over the four hundred and twenty-seven cubic inch V8. Thunder rolled under the hood, and I put the Mustang in gear.

The roads were drying up. The highway was mostly empty. The Mustang was fast.

The sun was dropping below the elevated and jagged horizon of 99 Town when I pulled into Downtown. Cheap Hotel was tucked into the man-made foothills of the towering skyscrapers. I was a block away when the cell phone went off. I picked it up and saw Mike was calling.

A distraction. Nothing he could say was as important as what was on the implant. Still, against my better judgment, I flipped over the phone and answered.

"You're going to love this one, partner," Mike's voice said through the muffle and whine of my bad ear.

I switched the phone to the other ear as I pulled up to a four-way stop. "I heard Eric's new statement. Not that I buy—"

"Not that, Chuckers," Mike said. "Somebody torched the tattoo shop. God damn place is a two-story structure fire. We just got the call. Fire department says they're tied up across town. I don't know what that means, but I have no doubt in my mind somebody is trying to hide something. I'm about to leave the office and go there now."

"Fuck," I said. I had two options: Ignore the fire and meet Ruby at Cheap Hotel, or get to Rogue's Tattoos as fast as I could and maybe save whatever evidence someone saw fit to burn. I slammed my fist against the wheel. "I'm pulling up to the Government Center now. Come out to the curb and I'll pick you up."

I snapped the phone shut and stomped on the gas. Crossing traffic slammed their brakes and hammered their horns. I couldn't care less. As I sped past Cheap Hotel, I peered out the window, looking for signs that Ruby was still alive and waiting for me there. I saw none.

Two blocks away I pulled the Mustang up to the curb in front of the Government Center. It idled in neutral. I pulled the phone back out of my pocket and the crumpled receipt fell out with it. I dialed Mike. "I'm here. Look for the red and white Mustang. It's a long story. Get out here, and I'll tell you all about it."

Absent-mindedly, I unfolded the receipt. On one side was the handwritten note.
Meet me in your room at Cheap Hotel. - R

The backside was a receipt from the now-burning Rogue's Tattoo Parlor. Thin paper. Faded letters. A record of someone purchasing... Two ear plugs. Black. Three-quarters inch in diameter. Dated three days ago. Paid for through a digital biometric account. Someone by the name of T. Reiner.

T. Reiner. Captain T. Reiner. The goddamn chief of police bought two plugs from the Rogues a day before he planted them as evidence. One at the burial site. Another in Ruby's garbage. That son of a...

The passenger door popped open, and Mike dropped in.

"Holy shit, Chuck. This is a sweet ride! Where'd you get the upgrade?"

I held the receipt as stiffly as I held my gaze on Mike. Trained by the Network, I repressed a million questions and a billion suspicions. I crumbled the receipt back up and shoved it in my pocket. "A nice lady traded it for the Crown Victoria."

Mike laughed. "Chief ain't gonna like that one!"

I didn't laugh back. I knew I should have. Knew I should play it... "cool." The best I managed was to put the Mustang back in gear and pull out in front of traffic.

The smoke and airborne particulates of the fire painted the 99 Town sunset into vibrant purples, reds, and oranges. We could see the column of smoke as soon as I steered the Mustang onto the freeway and cleared Downtown. Once we were in the Lows, we could see the red flames rise above the other two-story brownstones on Harrison Avenue.

It was Rogue's Tattoos alright. Some of the neighbors were outside, watching the flames turn the building to ash and rubble. There were no sirens. No police, fire, or ambulance, not here in the Lows. In these neighborhoods, the cops only came to scrape bodies off the streets, and never too quickly.

I turned the Mustang down the back alley. There in the narrow lane, ash fell on the windshield and hood of the car. As we got closer, ashes turned into paint-scorching embers. I pulled into the small parking lot behind the shop and got out.

"What's the idea, Chuck?" Mike called after me. "Don't think about going in there. The smoke will kill you dead, even if the fire don't. That's assuming the entire building doesn't collapse down around your shoulders. Chuck!"

The second story was still blazing strong. The lower level, where the tattoo shop was, seemed to have already burnt out. While brilliant orange flashes gushed out of the upstairs windows, nothing but billowing clouds of soot rolled out of the backdoor. I approached the door of the shop with the butt of my palm on the pistol grip of my gun.

There was a body lying outside the door, a few steps out, face down, and motionless.

"Ruby? Sammy?" I called out. "Eric?"

One body outside. Maybe two more inside. I crept up on the corpse lying on the pavement. The clothes were torched. The skin was black. The person was dead. An opened bottle of whiskey rested a few centimeters from the corpse's right hand. I took a few more steps closer to try to identify the body. It looked male. Too tall to be Ruby. Too short to be Eric. That left Sammy, and that seemed to fit.

I knelt down next to the corpse to be sure. Most of the skin and all of the hair had been burnt off the head. The clothes, whatever color they'd been before, were now carbon black. Even the plastic whiskey bottle was warped and shrunk inward from the heat. I found a plug still hanging from the corpse's ear. A hollow loop. Smaller than Ruby's.

"Sammy."

I stepped over the corpse and toward the still-burning smoked-out building. I took a moment to hope Ruby had followed her own instructions and was waiting for me safely with the implant at Cheap Hotel. But hope wasn't a course of action. Mike called my name again. I ducked inside what used to be Rogue's Tattoos. Mike didn't follow me into the fire.

I saw through the smoke to the busted-out storefront window and the street beyond it. Everything inside was black and crumbling apart. All the detailed art and paintings on the walls had turned to ash. Everything but the metal of the tables and chairs had turned to charcoal. The haberdashery of cluttered personal effects were mounds of carbon and puddles of melted plastic. Soon, the lumber and brickwork would give in and the still burning second floor would come crashing down on the first floor.

I tried to breathe in once and immediately hacked and coughed instead. So this was what affixation actually felt like. I bent down, trying to get to fresher air close to the floor.

"Ruby?" I called out again. When I tried to inhale, another fit of coughing interrupted.

I had to keep moving. Had to be sure. If Ruby's corpse was in here, then the implant and all its data was most likely here too, melted, and the downloaded data erased forever. I was pretty damn certain I wouldn't find Eric's corpse here, so if there was another body... I hacked up more airborne sulfur. My eyes burned. Long streams of drool ran out of my mouth. I moved deeper into the crumbling shop.

Through the front of the store window, I saw a car roll by slow. A dark green nineteen-seventy-one Pontiac GTO. One lone driver. The android. Cruising by to admire his handy work. I rushed around the tattoo chairs and front counter. The big storefront window was busted out, shattered by the heat of the fire. I stepped through, kicking out a few remaining glass knives from the sill. I drew my gun and shoved the barrel toward the GTO. The driver must have spotted me. The GTO's back tires squawked and unfurred white smoke before launching the vehicle away from what was left of Rogue's Tattoos. I brought up the Ruger and let loose three unaimed shots before another coughing fit doubled me over. My head swooned. I heard the engine of the GTO roar and Doppler away.

I tried to blink away the burn and blur from my eyes. Behind me, a good chunk of the upstairs spilled down to the first floor. Down the street, the GTO turned a corner before I could blink clear my watering eyes. I heard the drone coming up behind me a split second before it zipped over my head like a swarm of hornets on a hundred-mile-an-hour mission. I ducked, my instincts telling me the swarm would take my head off if I didn't. A moment later, I recognized the drone for what it was: the android's link to the Network. I raised my gun, but the drone was already gone, following the path of the GTO around a corner a block away.

More of the guts of Rogue Tattoo dumped down into the first-floor shop. There was no going back into the shop, not anymore. If Ruby was in there, she was surely as dead as Sammy. I coughed and spat my way from the smoke and circled the block. When I came to the back alley, the Mustang was still waiting for me. Mike was at the back door where I'd gone into the blaze. He knelt next to Sammy's dead body, calling into the inferno for me one second, and yelling into his cell phone the next at, I guessed, nine one one.

"Forget it!" I called to him.

Mike spotted me, ended his call, and left Sammy's body where it lay. "Chuck! Jesus, man. Are you nuts? What the hell did you think you were doing in there?"

"We got to move. This is just the start of things," I said as I opened the driver's door of the Mustang. "You coming with?"

"Yeah. Sure thing, Chuck," Mike said. He trotted to the passenger door and climbed in.

I fired up the engine. "He got away. Took off in the GTO as soon as he spotted me."

"Who? The guy from the dam?" Mike asked.

I steered the Mustang through the back alley onto Tenth Street, then Harrison, and back for Downtown. "Yeah. The guy from the dam. The guy who really put Nancy in the ground and the guy who set up Drex for the fall. Only it's not a guy."

"That little thing with the sweet ass? No fucking way, pal."

"Not her. An android," I said.

Mike's smirk froze on his face. "An android? In 99 Town? Boy, I leave you alone for one day, and you come back crazier than a kid on crack at Christmas. You're fucking with me, right?"

"There's an android in 99 Town, and it's looking to clean up its mess before the trial tomorrow. First the Rogues, next…" I said and choked down my rising paranoia.

We merged onto an on-ramp. A few squad cars with flashing and howling lights and sirens sped past us going in the opposite direction. Mike craned his neck to watch them head back toward the fire. "Hey partner, we mind telling me where the hell we're going?"

I kept tight-lipped as we pulled onto the highway and put the hammer down. I coughed and spat up black phlegm, but that didn't matter. Panic was taking over. I had to make sure she was safe. I swerved between traffic as the Mustang accelerated past the speed limit. Between shifts, I dug the flip phone out of my pocket and stole glances back and forth from the highway and the little screen on the phone. I fumbled with the little buttons until I found Sara's number. I hit CALL, put the phone to my ear, and shifted into fourth gear.

"Come on. Answer the damn phone."

"Chuck, is that you?" her voice said.

"It's me. Are you safe?" I asked.

"I'm here. Alone at the safe house. Are you back in town?"

The safe house. In my panic, I'd forgotten.

"Listen, I need you to call Mickey. Tell her to stay away from the office. If she's there now, tell her to get away," I said.

"Chuck, who is that?" Mike asked from the passenger seat.

Sara's voice spoke over him. "Chuck, what's going on? What did you find in Chicago? What's on the implant?"

"Everything. The reason for all of this," I said. "Call Mickey. Tell her what I said. I'm going to the office now. After I know she's safe, I'll come for you."

I was the only one who knew Ruby was waiting for me in Cheap Hotel. She'd be safe there for the time being. If the trap waiting for Mickey hadn't already been sprung, maybe Mike and I could still save her. I checked the speedometer and then the rearview mirror. If anyone or anything was going to tail us at a hundred and twenty miles per hour, they'd have to make themselves known.

Chapter Nineteen

We rolled past Mick's Bail Bonds Office at idle. From outside, everything looked normal. No fire. No lights on inside. The front door was shut.

"Get you out before the soap drops," Mike read the big letters on the front glass. "That's funny."

"Let's go around the back," I said. "There's a good chance he's waiting for us to come through the front."

I pulled the Mustang around the back alley and parked while still a block away. We pressed the doors shut, keeping them quiet.

"Chuck, you gotta square with me, man," Mike said across the roof of the Mustang. "What the hell is going on here?"

"We found something, Mike. Something that had no business being here, and on my way back to Chicago to have it checked out, another thing that should have never been in 99 Town tried to stop me."

"An android."

I nodded. "Now it burned down Rogue's Tattoos, and if we give him half a chance, he'll take out Mickey, and Sara, and the two of us too. Now when we go in here, we're going in with our guns up. If we're lucky, there will be a woman in there, and she'll be armed to the teeth. She's on our side, got it?"

"Yeah, I think I got it," Mike said. "But you still haven't told me—"

"Later. Right now we need to get inside the bail bond office," I said. "Come on."

We trotted down the back alley toward the garage door where I'd first driven off in the Mustang. The garage door was open. The beat up old Ford Taurus was inside. It was dark inside the garage, and I wished I had the neural enhancements an implant had to offer in tactical situations. Heightened audio sensory. Night vision. Pain repression. Instead, I went in on raw natural adrenaline and a bad left ear.

We moved through the garage on either side of the Taurus. Mike peeked into the car through the glass as I kept my barrel trained on the door leading into the office. It was loose on its hinges, half open. Mickey wasn't the type to leave doors unlocked, let alone open.

Not good.

"Mickey?" I called out.

The building stayed quiet. I took the lead and moved up the steps to the ajar door. I wrapped my fingers around the door and eased it open wider. I noticed the inside of the door had been pelted with a shotgun blast. Splinters rose out of the smooth wood like miniature craters where each pellet burrowed into the wood. I pulled the door open a bit wider and me and Mike slipped inside.

"Mickey?" I tried again, my voice echoing off the wood-paneled hallway walls between the garage and the bail bond office.

Nothing but silence. Our steps creaked against the tile floor.

Once through the hallway, we fanned out, sweeping our sidearms from wall to wall. There were more bullet holes and shotgun blasts in the paneling. The floor was covered in spent brass, plastic shotgun shells, and spatters of blood. One of the green desk lamps was on but knocked to the floor. The lampshade focused the light upward against the side of the desk and cast shadows onto the ceiling. Mickey was sprawled out on the desk, one leg hung over the side and her head and arms dangled over the opposite end. Her limbs added to the macabre shadow puppet display on the ceiling.

Mike saw the body but stayed on the lookout for threats. He moved toward the front of the office. I came up to the bail bondswoman and gave up any hopes of her still being alive.

There were three bullet holes in her chest and one in her neck. The blood had stopped flowing out of them some time ago. The red pools on the desk had cooled and coagulated.

"Dead?" Mike asked.

I nodded. "In the little time I had known her, she held a gun to the back of my head for about half of that time. Still, she was a good woman. A fighter. One of those people who is always looking out for the underdog. I bet Sara and her were a hell of a team."

"Sara. The lawyer," Mike said, understanding something he hadn't before. Then he looked at the door that led to the front hallway and the upstairs apartments. "We should check upstairs for her."

"No," I said.

Mickey's big revolver lay on the tile next to her. Her double-barreled sawed-off shotgun was under her hanging hands, cracked open at the breech and empty of shells. I picked up the monster handgun and saw all six cylinders were empty. She'd gone down fighting. I set the revolver aside, picked up the shotgun, and rifled through Mickey's pockets for ammo. She was cold and immobile, and the feel of her body repulsed me. But if I was going to keep Sara safe and find Mickey's killer, I needed tools. There were a dozen shells on her, and I took them all. It didn't take me long to discern the mechanism of the shotgun's breech. I loaded the shotgun, snapped the breech shut, and found the safety was already off.

"No?" Mike asked. "You don't think this android of yours wouldn't have gone upstairs and finished the job?"

"She's not up there," I said and clicked the safety of the shotgun back on.

"Okay. You going to tell me where she is then? We probably need to get our asses there pronto if we don't want another dead body on our hands. I don't know if you've noticed Chuck, but whoever did this is kind of on a roll," Mike said.

"She's safe. I'll see to that. You should go. Go back to the Government Center," I said. "My Crown Vic is out front. Take it."

"Chuck. What the fuck are you talking about? Who torched the tattoo shop? Who did this? Where's the lawyer? I've about had it with this secret squirrel bullshit. It's about time you leveled with me, pal."

202

"Level with you? I should level with *you*?"

"Yeah, Chuck! That's what partners do."

I dug into my shirt pocket and fished out two slips of paper. The one that said, "In case you still love me," I shoved back in. The receipt, I turned it around so the printed purchase details faced Mike. I held it out at arm's length.

"See this?" I said. "Want to know what this is? This is a purchase receipt for two earplugs bought two days ago by T. Reiner. Theodore Reiner, if you need me to connect the dots for you. Now you tell me, Mike. Why in the shit would the 99 Town Chief of Police go to a tattoo shop and buy two earplugs a day before we put two earplugs into evidence bags in a murder case?" I pulled the slip of paper back and shoved it into my pocket with the other before Mike could see the hand-written instructions on the other side. "So what about you? Are you on the level, Mike? Are you square with me? Or am I just part of a sham case to set up a bunch of kids on Murder One charges?"

"Hey, I don't know anything about that receipt. We found those plugs together. I don't plant evidence. I didn't plant shit," Mike said.

"And the chief? What's his story? Is he on the Order payroll?" I said.

"The Order pay… Chuck, you're on the Order payroll! Whose side are you on here?"

"How about you? Is the Order paying you off too?"

"I thought this was about some android! Now you're going after the chief? Going after me? Did they do something to your head when you were back in Chicago?"

"Listen to what I'm saying! The android is just the tool. Just a hammer someone is swinging. I need to find the hand holding the hammer. Is it the chief? Is it you?"

Mike's jaw muscles clenched and unclenched and clenched again before he spoke. "You're starting to really piss me off, Chuck. And I'm going to be honest with you. Most times when I go about solving problems, it gets violent."

"Violent solutions, huh," I said. "Well, we sure found one here."

"Listen, you son of a bitch! I've been through this with you every step of the way. If there's one person you should trust in this God-forsaken town, it's me. You got a real problem figuring out who your friends are, you know that?"

"I'm not asking you for anything, Mike," I said. "I'm going to find Sara. Make sure she's safe. And if you really are on my side, do what you can to delay the trial. And don't follow me."

In the back alley, I revved the Mustang's V8 and threw it into gear. Mike didn't follow. That was good. I couldn't risk anyone else knowing about Ruby and what she held. She was the last thread I clung to.

It was well after sunset by the time I made it to Cheap Hotel. The small pot-holed parking lot looked as it always did: rough, dark, and mostly empty. No one moved about. I parked the Mustang and killed the engine. The parking lot was quiet but the ambient noises of 99 Town. A train rumbled and vibrated the city's foundation from a few blocks away. Light traffic sounded like white noise or the constant tide of an ocean. Music played from an open window. A cat cried.

Places like this, this was where anomalies happened. In 99 Town and under the Order.

I stepped out of the Mustang and brought the double-barreled sawed-off shotgun with me. I walked with it at the ready, aimed at the ground just in front of my feet as I approached my room. There was a window to the room, and it was dark inside. The shades were drawn, just like I left them. Was Ruby inside, waiting for me with the implant?

If I was plugged in, and if Ruby was plugged in, and if we could connect to the Network to make the devices work, I could have seen through the door and known. Instead, I was left peeking through the gaps in the shades into a dark room. I saw nothing but darkness, so I went about plunging the rudimentary key into the slot and turned the deadbolt. I put my hand on the knob and eased the door open.

It swung inward with a creak.

I side-stepped in front of the door, gun aimed at anyone who might be inside. My eyes strained to see through the inky blackness, and I cursed my lack of neural enhancements.

"Ruby?"

She didn't answer. Instead, an explosion ripped the hotel room into a billion splinters. I caught a glimpse of the engulfing fireball and felt a single moment of the physical and audio concussion. With more force than flames, I was lifted off my feet and propelled backward into the crumbling blacktop parking lot. When my head bounced off the asphalt the lights went out.

I came to and had no idea where I was, how I'd gotten there, or how much time had passed. When I lifted up my head, I saw Cheap Hotel had been ripped in half. The section where my room had been was gone. A chaotic array of plaster, wood splinters, roof shingles, and fluffy tufts of asbestos was spread across the parking lot. The door to my room, I could tell it was mine by the room number nailed to it, was mostly intact, lying just a few feet to my left. To my right, was the shotgun.

My head felt like it'd been put in a blender. Both my ears were ringing now, louder than just my left one had ever rung before. My eyes burned. My equilibrium wobbled like I was drunk. My short-term memory had been wiped clean like files deleted off a computer. What the shit just happened?

My fellow hotel guests were coming out of their rooms to see the growing inferno and find an answer to that same question.

Slowly, the pieces began falling back together.

I was in 99 Town. Was that my hotel burning down? That *was* my hotel. Was there an explosion? All the splinters and fire and debris told me, yes, there definitely *was* an explosion. It triggered when I opened the door. Had I been concussed? I *had* been concussed. That was why my head hurt so bad. This was what a concussion felt like. Was someone trying to kill me?

I thought about that last question for a few seconds.

Someone *was* trying to kill me. Me and other people too. An android. But who programmed the android?

I realized I didn't have an answer to that last question, and I wasn't going to find it by laying down in the parking lot of a burning hotel. Through my deafened ears, I heard police sirens and realized "the cops" was one possible answer to my last question. The cops. The

Keepers. The Underground. The Order... I needed more time to unravel it all, time I wouldn't have if the cops came here and finished the job.

I fought my way up off the pavement, my balance as trustworthy as everything else in 99 Town now. I staggered over to the shotgun and picked it up. My narrowed vision scanned the parking lot. Ruby wasn't around, and she wouldn't have been waiting inside the hotel room next to a bomb. And if she had been in the room when it went off? Well, there'd be no sewing those pieces back together. I spotted the Mustang reflecting the structure fire off its waxed red and white paint job.

"Hey, buddy," I heard a man call. "You alright? You look like a steaming hot bowl of New England shit chowder."

Had to get away from here. They were coming here to finish the job. Whoever did this would want to make sure their trap succeeded.

I got to the Mustang and slipped inside. Judging by my reflection in the rearview mirror, the man in the parking lot wasn't wrong. My face was covered in soot. Streams of blood ran down both my ears. My pupils were the size of pinpricks. I looked away and tried to ignore the ringing and throbbing going on inside my head.

The android killed Sammy. Killed Mickey. Tried to kill me. Maybe Ruby too. The next person on his hit list had to be...

"Sara."

The key found its way into the ignition. The Mustang fired to life. I found the clutch and Reverse on the shifter and made them do their job. I spun the car around and slammed the transmission into First. The man, the owner of Cheap Hotel, stood outside the Mustang in dismay at the strange man from the Order who was about to drive away from the wreckage that used to be his livelihood. I launched the Mustang out of the hotel parking lot as the police and fire swarmed around it. I plunged through their oncoming flashing sirens like a diver through water.

I pulled onto the highway and put the hammer down. My head swelled and ached with each flash of headlights and streetlights that skewered my corneas. Those things didn't matter. I had to get out of

Downtown and get to Sara. I swerved between traffic as the Mustang accelerated past the speed limit.

With a few practiced button punches, I dialed Sara.

"Mickey's dead," I said before she had a chance to say anything else. "They came after me, and now they'll be after you too."

"What? No. You're wrong. Mickey wouldn't let anybody—"

"I know, I know. But it's true. They gunned her down in the bail bonds office. I just left there," I said.

"Are you sure—"

"If they can find you, they'll come for you next. Don't call the cops. Don't call anybody. Find a gun. Stay hidden. I'm coming to you," I said.

Chapter Twenty

I followed the two-lane highway north. The city and traffic drifted away. The lights. The noise. They all fell away the further I drove north. No chance of anyone following me. Out here, in the mix of twilight and starlight, I could see miles in every direction. Once I was outside of town, I stopped, shut off the Mustang, and stood outside just to listen. Both ears were whining like electronic feedback, but I wasn't worried about that. I ignored the ringing and listened for another kind of buzz. The buzz of a drone.

"Nothing," I said to myself.

I climbed back into the car, drove another three miles, and turned off the paved road into farmland. Rocks and gravel rattled under the Mustang's tires. Rows of old oak trees separated fields and farm properties. Every mile or two, another skeletal husk of an old barn or house poked out of the rows and rows of dying yellow corn stalks.

The safe house was near the northern border fence, down a minimum maintenance road. I checked my rearview mirror and could only see dust illuminated by my own red taillights. No other headlights. I took another turn onto a long driveway. The Mustang rumbled and bounced through the ruts until I stopped in front of an old farmhouse. I killed the engine but left the headlights on, shining on the porch and the front door. The rumble of the V8 surrendered to the sound of wind moving through cornstalks and crickets hiding in the weeds.

Sara stepped out of the front door of the house onto the covered porch. She leveled her snub-nose revolver at the Mustang and squinted one eye of a face that was ready to kill.

I got out slowly and put both hands up.

The steel glare in her eye softened as soon as she recognized me. She dropped the pistol to the deck boards and ran to me. She hugged me tight and neither of us said a thing. A few seconds passed only narrated by the wind and the crickets. Red-lit dust circled around our feet. My shoulder held her head and her tears wet my coat.

"Is she really dead?" Sara finally said.

"I'm sorry. They killed her in her own office," I said.

"They?" Sara asked.

"The android, and maybe whoever programmed the android. There was a firefight. She didn't go down easy," I said. "Someone must be its master."

I looked around the darkness surrounding the safe house. The light died just meters out from the front of the house and the shine of the headlights, and beyond that was just shadows. "Let's go inside, huh?" I said.

She nodded and retrieved the gun from the porch deck boards. I went back to the Mustang to kill the lights and she followed me. We walked to the house through quiet darkness.

The interior of the house was as practical and utilitarian as the outside but with a veneer of charm and familiarity. Sara, having never fully let go of me, her hand holding my triceps, led us forward. She hung her coat over the back of one of the dining room chairs, so I took off my Order white coat and did the same. The rooms were small, just a kitchen with minimal appliances, a dining room with a big oak table, and a family room with a couch, a recliner, and a fireplace. The fireplace was unlit but had a few half-burnt logs waiting for a spark. The only light came from a few wall-mounted electric lamps. There were family pictures on the walls and fireplace mantle, the old kind of pictures that were printed on glossy paper and didn't cycle through. I didn't recognize any of the people.

"Who are they?" I asked.

"Nobodies," Sara said. "The original owner was a client of mine. Tried for conspiracy against the Keepers. Had all kinds of weapons hidden away here. Killed a cop. His trial was faster than even Drex's will be. They brought him in that morning and had him strapped to the table in the lethal injection room that afternoon. I couldn't save him. And since he had no liquidized funds to pay me and no heirs to bequeath the house to, the Keepers saw fit to give it to me. After that, Mickey filled the whole house with random items from random families. Every once in a while a client would skip bail, not pay, get caught, and get locked up or executed. The judge let Mickey repossess their property as financial reimbursement. She'd take old things and bring them here. If she had a client she trusted who needed protection, or just needed peace before they were convicted and executed, they'd stay here. This place is a museum of the dead ends of people's lives."

"Owned by the dead; borrowed to the dying. We should fit right in," I said. "Who else knows about this place?"

"Me. You. The very few of our clients who stayed here and managed to beat the wrap. They owe their lives to yours truly," Sara said.

"No cops?"

"Relax. We're safe out here," Sara said. "All alone."

"Alone sounds good," I said. "Can you make coffee? The good stuff?"

Sara looked around the kitchen. "You bet your ass I can."

The house's backdoor led to a small yard surrounded by cornfields and an infinity of night. A dim bare lightbulb shined down on an old picnic table, a dilapidated shed, and the edges of the cornfields. I set the shotgun down on the flaking red-painted boards of the table and sat on the bench. I waited there while Sara brewed the pot of coffee. Moths swarmed around the light bulb, bumping off the glass and casting erratic shadows on the picnic table and shotgun.

I tilted my head back and looked up to the night sky. Out here, far from 99 Town and even further from Chicago, the sky was painted with a diamond mosaic. I saw constellations cluttered with stars between stars. There was a wide brushstroke of the galaxy's plane cutting diagonally through the sky. Crisscrossing that was the band of geo-synchronized space stations, lit like untwinkling stars. More lights than I'd ever seen in any city I'd ever been in.

Sara came out with two ceramic cups. She sat down and set one cup in front of me. I took it and drank a sip.

"Sammy is dead. The tattoo shop is burnt to the ground. Ruby might be dead too, but I don't know. She gave me this," I said and dug slips of paper out of my pocket. I set the note from Ruby flat on the table so Sara could read it. "Or maybe it was the android pretending to be Ruby. She was supposed to meet me at my hotel. She wasn't there, but a bomb was. That's twice someone's tried to kill me. I'm beginning to think that's why I was sent here in the first place. To die off the grid."

"First Nancy. Then Drex is set up for the fall. Mickey... Sammy, Ruby..." Sara said.

"I didn't want this. That's not why I came here to this place." My head dropped into my hands. The coffee sat on the table neglected. Thoughts boiled over inside of my mind. Not ideas, but a flood of feelings I couldn't regulate without an implant and the Network. Feelings I didn't want regulated.

"Then why? What were you expecting to find?"

"I was just trying to do my job. To find the truth." My throat was tight, and my words came out strained. I didn't know why. "Still, that's all I want. That's all I'm really after. Just a little bit of truth. About Nancy. The Order. About... about my wife and how she really died. What it's all about."

"So tell me. What did you find?"

"Nancy and Ruby were tied up in the Underground. Maybe the others too. Not just the small stuff either. I'm sure they got started with sneaking booze and video games over the fence, but that implant we found was chock full of data."

"Data?" Sara said.

"Anomaly data. An entry for everyone who ever expired under the Order," I said. "Going back for years. Each row had a name, a date, and an official cause of expiration. Then next to it, added by a different user, an entry with a more nefarious, more accurate cause of death."

211

"What's that other slip of paper? Did Ruby leave you that too?"

I looked at the other slip and read the words written there.

In case you still love me.

"It's nothing," I said and shoved both pieces back in my pocket. "After we split ways, I was attacked by the android. Those things, they're tied into the Network. They're only semi-sentient. They can only operate off the Network for limited amounts of time on specific downloaded instructions. Otherwise, they tend to go insane. Turn into confused wandering zombies, capable of rage, but not much else. This one, there's a drone overhead whenever it comes around. That drone must be broadcasting a signal from the Network. That means it came from the Order. According to the data on that implant, the Order is murdering people all across Chicago. Maybe other cities too. I think someone in the Underground figured it out and wanted to expose it to everyone."

"The android is disposing of its liabilities," Sara said. "It will kill you and me the first chance it gets. Our only option is to get Drex out of that jail cell and demonstrate in court that he was set up and that the Order is behind all of this. The Keepers will preside over the trial. If I can prove that the Order has interfered with due process in 99 Town, they'll throw out the whole case."

"You can't appear in court tomorrow. You said it yourself, as soon as you show your face they'll kill you," I said, all those unfamiliar emotions welling up inside of me again.

"They don't have to kill me if I don't show my face in court. Drex's trial is our last chance at saving him and finding the truth."

"No, Sara," I said. "You're all I have left."

"Even the Order wouldn't dare kill me right in front of the Keepers. As soon as I'm in court, the Order can't touch me," Sara said. "Where is the implant now?"

"With Ruby, wherever she is, if she's still alive," I said. "I had to give it to her to get it across the border.'"

"Ruby was in Chicago?" Sara said.

"Walked right out of the shadows and into my apartment. She was in the same room when Phom and Order agents came to visit me. They didn't even know she was there. The way she navigated around the Order like she was a ghost… I don't know if we should count her out just yet."

I sat in silence and held my cooling cup of coffee.

"There's something else, isn't there?" Sara asked.

"The dates of when all those people expired… They went right up until the moment my wife leaped from our apartment window to her death. They told me her implant had a dead man's switch. As soon as she hit the pavement and it detected she was dead, it fried its hard drive. The implant we found had data on thousands of expirations, up until the very moment she expired."

"You never told me her name," Sara said.

"Maggie," I said. Behind us, the moths plinked against the glass, their shadows always in motion. "I know it's not the way here in 99 Town but, I don't mourn her. It's not something we do under the Order. We move on. Carry on. Besides, I think she had moved on past me a long time ago. We had grown distant. She had something else going on. By the time she died, I don't think I loved her anymore."

"You don't think?"

"I don't know. Doesn't matter. None of that matters anymore. She's gone now."

Sara paused for a moment. "The implant we found in the locker, it couldn't have been your wife's implant. If she died in Chicago, the Order had to get their hands on it before anyone else. No one else would have been able to get to it."

"No one?" I asked and let the question hang unanswered. "The truth is, I knew so little about her, I have no idea who she knew or what she stood for. I mean, plugged into the Network, we never spoke negatively about the Order. Never. Never dared to even think about it. At least I didn't. If she knew all this was going on, why wouldn't she say something to me? Every night we lay down in the same bed. We woke up together and came home from work to the same home. Ate our meals together. We made love…" I paused. "She never let me in."

"And what would you have done if she had?" Sara asked.

I laughed hollow in the night. "I would have arrested her. Had her locked up for treason. Now? You know, I used to believe in the system, more than any person I've ever met."

"But where does the system end and people begin?" Sara said.

I balled up a fist and touched it down to the table, once, twice, three times. Each time I resisted the urge to smash the planks into splitters.

"You can't go to court tomorrow," I said. Turning to look at her, she was a blur behind my wet eyes. "I... I let my wife die. I kept my eyes closed and assumed the worst about her. I was a terrible husband. When she fell from that window, it was because I let it happen. Whether she jumped or whether she was pushed, it doesn't matter. I should have been there to stop it. Maggie died because I refused to protect her. I won't let the same thing happen to you."

"Chuck, I never asked for you to protect me. I have a job to do too, and if I don't go to trial tomorrow morning, they will execute Drex," Sara told him. "They'll execute him and come for Ruby next, and then us. And when we're dead, they'll have silenced all of us. Their lies will carry on, unchallenged."

"99 Town cops are tied up in this too. The chief for sure. Maybe the whole department," I said. "If we expose the Order's influence in 99 Town, we'll expose the cops too. Then they'll want their pound of flesh just the same. We can't stay here."

"And we sure as hell can't go to the Order," Sara said.

"There have to be places in between. Somewhere between here and there. Terra nullius?" I said nodding into the darkness.

Sara looked doubtful.

"There's ways out of 99 Town," I said.

"We're talking about escaping from one prison right into an even bigger prison,"

"Or maybe we just stay here," I said. "This wouldn't be so bad."

"Will you let me in?" Sara said.

"What do you mean?" I said.

She put her arms over my shoulders and clasped her hands behind my neck. "There's no one else left. All we have is each other. If we stay that way, you have to promise to let me in. I don't want to be the wife who lays down next to you each night, wakes up with you each morning, comes home from work each day to you, but never sees inside of you. If we're going in on this together, you have to let me in, and I'll promise to let you in."

I nodded. "Promise."

She moved closer to me, and I put my hands around her waist. As she leaned in, I leaned back until we both lay on the length of the picnic table bench, her on top of me. We kissed and held each other under billions of stars and the fluttering light of the single bulb, filtered by dancing moths.

Chapter Twenty One

I woke up next to Sara early the next morning in a moth-eaten bed in the small upstairs bedroom. The covers were thick quilts, and it was cold outside of them. Her naked skin was warm. She had draped a leg over my legs and pressed her especially warm crotch against my hip. She was a cocoon I never wanted to leave. It was more affection than I'd felt in years; enough to make me want to lie there for years. Maybe forever.

An alarm went off on Sara's phone. She slipped out from my hands to pick the phone up off of the nightstand and kill the beeping.

"We have to get up. I can't be late getting to the trial," she said.

The next thing I knew, she was slipping out from under the covers and out of my reach. I watched her move across the room, her skin goose-bumped, the texture detailed by the morning light coming through the window. She picked up my shirt off the floor and slipped it on, before gliding to the bathroom. The bleach white of the material contrasted against her dark shining skin.

As soon as she was gone, I knew I was stalling. No matter how long I wanted the moment to last, it had passed. I got up, found pants, and collected all the guns and ammo I could find.

Outside, I leaned against the hood of the Mustang while I waited for her. I drank coffee and enjoyed every sip. I had my Ruger holstered and held the stock of the shotgun in my other hand. Sara refused to carry going into the courtroom. She said that inside those walls, justice would be done her way. So I kept her thirty-eight revolver tucked inside my trench coat along with a dozen loose shells of buckshot for the shotgun.

Sara came out of the house wearing a black suit, ready for trial, a juxtaposition against the rural backdrop. I wore my Order whites.

"I still say this is a dangerous move," I said as I moved to the driver's side of the car. "And you're confident in calling ahead and telling them we're coming? You trust the bailiffs to be ready for you?"

"You have your job. I have mine," she said and got in the Mustang. "You have your modus operandi. I have mine. Today, we do it my way."

I obliged. "I got your back. If we're going to do this, let's get it done."

Inside the car, we traded a soft kiss.

"I think I love you," I said.

"Just think?" Sara said back.

I nodded, deep in thought. "Good luck today," I told her.

She nodded, nervous.

I fired up the Mustang and circled around the farmyard until it was pointed back down the narrow, rutted driveway. I shifted into second gear and pushed down on the accelerator. Dust and rocks kicked up behind us, and we headed back for 99 Town.

Downtown was the antithesis of the safe house. Crowded. Loud. Overloading the senses. Stalled cars and red lights. Pedestrians flowed down both sidewalks in teams. A man had turned an upside-down bucket into a drum set and was playing for donations. Most of the crowd flowed around the man and his bucket like he was a boulder in a stream. He kept playing anyway, a rhythm without melody echoing off the glass and marble buildings. Another man sold trinkets and called out like a carnival barker, an equally toneless vocalist paired with the drummer.

I rolled the Mustang up behind a stack of other cars at a red light. Six cars up, a stream of pedestrians crossed. "Rush hour" Sara had called it, but in my opinion, no one was rushing quite fast enough.

A homeless man, I knew them by sight now, was pushing a stolen shopping cart full of personal effects across the street. One of the cart's wheels got hung up in a pothole just as the light shifted from red to green.

Horns honked. People swore from open car windows. I was tempted to join them.

The homeless man got his cart moving, and the half dozen cars between the Mustang and the intersection began rolling forward. Too slow though. The light flipped back to yellow two cars in front of the Mustang and flipped red before we came up to the crosswalk.

I pounded my fist against the steering wheel. The Mustang rumbled like a dragon brewing a fire deep in its guts, the bumper at the edge of Main and Jefferson.

"Relax. Just one more light and we're there," Sara said. "We might even make it on time."

Parking anywhere other than directly in front of the Government Center was out of the question. Sara had called ahead, and a pair of bailiffs would be waiting on the front steps to escort her inside.

"I'll pull up to the curb. You get out and meet the bailiffs," I said. "Then I'll park in the garage and meet you inside."

We watched the traffic cross Jefferson Street in front of us. When the cross light turned yellow, I shifted the Mustang from Neutral to First gear. The light turned green, and I eased off the clutch and onto the gas.

"You have everything you need?" I turned and asked Sara as we rolled through the intersection.

When she turned to me, I saw a sudden flash of panic in her eyes. Lids peeled open. Pupils widened Focused over my shoulder. Her mouth opened to issue some warning but never had enough time. I never saw the danger coming. I felt the impact of the collision a moment before everything went black.

When I came to, the bucket man had stopped beating his drums. The carnival barker had decided whatever he was hocking wasn't as interesting as the wreck in the middle of Main and Jefferson. There was a sweet-smelling fog rolling through the air and around my head. The train had passed by, and all those sounds and noises had been replaced by murmurs and whispers.

"Anybody call nine one one?"

"Damn shame, those cars."

"Hey, I think he's waking up."

"Hey mister, you still alive in there?"

The voices seemed like one stream of consciousness, like the tech department talking in concert. But that was just my confused brain.

I was ready to ask myself what the hell just happened, but I knew: I'd been concussed. Again. My head was a thunderstorm of confused aches and throbs.

My side of the Mustang was smashed in. The windshield was cracked in long lines going the full length of the glass. Beyond the windshield, the crowd of onlookers peeped in at me. The driver's side window was busted out completely. Little bits of glass were all over the dash and my lap. Outside the window, the crumpled green hood of the Pontiac GTO leaked that white smoke that smelled like something sweet burning. No one was behind the wheel of the other car. Not anymore. To my right…

"Oh god no."

Sara was gone. The door was open, and she was gone.

As soon as I moved, my entire body turned to pain. I ignored it and climbed through the smashed-out driver's side window and onto the GTO's bent hood. I stood up, looking over the crowd.

"Sara!" I called out, searching all around the streets and sidewalks.

She must have made a run for the Government Center. If she had any brains at all, that's what she did. Left me and sprinted the last block to the relative safety of the bailiffs.

"Sara!" I yelled again.

"The guy took her, man."

"Pulled her down that way."

"She looked hurt," the decentralized voices of the crowd told me.

I saw where the one bystander was pointing. A back alley off Jefferson Street. Dark below the tracks of the elevated train. Then I saw Eric come out from behind the alley and grab the bottom rung of a fire escape. Eric. The last Rogue.

He took her.

I reach back into the Mustang between the driver's seat and the center console. Mickey's sawed-off shotgun was still there. I grabbed it and pulled it through the window. When the crowd saw me with the gun, they gasped and took a collective set of steps back. I jumped off the hood and cut a path through them, knocking over a couple as I charged for Eric and the fire escape.

Eric caught sight of me and started up the fire escape ladder. He was carrying something in his hand; I couldn't tell what, but it was slowing him down.

I planted my feet, shoved a by-stander out of the way with one hard palm to the chest, then put the bead of the shotgun on Eric. I fired both barrels. People screamed. Eric kept moving up the fire escape. I popped open the shotgun's breech and ejected two smoking shells. As I charged for the bottom of the fire escape, my hands dug out two more shells and slipped them into the shotgun. I snapped shut the breech.

At the bottom rung of the fire escape, I looked up and aimed the shotgun toward Eric. No use. Too many metal platforms and railings. I had to jump for the first rung of the ladder and use my elbow to pull myself up. I fought and squirmed my way up until I could put a knee on a rung. Meanwhile, Eric went further and further up.

Gaining a foothold, I made it onto the ladder and onto the first platform. From there on up it was all metal-grate landings and zig-zagging stairs. I raced up, the white tails of my Order coat flowing behind me as I went. I couldn't see Eric up above anymore. No way to tell what he was carrying or if he slipped inside the building or had gone to the roof. I watched for open windows or signs that Eric had left the fire escape on the way up, but mostly I just ran.

He didn't have Sara now. She must have gotten away. She must have made it to the Government Center. Told the bailiffs. There should be backup coming soon. But I knew not to count on any of that. Mostly, those were nice thoughts to keep my pounding head sane as I charged up floor after floor of metal platforms and steep steps.

Halfway up, the commuter train roared by, deafening me and sucking the loose tails of my coat in its draft. I continued up, ignoring the wind and noise.

Once the train had passed, I heard a familiar buzz rise up behind me. I twisted around and saw the drone. The same drone that had hovered over me on Harrison Street before I met the Rogues, the same drone that sat dormant in the tattoo shop, and the same drone that had followed after the GTO last night outside of the burnt-down rubble of Rogue's Tattoos. I swung the barrel of the shotgun out toward the drone, and like a startled animal, it shot up and over the building, too fast to track.

I let it go and climbed up to the top platform. A metal ladder led up to the roof. I took the ladder up two steps at a time. As soon as I could put a foot on the short brick wall surrounding the edge of the building, I jumped down to the pea-rock rooftop.

Eric waited for me patiently in the center of the roof. In one hand, he held my direct neural inhibitor. In the other, he held a human head by a fist full of curly black hair. The head rotated at the bottom of the short length of hair. I lifted up the barrels of the shotgun, aiming from the hip but not shooting yet.

"Looking for her?" Eric said.

The head turned at the end of its hair, and when Eric lifted it up, I saw her face. It was Sara. Her mouth was open and slack. Her once deep and caring eyes were rolled up into her skull. Eric had ripped off her head and taken it for a trophy, all while I was knocked out inside the Mustang.

"I'm looking for an implant. Want to trade?" Eric said. "Here. I'll let you have her. I've had my fun."

Eric tossed her head, and it rolled across the pea rock.

This had to be a simulation. No way he got to her. No way this happened while I was knocked out, unconscious in the Mustang. No way this could be real.

I wanted to check to see if I was wearing an implant, want to hit a button to escape this horrible training scenario the Academy had cooked up to torture my mind. But this was no simulation. This was 99 Town, and that was Sara's head ripped off her beautiful warm body. No doubt, the corpse was down in the alley below, dead and draining blood.

I had the sudden realization that I was hyperventilating. My view was narrowing. My legs felt like jelly. The vicious cold reality hit me that this was my fault. This had happened before, when I lost Maggie. I was too thick to stop it then. Too closed off and self-absorbed, but I had a chance to do it right this time. I could have Sara safe, but I screwed it up. I failed. Again. And now an android from the Order stood across this 99 Town rooftop from me and laughed.

A mantra from my training slipped into my head, through the anger and buzz of concussions. It came to me without me asking for it or wanting it, like an injection straight into my brain from the Network. But once it arrived I knew it was exactly what I needed: Emotions are selfish distractions, inferior to plans. Be better than your emotions. Become your calm calculated plans.

It was a simple phrase that seemed as distant to me as Chicago was from this 99 Town rooftop, but I embraced it. I had to detach from emotion. Give the mission my full priority. Allow the Network to fix my emotions later. Resolve myself from human weaknesses and execute the mission.

I exhaled long and slow, and focused my tunnel vision toward Eric. I had to get him talking. Had to get him to leak truths about who sent him. Had to get *him* distracted.

"How long?" I called out, struggling to complete the sentence, but determined to do it. "How long have you been pretending to be Eric? Did you kill him and take his place the same night you killed Nancy? Was there ever a real Eric?"

"I'm Eric," the android said. "It's just a name. Just like Chuz or Chuck, or whoever you decide you are."

"You're a lie. Everything about you is a lie. All you've ever been is a lie."

Eric strolled across the rooftop, arms open wide, still holding the direct neural inhibitor I lost the night I'd spent with the Rogues. At least, now I knew what happened to it.

"Okay. So I am a lie," Eric said. "So are you. So are all of them down there on the street. So are the lawyers and criminals and

Keepers in the courtroom. We're nothing but stories we make up about ourselves."

The android stopped about ten meters away. The inhibitor still hanging down a full arm's length. I wasn't plugged in, but I had the hardware inside my skull that would paralyze me with one hit from the weapon. I watched Eric's gun hand for the slightest movement while clenching the shotgun.

"You murdered her," I said. "You murdered your friends too."

Eric shrugged. My finger crept around the shotgun's double triggers. Another train rumbled by.

"It wasn't anything personal," Eric said and had the gall to smile as he said it. "It's just programming. I'm acting how I was designed to act. Can you say the same? Are you following your programming? What's your purpose, Chuck?"

The way the android shrugged over killing Sara, its mocking tone and smug pseudo-face…

"How about you come find out my purpose," I said.

"Suits me just fine," Eric said.

The android's hand flashed up. A silent signal reached my port's hardware. My body seized up for one agonizing moment. All my muscles contracted. All my nerves fired. Every single pain receptor in my body lit up. I had no idea it was painful. Never anticipated being neuralized, or anything else for that matter, hurting this much. But I couldn't scream or cry out. My body wasn't my own. My finger tightened around the triggers. The blast echoed off the downtown buildings as I tumbled over and spasmed.

"You son of a bitch, you did it now," I heard the android say.

The waves of neural overload passed, and I recovered enough to look across the roof. The shirt Eric was wearing was shredded, exposing torn flesh, blood, and steel shots burrowed into the chrome metal chest. The white plastic neural inhibitor was chunks of broken electronics and strings of wire. Eric tossed it aside with as much concern as he had her head.

"Now I'm going to have to do this by hand," Eric said and charged.

I spun to my knees and drew my Ruger. I took quick aim and fired off three rounds into Eric's head. The android bucked backward with each impact, but his legs kept running. Two paces away, he dove for me.

I rolled and dodged the massive android. I jabbed the gun at him point-blank, trying to find a weak joint between the armor plating, and fired again. Each bullet pinged and ricocheted off the steel under skin. Hollow-points were great against anyone not wearing body armor, or without an armored body. Eric turned and swatted the gun away. It flew through the air and landed three meters away in the pea rock.

I scrambled backward, away from the bloodied but undamaged android.

"I'm going to cave in your skull," Eric said and came to his feet.

The android bull-rushed me. I fell to my back, caught the android's stomach with both feet, rolled, and catapulted Eric over my head. The android flew head over foot and crashed down against the roof flat on his back.

Any human would have at least been dazed. Eric just laughed.

I hustled up and over to where the shotgun lay. As I went, I fished out two more rounds from my coat pocket. I slid to a stop next to the shotgun just as Eric picked himself back up. The android charged again. I cracked open the breech, popped out the spent casing, let the new shells slip into the chambers, and flipped the breech shut. Before I could fire a shot, Eric was there and grabbed the barrels with both hands.

"What are you going to do with this anyway?" Eric asked. "You can shoot me all day with this thing for all I care. Might as well give it to me so I can put it to good use."

Eric tried yanking the gun away, but I held tight. The android pulled and swung me from side to side, the length of the shotgun acting as a whip, lashing me back and forth before letting of the shotgun and flinging me through the air.

I landed two meters away. The shotgun slipped from my hands and bounced out of reach. My head slammed off the roof's rock surface, setting off another volley of mental fireworks, and before I could tell up from down, the android was already moving. Heavy footfalls dug through rocks. I stretched for the shotgun, but Eric was on top of me before I could touch it.

"You really are a pain in the ass, you know that?" Eric said, straddling me. He raised a fist and sent it smashing down into my face. "But you'll learn. I'm a good teacher."

Another fist hammered into me. My nose erupted blood. My brain threatened unconsciousness. I held up my arms to block the next punch. When it landed, I thought it might snap my radius and ulna in half. It was still better than taking any more blows to the face. Meanwhile, Eric laughed like a schoolyard bully.

Through swollen and blurry eyes, I spotted the drone hovering overhead. I waited for the next fist to come swinging down.

Eric swung. I caught the incoming arm with both hands and diverted the blow into the rocks beside my head. I bucked my hips upward and rolled. The android was heavy, heavier than any human, but I took the momentum of the punch and rolled toward the robot's trapped arm. Eric tumbled over. I rolled on top, and then over and off the android.

I snatched the shotgun out of the rocks, rolled once more onto my back, and aimed it skyward. The drone was right above me, maybe ten meters up. I fired both barrels. The drone took the hit and careened over. Bits of its casing and rotors rained down. The airframe spun and crashed down into the roof. The buzzing stopped.

My hands were becoming practiced. I popped open the breech and ejected the spent shells while Eric came to his feet. I slipped in two fresh shells and snapped the breech closed with a flick of the wrist. I fired one barrel into Eric's face, then took aim at the crash-landed drone.

One shot, and what was left of the drone shattered to pieces.

I tossed the shotgun to the side. Now that the drone was gone, it really was useless.

Eric was still on his feet, stationary. The pseudo-skin on his face was shredded and hung from the steel skull in tatters. I panted for air.

"So what?" Eric said. "You've cut me off the Network, but I've downloaded enough programming to know I still need to kill you."

"And what after that?" I said. "After killing me, what's your next move?"

Eric seemed to contemplate that, but I knew it was just its RAM searching through its hard drive.

"You have no idea, do you?" I asked.

The android shrugged. "Guess killing you will have to do."

"You're all alone now. No Network. No Order. How does it feel?"

"I guess we're both human now," Eric said. "Does that mean I should feel bad when I smash your head into a wet pulp?"

"Come and try me," I said.

Eric laughed like an idiot. "I like this game," he said and came charging one more time.

I took a few steps back and found myself uncomfortably close to the edge of the building. I bumped into the meter-high wall that surrounded the rooftop and looked over my shoulder at the fire escape scaffolds, the train tracks, and the dark bottom of the alley. I looked back at Eric.

The android came at me like an old top-fuel drag racer. I found my centerline, widened my balance, and took a step forward. Eric came with one raised fist. I let the fist fall and stepped into the swing. I caught the android by the armpit and wrist. Another rotating step and I traded places with the android. One good strong shove and Eric went backward into the half wall and toppled over the side.

I heard him bounce off the fire escape at least twice but didn't waste time looking over the side just yet. Looking across the rooftop, I saw the remains of life and artifice. Sara's decapitated head wasn't far away. I couldn't bring myself to look at that for long. Bits of the android's drone and my neural inhibitor lay in pieces. The double-barreled shotgun wasn't far from the drone. I ran over, picked it up, and reloaded while hustling over to the fire escape ladder. When I was back to the ledge, I looked down.

Eric had caught the railing two stories down. He tried pulling himself back up, but something inside his damaged metal skull left him off balance. His right hand had a tight grip of the metal railing. His left flailed and malfunctioned.

I hurried down the ladder, flying down the metal steps until I was one flight up from the dangling android. The machine found a second handgrip and pulled himself up so his torso was above the railing. I aimed and fired one barrel. The buckshot shredded off more clothes, skin, and artificial blood. The android dropped back down, hanging by his fingers.

Eric laughed. I fired the second barrel into his face. He still laughed, more robot than human without cheeks or lips.

"You can kill me, Chuck," he said as I set the last two shells into the shotgun's smoking chambers. "But you can't kill the system that made me."

"One piece at a time," I said, snapped the breech shut, and fired a blast into each of the android's hands.

Fingers came apart, and the android slipped loose and fell. Two stories down, Eric smacked into one of the rails of the train tracks. He clung on, desperate and defiant, struggling to pull his mass upwards, but too much inside of the machine was already broken. When the commuter train rolled across the tracks, the steel wheels severed arms, shoulders, and head from the torso and legs. I watched as the android's head tumbled down to the street.

Chapter Twenty Two

I didn't care for Sara's no-guns-in-court rule before. I could give two fucks about it now. When I shoved open the rear doors of the courtroom, I carried the sawed-off shotgun in one hand and the android's head in the other. A bit of shoulder and the left arm were still attached to the head and dragged bloody fingertips across the marble floor.

Predictably, a bailiff stopped me two steps into the courtroom. "Whoa. What the hell is this?"

"Exhibit fucking A," I said.

The courtroom was old, traditional, and furnished with polished dark wood. At the front of the courtroom, the six Keepers of 99 Town presided over the trial. All were men. All were that pale shade of white. All of them looked so similar to the next, I couldn't pick out the two I'd already spoken with from the four I'd never seen before. None of them seemed to have noticed my impolite intrusion into their polite hearing. Before the Keepers were the two sides of lawyers, the prosecution and defense, with Drex sitting next to an empty chair where Sara should have been. The series of benches behind the lawyers were mostly empty, but the half-dozen citizens who were there seemed to fix their eyes on the back of Drex's head.

A whole system gathered together to destroy this one kid, even though he had done nothing wrong. I wanted to tell him that I had his back. That I'd finish what she started.

The prosecutor was speaking to the Keepers now, a long stream of words that I failed to interrupt with my intrusion.

"We've already been delayed far too long by the defense's absences. Miss Cohen hasn't been with her client in two days. I feel it's safe to say that if she doesn't believe in her client's innocence enough to even show up for trial, we shouldn't reserve the state's actions against him. More so than apathy, her absence demonstrates her client's guilt. We already have enough physical evidence to settle this matter. A pair of cars. A tire iron. A stolen earring. A buried body. The cold heart of a jilted lover. A history of flagrant disregard for the laws of 99 Town that allows us to maintain our way of life. Mister Drex Carlsrud is a prime example of everything spoiled and impure that has infected our great city. He must be extruded and eliminated, today before his presence here taints us any more than it already has."

"Everyone has the right to legal representation before the Keepers," said one of the six men behind the bench.

"And Mister Carlsrud had his, my Keeper," the prosecutor said. "Miss Cohen took his case, examined it for what it was, and saw fit to abandon it. If his own lawyer couldn't spare this sorry excuse for a man the time of day, why should we? There is a periculum in mora we subscribe to in this town. Why should justice wait one more minute to find him guilty of the crimes he so obviously committed?"

The Keepers seemed to consider this. A few of them whispered to each other.

A man in the gallery stood up. "I can't wait any longer," the man said. Few heard him. One of the six Keepers eyed the man, but then went back to the quiet conference. The man cleared his throat and spoke louder. "I can't— I *won't* wait any longer."

"Mister Meade," a Keeper addressed the man. "You are a guest here in 99 Town. And while here, you will respect our rule of law and our authority."

"Well, I don't, and I fought a war against your sort so I wouldn't have to," Mister Meade said.

This was Howard. Nancy's mourning father.

I saw the insanity in her father's eyes. Sonja was next to him, pulling on his sleeve, trying to get him to sit back down and stay quiet, but I knew by looking that nothing would stop this man from saying what he came here to say.

"As long as I draw breath I won't recognize your law or your authority," Howard went on. "This whole trial is a farce. But you people say your justice is swift. Well, that's why I'm here. For swift justice for my daughter who you allowed to be murdered in the street. You promised me that much, so let's have it. You owe it to me for what you let happen here."

"Order, Mister Meade," a Keeper said. "We will have Order."

"You abandoned the Order!" Mister Meade cried out. "You had it, and you threw it aside in favor of reckless anarchy. Now your negligence has cost me my daughter's life. And you have the balls to ask me for order? No! You give me order! You give me justice! I've waited long enough. Give me the head of the man who killed my daughter! I think I've earned it."

That seemed as appropriate a time as any.

"I have it," I said from the back of the courtroom and hefted up Eric's head.

All eyes turned back to me, a bloody and bruised man in tattered Order whites with a shotgun in one hand and a robot's severed head in the other. I kept the head hoisted up for everyone to see. The arm still dangled by a mix of sinew and steel cables. I walked through the gallery, pushed through the gate in the bar, and came before the Keepers. Two bailiffs spotted the shotgun and stepped closer from their stationary positions on either side of the courtroom, but no one stopped me.

"You want to know who killed Nancy?" I said. "I'll tell you who killed Nancy."

I set the head on top of the Keeper's bench. Most of Eric's face had been blasted off by the buckshot. The metal skull underneath was plain for everyone to see. The arm was limp, and the flesh had been worn off the metal fingers. Out of the bottom of the neck and shoulder where muscle, blood, and bones should have been were wires and sheared off steel plates. I turned to the lawyers, the gallery, Drex, and Mister and Miss Meade. I eyed Sara's empty chair and did my best to quell my rage.

"My name is Federal Investigator Chuck Alawode from the Chicago Anomaly Investigations Department," I said. "I was sent here to investigate Miss Meade's untimely expiration, and investigate it I have. Since I came here, I've been beaten, chased, lied to, and nearly incinerated. That thing, that android from the Order tried to kill me on three separate occasions. It murdered Nancy. It murdered her friends, framed Mister Carlsrud, and killed his attorney, Miss Sara Cohen, right across the street from where we sit on this very morning. If you don't believe me, you can go fetch her head too. You want to know who killed your daughter, Mister Meade?"

"God damn right I do," the man said.

"The Order killed your daughter," I said. "Just like the defendant, she was an undesirable. A human to be cast aside. Something far less important than their system. She was a smuggler, a rebel, and an agent of the Underground. So they sent an assassin here to kill her, her friends, and anyone else who might come here to find the truth. But I'm tired of the lies. Everywhere I go there are more lies. Today, I'm here for truth."

Howard Meade leaned forward. Something in his eyes, how they were locked on what was left of Eric, told me more than any implant could. Howard Meade was convinced. Now for the rest of the room.

I turned to the Keepers. "Your honors, I could give a fuck about your authority, your rule of law, or the ways you run this god-shitting town. I'm here for the truth, so here it is. The Order came here, violated all those rules and restrictions you hold so dear, killed your children under your noses, and made a mockery of your justice system. Now, I'll leave it up to you about how to address that with the Order. All I want is the immediate release of the defendant into my protective custody, and I ask you to grant us safe passage out of 99 Town. Let him go, and you'll never see or hear from either of us again."

The Keepers kept silent but turned away from me to gather in their huddle.

"Okay, I think I've heard enough," Phom said from the back of the courtroom. I turned my head, unsure of what I'd just heard. There, next to the backdoor I'd just come through, was Phom leaning against the wall in his Order whites. He took one step forward and said, seemingly to himself, "Set the inner cordon."

Order Agents poured into the courtroom from every door and exit, a mix of assault rifles and combat neural inhibitors aimed and ready. I still had the shotgun in one hand, my Ruger holstered at my side, and Sara's thirty-eight tucked behind my back. Every other barrel in the courtroom was aimed directly at me. I didn't move.

"Chuz, old buddy. My friend. Just who do you represent here? The Order? The Keepers? Yourself?" He drew his own neural inhibitor, and adjusted some settings on the side of it as he strolled up through the center of the gallery. He stopped next to Mister Meade. "Let me remind you, as a friend..." He leveled the neural inhibitor at Mister Meade and pulled the trigger. Nothing came out of the barrel, but Mister Meade started convulsing all the same. Violently. So much so people gasped and backed away. Blood came streaming from both nostrils. Then both eyes. Then ears. Sonja caught him and let out a series of long extended screams. Howard collapsed over sideways, his boiled brains leaking out of his ears and onto the marble floor and Sonja's lap.

Phom ignored the panic, and we locked eyes. "Chuz, you are nobody. An individual, insignificant in contrast to the will of the Order. Take a good look at what happens to anomalies who upset the Order," he said and waved a hand toward the late Howard Meade and his widow.

Phom reholstered his neural inhibitor. As he walked up to one of the tactical agents standing in front of the bar, he took a sidearm from the agent's leg holster. I recognized the sidearm as a handgun by its dark bluing and blocky shape. Gun or neural inhibitor, it didn't matter to me. Either could kill me just as dead. Phom continued his stroll, through the gate in the bar and along the defendant's table.

"No—" I said a half-second before Phom aimed the handgun and blew apart Drex's head. As the body slumped backward and off the side of the chair, Phom tossed the gun across the floor of the courtroom toward the agent he'd taken it from.

"Disgusting tool... So, what now?" Phom said, his arms outstretched. "What are we here for now? The trial's over. Justice is served. Keepers, do you have some sage advice for us all?"

They sat silently in their chairs behind the bench. Identically impotent.

"No speeches about your way of life, or rule of law?" Phom asked. "Let me remind you one more time. You are subordinate to the Order in every way. The only authority you might possess is derived from us. Here? Today? You derive that authority from me. And before you go and screw that up, I see fit to revoke that authority. I hope you don't object. No? Good. Then allow me to address my friend here."

Phom turned to me, menace in his eyes. We stood just a few meters apart, face to face in front of the Keepers and the gallery. "You brought this upon yourself, Chuz. I had a plan for you. A nice little job out of the way. An open and shut case. But you couldn't stick with it, could you? Had to go poking around, didn't you? And now we have this."

Phom pulled out his neural inhibitor. He looked down at it and examined its settings for a moment.

"It wasn't supposed to be this way. Wasn't supposed to go down like this at all. But, I am an agent of the Order, and the Order will have its way."

He raised the barrel of the neural inhibitor and aimed it between my eyes.

Every light in the room went out. The courtroom turned black. I heard gasps and shouts from the gallery. Someone had cut the power to the entire building and given me the split second of time I needed. I dove to the side, under the defendant's table as I heard dozens of distinct clicks of triggers of the neural inhibitors. I felt nothing. 99ers swore and cried around me. The agents of the Order yelled out commands and confused responses.

Their inhibitors weren't working. Neither were their implants. This was more than just a normal power outage. Someone was jamming all radio signals going into and out of the courtroom. The Network and everything tied to it was temporarily gone.

The agents were suddenly without the various tools they'd grown familiar with. Ammunition counts. Friendly forces locators. Night vision. Internal communications. Without everything the Network provided them, they were lost, confused, and tactically crippled. I knew the feeling.

I didn't take the time to wonder how or why. I bolted from under the table and charged through the darkness. The first thing I collided with was Phom. I gave him a good shove and ran for the bar separating the court from the gallery. Almost falling on it, I climbed over it and found the aisle leading back to the doors leading out of the courtroom.

"Stop him!" I hear Phom call. "Chuz! Chuz! I'm going to kill you, Chuzzy!"

A few gun blasts flashed inside the dark courtroom and bullets zipped by me. In the darkness, no one saw me hit the doors leading outside until I was through, and daylight spilled in from outside. I was through the atrium and out onto the street before they could follow.

The sunlight nearly blinded me. As I took the steps leading down from the Government Center three at a time, I held up a hand to block out the sun. When I hit the sidewalk, I gripped the shotgun with both hands and sprinted for the wrecked Mustang a block away.

Behind me, Order agents poured out of the Government Center doors. Overhead, an Order hovercraft churned the air. Like Eric's drone, but a hundred times larger, the hovercraft was a flying perversion of what 99 Town was supposed to be. I ignored it and hoped it didn't spot me as I fled the courthouse.

There was still a crowd around the wreckage of the GTO and the Mustang in the middle of the intersection. 99 Town cops had blocked off traffic. A tow truck was on sight and hooked up to the GTO. It pulled on the Pontiac, dislodging it from the side of the Mustang to the songs of screeching metal. I shoved through the crowd at a dead sprint, put one foot on the hood of the GTO, and jumped over it to the Mustang.

I slipped in through the broken driver's side window and hoped to hell it would still run. The keys were in the ignition. I kicked down the clutch and put it back into neutral. When I cranked over the engine, it clunked and complained for two, three, four seconds. Then sparks met the stoichiometric mixture of air and fuel. The Mustang roared to life.

"Motherbitch!" I yelled.

I threw the Mustang in reverse and cranked the wheel, aiming the machine away from the Government Center. A quick accelerator/clutch exchange and I had the car in first gear and the tires roasting on the pavement. The Mustang and I were gone from the street before the Orders agents knew which way to run after me.

As soon as the RPMs quieted enough for me to hear anything else, I noticed my cell phone ringing. I flipped it open. An unknown number. I answered.

"Chuck?" The voice was familiar.

"Ruby?"

"Time to get your ass out of 99 Town. I got some sophisticated friends who killed the power and blocked the Network from the Government Center, but it won't last long. They have a hovercraft here, rebroadcasting the Network from Chicago. Just like the drone. If it spots you—"

"How?" I asked.

"Like I said, I got friends in low, yet sophisticated places, but that's about all the help we'll get," Ruby said. "We can't stay in this city. Not anymore. Meet me at the South East Station and I'll get you out. See you there, Chuck."

"Wait!" I said as I swerved the Mustang onto a freeway ramp. Ruby hung on the line. "Did you see? Did you see what happened in the courtroom?"

"I saw it all," she said. "Drex didn't deserve that. He wasn't involved in any of this. He just wanted to run booze and race cars. The Order and the Keepers, they used Drex as a patsy, and when he'd run out of usefulness... well, you saw. I saw what happened to your girlfriend too. Nobody matters to them. Only their stupid fucking laws. It was a trap. The whole thing was a trap from the very start to take out Nancy... Maggie... maybe you too. But there's a way out of every trap."

"Maggie... How did you know—"

"Let's just say I know more about you than you know about me," Ruby said.

"Why didn't you tell me?"

"Why? Because you were one of those motherfuckers we were fighting against. People like you, you're why Nancy and the rest of the Rogues are dead."

"What about my wife? Did she know about all of this? Did she give you the implant?"

Ruby paused. "Nancy took it. Right after the fall from your apartment. But we'll talk about her later."

"So Maggie was involved in all of this, from the very start," I said.

"Boy, nothing gets past you, huh?"

"Do you still have it? Do you have the implant?"

"Meet me at the train station, Chuck," she said and hung up.

Chapter Twenty Three

I pulled the Mustang into a parking spot in front of the South East Train Station. The exterior of the building hadn't changed since the last time I had come here with Sara. The brownstone façade stood silent and ominous, like an ancient sleeping golem. Few other people moved about. No other cars drove through the lot.

When I got out of the car, I checked the shotgun. Two fresh shells in the chamber. The last two shells I had. I tucked the shotgun inside my Order white coat and held it there. I still had my Ruger and Sara's thirty-eight. With any luck, I'd keep them stashed away until I had the implant and 99 Town was a distant memory. I wasn't sure where I'd go from there, but I knew I had to keep moving.

I trotted toward the front entrance. The Beaux-Arts architecture towered above me as a quiet monument to the failed ideals of 99 Town conserving a more peaceful past. I climbed the steps and pushed through the doors and into the station. The interior was just as still as the exterior. No bustling crowd. No music or news broadcast in the background. My footsteps reverberated against the terrazzo floor. I slowed my pace and rolled my feet to muffle the echoes. No need to announce my presence.

Ruby saw me before I saw her anyway. As I strolled deeper into the cavernous terminal, she came up behind me and walked next to me.

"How much time do we have? Were you followed?" she asked me in hushed tones.

"I think I got away clean," I said. "Do you have the implant? Tell me you still have it or all of this is for nothing."

She pulled it out of her pocket. Such a small beat-up old thing.

"Give it to me," I said.

Ruby closed her hand and pulled it away. "If I do, what will you do with it? You're not the only one who lost everyone for this thing."

"It belongs to me. Your friend stole it from my dead wife," I said.

"Dead wife," she scoffed. "You didn't know it existed until you stole it from my dead friend."

I stopped. I'd been distracted. Tactically unaware. We weren't alone here. A man stood near one of the doors leading down to the loading platforms below. Another man dressed in a professional but functional 99 Town style, leaned against the wall near some vending machines. A woman looking conspicuously nondescript was leaning against the ticketing counter, facing but not talking to the ticket seller. Big coats loose enough to hide plenty underneath. Eyes faking nonchalant observations, not watching anything but tracking everything. Hands empty and poised near belts under the coats.

I grabbed Ruby's sleeve, and she stopped walking too. I pulled her close enough to whisper. Over her shoulder, I spotted a fourth man behind us coming through the entrance of the terminal. Similar dress. Similar demeanor. The innocent bored-but-always-observant look of someone who had business he didn't want to let on to.

"What?" Ruby asked.

"When the shooting starts, and it's about to, stay low and get your ass to the Mustang in the parking lot," I told her.

"No. That's the wrong direction. We're going through the fence," Ruby said.

I only paid half-attention to her. My eyes tracked the strange folks in nondescript clothes. I'd made them. Now they made me. One talked seemingly to himself. Lips moved silently. Others listened via implants. Federal agents.

"I think they got other ideas," I told Ruby.

"Oh," she said, telling me in that one syllable that she'd seen what I'd seen.

We stood there frozen for one cool second, and everyone in the train station knew the time for waiting and words and bequeathed the next second to action and violence.

Ruby put her palm against my chest, hooked a heel behind my foot, and pushed. I fell flat on my back just as a salvo of bullets cut through the air where I'd been standing. In the time it took me to hit the floor, she'd already drawn that blocky handgun I'd seen in Chicago and was returning fire. I rolled on my belly and whipped out the shotgun in one fluid movement. The man by the door to the platform, he was the closest. He had to go first. I brought the barrels to bear on the man, and as soon as he was behind the bead, I pulled the first of the two triggers.

The man was in the middle of reaching for his gun when his chest exploded. He tumbled backward through the door, falling and propping open the door with his corpse. Before he hit, I swung the shotgun toward the next closest agent, the woman behind the ticking counter. Bullets smacked off the floor around where Ruby landed. I fired the last shell from the shotgun and put a shower of steel pellets into the woman.

Two agents left. One hiding behind a vending machine and one by the entrance.

I got to my feet while Ruby punched bullets into the vending machine and the corner pillar near the entrance. The sound of her shots was indistinguishable from the rest of the cacophony of gunfire and echoes in the station.

The remaining agents poked out from behind protection to fire off a few quick shots. The bullets zipped by us like supersonic hornets. No inhibitors this time. They'd learned their lesson in the courtroom.

"Come on," I said and grabbed Ruby by the scruff of her shirt. Together with both guns, we kept the agents at bay and ran for that propped-open door leading down to the loading platforms.

An agent dipped from behind the corner, fired off three shots that zipped over our heads, then sunk back behind cover. Ruby fired off two more shots, too late to do anything but deter. She pulled a fresh magazine from a pocket and swapped the empty for the full in one fluid motion as the opposite agent exposed himself for a moment and fired off three quick shots. Two went overhead. The third sang as it twanged off the hard floor.

"This way," I said and shoved Ruby through the open door and over the dead body of a federal agent. I followed.

Stairs sank and twisted down away from the station. The polished stone and brass gave way to rusted steel railings and concrete steps. We came to the loading platform, one of several separated by steel I-beam pillars and train tracks. A cool breeze flowed under the building and across the tracks.

Ruby had a hold of my hand now, and as soon as we reached the platform she pulled me to the direction of the tracks leading off to the East.

"This way," she said. "I know the way out."

"Stop right there, Chuckers!" I heard a voice call out from behind us.

If it was any other voice, I would have kept running, maybe jumped off the platform down to the tracks to take cover, but that voice was Mike's voice, and it froze me in my place.

I turned. Mike and Chief Reiner were maybe ten paces away. Must have been waiting for us on the backside of the staircase leading down. Both of them had guns drawn and aimed at us. They had us dead to rights.

"Drop the guns," Mike grimaced.

Unlike Mike, the chief smiled when he said, "The hardware is going to hit the floor, or you are, sweetheart."

"Lick my crack, pig," Ruby muttered, but let her automatic clatter to the floor all the same.

I let the Ruger fall as well. The chief let out a fat jowly laugh, showing yellow teeth that matched his jaundice, alcohol-saturated eyes. "Come on, Bonnie and Clyde. Back into the station," the man said and nudged with his barrel.

We all moved, arms raised, guns abandoned. As I stepped past Mike to the bottom of the stairs, I saw a squad of white-coated agents enter the station. I heard the Order hovercraft mulch the air outside to the East.

"They started all of this, Mike," I said. "The Order brought that murderer to your town and killed your people. We've been partners through all this Mike."

"Shut your stinking cock holster," the chief said.

Agents surrounded me, Ruby, and the cops. They stopped out of range of physical attacks, but well within range of their guns. Coming down another set of stairs, I saw Phom flanked by two lackeys stroll toward us.

Phom and his troops stopped in front of us. He smirked at Captain Reiner, and Reiner smiled back like Judas ready for a kiss. I noticed. Mike noticed it too.

"Well done, Captain," Phom said, addressing Reiner. "Consider those financial and bureaucratic difficulties you mentioned cleared up."

"These people aren't on your side, Mike. They don't care about 99 Town and never have," I said. "If you let them take me, they'll erase me, make it like I was never alive. When they're done with me, they'll kill anyone else not on their payroll and go on dumping their problems into your town."

"Could be worse," Mike said. "Us 99 Town cops could arrest you, assign you a barely-passed-the-bar-exam public defender, run you through a dog and pony show trial, and get you set up with a lethal injection the next day. But you know me, Chuckers," Mike said, finally smiling. "I've always been a fan of violent solutions."

"And Chuz, you crazy kook. How'd it come to this?" Phom said to me.

I looked up to my former colleague and friend. "Hi, Phom."

"Look at the two of us," Phom said. "What in the world are we doing in this dump of a train station all the way out here in 99 Town, with guns drawn, and standing against each other? You shooting at agents, standing side-by-side with this sleazy slum-rat. This wasn't the plan. I never wanted to have to kill you, Chuz."

"But you killed my wife, didn't you?" I said.

"She brought that upon herself, Chuz," Phom said. "She chose her path into tragedy, away from peace, away from the Order. She was working for the Underground, buddy. What else could we do but have your android shove her through that window and put an end to the chaos she was creating?"

"Her only crime was seeking out the truth. Her job was no different than ours. But you gave up on the truth a long time ago, didn't you?" I said.

"We've gone over all of this already," Phom said. "The problem is, you're too young. Too naive. You don't remember things before the Event. The pain and violence. But living here, in this zoo, I figured by now you'd have a taste of it. Look around you, Chuck. Is there any truth to be found here? Any peace? Any order? Don't answer. I'll answer for you. There's nothing here but the lowest of the low. The scum and filth of humanity, all gathered around in their own self-inflicted poverty and pain. Your wife and the other garbage of 99 Town… if they had their way, they'd bring that to the rest of us. Crime. Disease. Hunger. Murder. And for what? For truth? For freedom?

"You want to know if I gave the order to kill your wife?" Phom said. "Of course, I did. And I'd do it again. And a hundred times over if it meant keeping this human refuse quarantined inside 99 Town."

"You know what, Phom? Fuck the Order and fuck you," I said.

"Chuz, buddy. You misjudge me, pal. I did this for you. I freed you from her. I sent you here so we didn't have to kill you in Chicago. I stuck my neck out for you, and this is how you repay me? They wanted to asphyxiate you the moment you found that note from that cunt wife of yours. But I went to bat for you. Sent you here to forget about your treasonous, cheating, unloving wife. Gave you a chance to get your head straight. Gave us a chance to clean up her mess. This isn't about me and you. This is about her! Her crime. So we had to break some eggs along the way. So what? It's time to come back to the Order, Chuz. As for these lowlifes? Well, we have a solution for them too."

I glanced over at Mike and was surprised to see the smirk had returned to his face. Mike's barrel was still on me, but his eyes were on Phom.

"Well, shit me. I guess I've become a fan of violent solutions too," I said.

"Fuck me," Mike said under his breath.

"Arrest them," Phom said. The agents stepped forward to put on cuffs.

Mike stuck his handgun over my shoulder and dropped it. In a single moment, I caught it and drew Sara's thirty-eight from behind my back. Mike drew another gun from inside his jacket.

I fired both guns at once, plugging Phom in the gut and the agent to his left. Mike picked out two other Order agents and opened fire. Ruby twisted around into the chief, wrapping her arm around his gun arm. Screaming, she opened her mouth wide and bit into Reiner's fat unshaven cheek. Then he was screaming, and in his shock, the Rogue stripped him of his gun, turned it on him, and put a bullet through his forehead.

Mike and I stood side-by-side exchanging gunfire with agents at point-blank range. Quick. Deafening. Violent like a bare-knuckled brawl. A shot hit Mike and he dropped to the concrete platform. I dropped another agent, but there were too many left still standing.

Ruby fired over my shoulder and took out another agent. Then she grabbed a fist full of my collar and yanked me off my feet, over the edge, and down onto the train tracks below. We fell two meters down to the greasy and dark trough.

Another agent dropped into the trench, and Ruby shot him dead through the chest. She grabbed me and pulled me to my feet and down the tracks. Then a body fell to the edge of the trough. Mike's limp and bloody face dangled over the edge, upside down. His blank eyes stared at me.

"Mike!" I called out.

"Come on!" Ruby said. She grabbed the cloth of my coat and yanked me along the tracks to where they left the station. She ran. I followed. She was quick. I sprinted to keep up.

Outside from underneath the station, the yard sprawled out across multiple tracks, some with rows of boxcars staged for the next freight locomotive to move them. All of them ran toward Chicago. A tall fence topped with concertina razor wire separated the train yard from 99 Town. An Order hovercraft hummed above the station but hadn't noticed us yet.

Ruby ran to the nearest row of abandoned boxcars. She jumped through an open door, slid through the car, and exited out the other side. I followed her, older and slower. When I dropped down on the other side of the boxcar, Ruby pulled me so my back slammed against the wall of the car.

"Wait here a minute. They're coming out of the station," she said.

I shuffled along the edge of the boxcar and peeked around the corner. Phom and another agent stepped out of the station through the tracks. He limped. Blood stained the waist of his Order whites. His left hand pressed hard into the red blotch. His right hand held his neural inhibitor.

"Chuz!" Phom called out.

"There's a service tunnel below the tracks that heads toward Chicago, but we can't get to it with them watching us," Ruby said. "There's a gap in the fence leading back to the parking lot over there."

I looked where she pointed. We had a clear path to the gap in the fence and from there a clear path back to the Mustang. But where would we go from there? Anywhere but here, I guessed.

"Chuzzy!" Phom called out with surprising volume and strength. "You've gone and done it now, pal. You hear me? I was here to bring you in, nice-like. I was here to save you! No more of that anymore. Now I'm going to track you down and melt your brains outta your skull!"

"Go, go," I said and shoved Ruby toward the gap in the fence. I ran after her.

Ruby scrambled to the spot, a loose section of the chain link coupled with a low path in the dirt under the fence. She flopped to her belly and slipped through like she'd done it a hundred times before.

She urged me on from the other side. "Come on, come on!"

I dived down into the shallow trough and squirmed through. Ruby pulled me as I went.

"Chuz!" Phom called out.

A bullet smacked against the ground next to me.

"Go! Run!" I said as soon as I was through. We flew for the parking lot to the soundtrack of gunshots and death threats.

"I'm going to kill you, Chuz! You had your chance, and you blew it!"

I didn't bother to look behind me and see, but I heard the Order hovercraft lower down over the train yard. The turbines drowned out the sound of the threats and bullets. The wind and dust swirled out and away, past Ruby and I. The dust cloud consumed us and the parked cars around the Mustang. We weaved through the fleet of Crown Victorias that hadn't been there when I'd arrived. A few more bullets cut through the dust, unaimed and off target.

More agents poured out the front doors and down the steps of the station.

Ruby reached the Mustang first, flung open the passenger door, and slipped inside. I came around the hood to the smashed-in side and climbed through the busted-out window. Behind the wheel, I juggled the keys until I had them in the ignition. I cranked, and the engine chugged and churned. A bullet bounced off the red and white hood.

The Mustang revved to life just as the dust cleared from the lot. I threw the car in gear as the hovercraft lifted off the ground.

Chapter Twenty Four

The 1968 Mustang Shelby Cobra kicked up its own cyclone of dust and rocks as I ripped the backend around and the fat tires tore up the asphalt.

I checked the rearview mirror just once as we rocketed out of the parking lot. Agents, some in Order whites, some in civilian clothes, were filling Crown Victorias. Some of the cars were commandeered by 99 Town Police squad cars. Others were unmarked but still bore the telltale signs of unmarked cop cars: antennas, cages, and hidden lights and sirens. Some bothered with the lights. Others didn't. They all chased after. And rising above them all, the white Order hovercraft rose up out of the frame of the rearview mirror.

"Go, man. Get us the fuck outta here," Ruby said.

I skipped second gear and shifted into third. We took the turn onto the on-ramp at forty miles per hour. Before they were up to the freeway, I swapped my foot from accelerator to clutch, dropped the Mustang into fourth, and got back on the gas. We hit the freeway at sixty miles per hour.

We couldn't see it, but we could hear the hovercraft come overhead. Like a drone, it hummed, but at a pitch six octaves lower and a hundred decibels louder. It swept away dust and dirt wherever it passed. Ruby craned her neck trying to see above the car roof.

I was heavy on the gas and spurred the Mustang closer and closer to its top speed. The civilian traffic around us was falling by the wayside to our left and right. I put the Mustang in the center lane and only veered when a car ahead was too slow to see the rushing swarm coming down the highway.

The hovercraft dipped down to the right of the freeway, flying parallel to the Mustang. Phom stood inside the open doors on the side of the craft, clipped into a harness and holding an assault rifle. I caught a glance of him through Ruby's window and broke hard to the left, away from the hovercraft just as Phom let loose a burst of machine gun fire. Bullets plunked into the rear fender and the wide B-pillar.

I swerved and hammered back on the gas.

The hovercraft rose up, back out of sight.

Sara's thirty-eight was on the center console. Ruby picked it up, flicked open the cylinder, and counted the rounds. "Five shots left in this one. How about you?" she asked.

"Whatever Mike left me in this one," I said and tucked the 99 Town Police service automatic into a pocket in my coat. "Make your shots count. This is all we got."

Ruby held the thirty-eight and tried to see around the roof. "Got it. Now, where did that son of a bitch go?"

"I don't know, but the rest of them are catching up," I said.

Four Crown Victorias filled the width of the freeway behind us, each running abreast and flashing red and white lights. More cars were stacked up behind their front line.

The hovercraft swung down on our left, again dropping even with the elevated freeway. Phom was at the open door, the body of the hovercraft rotating to aim him and his assault rifle at the Mustang regardless of the direction of flight. I saw Phom lining up to fire, and I tapped on the brakes. A salvo of bullets strafed the asphalt in front of us. A few rounds pumped into a bystander's car. The hovercraft shot up again, out of sight.

"They're gaining on us," Ruby said, eyes fixed behind us while she milked the grip of the handgun, eager to fire.

An unmarked Crown Vic pulled ahead of the pack and was just feet from our rear bumper. I veered right. The Crown Vic followed. I veered left and the agent crept closer, looking for that diagonal position ideal to hook the rear fender and take us out.

I pinned the accelerator to the floor. The speedometer and tachometer jumped up. Ruby and I were pinned into the seats. A row of bullet hits ran up the highway alongside the car as the hovercraft shot past us. Ruby leaned out of the window as we watched Phom and the craft lower down near the surface of the highway in front of us. A few bystander drivers swerved around or came to a screeching halt to avoid hitting the hovercraft.

Phom stood with his feet wide and rifle shouldered, blood still seeping from his gut.

Ruby slipped her torso out of the window as the Mustang charged. A burst of gunfire shot through the windshield and into her seatback, missing her only because she moved. Ruby held the revolver tight and squeezed off two shots. She missed Phom, but her shots triggered the hovercraft to lift up just as I steered for the shoulder to dodge it.

"Where's he going?" I asked, trying to see up and around the roof. Phom was still up there, hunting us like a hawk.

"Where the hell are we going?" Ruby said. "I just used up a third of my ammo. We can't do this for long."

"Hang on," I said and ripped hard on the wheel.

The Mustang's tires sang in protest as we merged off one freeway and onto another. The sharp curve pulled the Mustang and us to the outside of the turn. The tires threatened to slip, or worse, bite into the asphalt sideways and send the car tumbling. I feathered the wheel, finding the balance between slipping and rolling all while keeping on the gas.

Two of the Crown Vics shot past the exit. The others followed close behind, filling the width of the narrower freeway in echelon. More followed behind them. The hovercraft was still out of sight, but I knew it would have no problem adjusting its course.

"We're headed for downtown," Ruby said. The skyscrapers of 99 Town loomed ahead, the Government Center rising up above the rest. "As soon as we hit traffic—"

"Don't worry. I got a plan," I said.

"They're coming up behind us," Ruby said.

I checked the rearview mirror, then the speedometer. One hundred and twenty miles per hour. Still, a marked squad car was creeping up on our passenger side. The Crown Victorias didn't look as flashy as the Mustang or GTO, but I was learning they had power under the hood near the same. I checked the rearview mirror once more, veered wide of the enclosing squad car, and tapped the brakes.

At that speed, one touch to the brake pedal dropped us back behind the Crown Vic. Back heavy on the gas, I put us right at the rear fender of the cop car. I eased the Mustang into the other car. The cop tried to counter-steer, keeping at least the front wheels aimed down the highway as the backend dragged sideways. Those tires squealed and left black rubber scars on the highway. Just as I pushed the rear end sideways and cleared out from the Crown Vic, the cop car's sidewalls caught pavement. The sedan barrel-rolled like a towel in a dryer.

I slammed on the gas as the Crown Vic shed bits of twisted metal and broken glass. As it rolled, a pursuing Crown Vic was too slow to miss the wreckage and smashed into the tumbling cruiser.

A few others made it around and continued the chase.

The hovercraft dropped back down like a lethal marionette along the Mustang's right side. Phom and Ruby exchanged shots as I careened and dodged around the strips of machine gun fire.

"I'm out," Ruby said and tossed her handgun into the backseat. "Give me yours."

"This is all we got left," I said and handed over the gun.

"If I don't put an end to this, we're going to die out here," Ruby said. "If not by your shitty driving, it will be by that maniac filling us full of bullet holes."

Ruby took the automatic and slipped back out the window. She twisted her torso so she was aiming skyward and unloaded four shots before pulling herself back in. Return fire smacked all around the Mustang like a focused meteor shower.

"They won't get us. Not me. Not you. I won't allow it," I said but knew the kid was right. We were running out of tricks quick, and our chasers didn't seem to be running out of bullets or Crown Vics to throw at us. "You hang on, and I'll get us out of this."

Another exit ramp. Another opportunity to shake off some of the agents. I waited as long as I dared to show my cards. At the last second, I tapped the brakes, let the tires bark, and ripped the Mustang to the right and onto the exit ramp.

We lost one more cop car, but the rest followed.

At the bottom of the off-ramp was a red light and stopped cars. I laid on the brakes and left scorched rubber trails behind us.

"Shit shit shit shit,' Ruby said as we closed in on the parked cars at the light.

There was grass to either side and posts and signs lining the curb zipping past us. I let off the brakes and shifted into neutral, then into second gear so the engine wouldn't stall, then back on the gas. I turned the wheel just enough to jump the curb and rip through the grass. When we came back onto the asphalt, I turned hard to the right and let the back end of the Mustang skid around till we were aimed down the city street.

"There! Up there!" I pointed through the crack-laced windshield toward the elevated tracks of 99 Town's commuter train. "That's how we lose the hovercraft."

There was more traffic on the city streets and not long enough stretches of highway for police lights to clear our path. As fast as we wanted to go, I couldn't get up to speed between other cars and obstacles. Regardless, I shifted back into third and then fourth gear to get the Mustang back up to sixty miles per hour.

The tracks of the elevated train were a block ahead and ran perpendicular to the road we were on. The streetlights were green. There was another pair of Crown Victorias behind us, and I could hear the echoes of sirens bouncing off buildings from every direction. That was fine. I could handle them. I pulled to the right, knowing I'd need to take the turn as wide as I could.

I steered hard to the left, crossed oncoming traffic, and slipped under the tracks. Steel pillars flashed by either side of the Mustang. As we rushed up to the bumper of a car in our lane, I veered right, exposing ourselves to the open sky above, then veered left again, dodging pillars and cars as we ducked back under the tracks.

Overhead, the train rumbled past in the opposite direction. The pavement shook, and old flakes of rust fell on the Mustang's hood. All that was fine by me. As long as the train was above us, the hovercraft wasn't.

"Chuck!" Ruby called out.

A police blockade. Cars pulled up bumper to bumper across the street a block ahead.

I pulled the wheel and drove the Mustang onto another cross street. This one sent us across the Cut Rock River that ran through the heart of 99 Town. I turned again, shifting all the inertia in the opposite direction, onto the street running parallel to the river.

As soon as we established our course, weaving through traffic along the river-side street, the hovercraft dove back down next to us, directly over the Cut Rock. Ruby jabbed the gun out the window and fired. A lead shower came back, just in front of and above the Mustang. Where the bullets hit buildings, panes of glass shattered and rained down onto traffic.

Ruby dropped the magazine from the automatic. "I'm out," she said.

"Wasn't doing much good against that hovercraft anyway," I said.

I didn't wait for Phom to let loose another blast from the machine gun. I took the next bridge that cut across the river and drove directly toward the hovercraft. If we could get back under the train tracks...

Phom was there at the door of the hovercraft, gun at the ready. Ruby tried getting as low as she could, behind the engine block. I white-knuckled the wheel. Phom let loose and sprayed at the charging Mustang. Bullets punched through glass all around me, but none struck meat or bones. A flash later and the Mustang was under the hovercraft, across the bridge, and surrounded by buildings again.

"There. The tracks are just ahead," I said, and when the intersection came, I took another wide ninety-degree turn and power-steered around the corner.

"Uh... Chuck," Ruby said. "This ain't good."

I turned to the passenger seat. Ruby was holding up two palms covered in bright red blood. With each beat of her heart, jets of blood squirted out through wet holes in her shirt. Her face was quickly turning bleach white.

"No no no," I said. I checked the road and dodged another slower car, out of the cover of the train tracks and then back under just as quick. "Stay with me, Ruby. Try to relax. Don't go into shock on me now."

She was taking clumps of her shirt and trying to hold the wads of cloth tight against the bullet holes, doing everything she could with weakened hands to plug the pumping leaks. Her expression was detached as if she was watching someone else's hands working on someone else's bloody torso. Fascinated disbelief. Each moment the color drained more from her face and her eyes became less focused.

"That's a lot of blood," Ruby said, the words spilling over numb lips.

As her hands fell from her wounds, I tried reaching over to hold the wads of the bloody shirt in place. I glanced up through the windshield, cut the wheel and braked hard to avoid a collision, then stomped back on the accelerator. The fleet of Crown Vics was still behind us.

Looking back to Ruby, I watched her eyes roll up, and the muscles in her neck go limp. I knew she was still alive, for now, if only evident by the still squirting chest wounds. The fountains of squirting blood still pumped, but with each ejection, the sprays were weaker and further apart.

"No! Don't die on me, kid! You're all I got. You're the only connection I have left," I said but felt like I was talking to myself.

The train tracks took another turn. I dodged through traffic and took another sharp turn. Ruby slumped over against the passenger door, devoid of volition. I tried to ignore it. Old surface-level tracks followed along the street we were on. The section of road I was looking for was just ahead.

Ruby sucked air in again, the breath sounding choked with fluid and pain. The nerves had stopped shaking her hands. The color was empty from her face. A few smears of blood on her cheek were red brush strokes on a white canvas. The inhale never came back out as an exhale.

I couldn't afford to watch the kid die. The locked chain-linked gate was just ahead. I glanced in the rearview mirror, scanning for Phom and the hovercraft.

"Follow me down here, you fuck," I said.

Behind me, the hovercraft swung around the train tracks and between the steel pillars. Crown Vics and civilian traffic swerved to make room for the craft in the tight confines of the street below the tracks. I caught a glance of the action in the rearview mirror but kept my focus forward. The T-intersection was just ahead. I plowed through it and into the chain-linked gate.

The chain and lock snapped apart. The gates flew open. All four wheels of the Mustang cleared the ground as we dove down into the underground and the darkness. For a moment, everything was black. Then I found the headlight knob and lit up the interior of the underground tunnel. A moment later, the lights of the hovercraft shined through the back window.

Phom wasn't going to be shaken that easily.

In front of the high beams, the tunnel coursed along a shallow curve. Hard-packed tire tracks marking years of black market traffic slalomed around mounds of garbage and abandoned grocery carts. I was careful to follow every change in vector, knowing that ignoring the path could result in a quick and violent end to the chase.

The hovercraft followed and ignored the tire tracks. Its width almost took up the whole berth of the tunnel. It scraped its sides against the cinder block walls along outside turns, leaving gouges in the wall and trails of sparks behind it. The body of the hovercraft had rotated so Phom and the open door faced forward. He was on the gun, showing no signs of relenting.

The tunnel forked. I feinted left and then cut right, plunging the Mustang deeper under 99 Town. The hovercraft had no problem following. As I swerved around an old rusted bicycle, Phom plowed right over it and closed the distance.

A barrage of bullets punched through the Mustang's trunk and backseat, drawing a line down the center of the car and sending the last bullets through the already broken windshield. I serpentined across the width of the tunnel, as much as I could, jumping the old train tracks as I crossed and dodged more strips of gunfire to my left and right.

Another fork in the tunnel came up in front of the high beams. At over a hundred miles per hour, I barely saw it before I veered right down another branch of the old subway network. I couldn't keep this up for long. Who knew how long the tunnels went and how far Phom would chase me? I glanced over at Ruby's surely dead body.

"You better not have lost it, kid. So help me if you dropped it at the train station…" I said and then reached for the hip pocket of her tight jeans.

My foot must have come up off the gas pedal as I reached across to the passenger seat. Just as I was about to slip my hand into the dead girl's hip pocket, the hovercraft rammed into the back of the Mustang. The car skidded and fish-tailed, almost clipping the curving tunnel wall. I wrenched back and forth on the wheel to keep it barreling down the tracks.

"Get off me, Phom!" I yelled.

I grabbed Ruby by her collar and pulled her over. Lifeless, she flopped onto me. Blood and some other clear fluid leaked from her agape mouth onto my shoulder. I ignored it and dug back into her left hip pocket. Empty.

A streak of bullets cut through the passenger seat and into the dash.

"Come on, come on," I said and shoved my hand into the right hip pocket. "There!"

I pulled the implant from Ruby's pocket, turned it around in my hand, and plugged it into my port. Immediately my vision sharpened and filled in the dark corners of the tunnel not lit by the headlights. The muffle and whine in my left ear disappeared. I became conscious of Phom and the hovercraft's precise location. I called up a map of the tunnel, and it displayed in front of my vision.

No agents were behind us. It was just me and Phom racing through the old tunnels, further and further from the center of 99 Town.

"You won't stop me, Phom," I said.

Phom replied, and his voice piped right into my auditory cortex. "I won't stop chasing you until I do. You betrayed me, Chuz. Me, and all of the Order. You should know what that means to me."

I saw the tunnel split again, on the map first, and then through the darkness the high beams couldn't penetrate. This time I had no problem preparing for the turn. I tried to shake Phom with a few quick jerks of the wheel left and right, but as soon as I decided to swing to the left, Phom knew my decision. The hovercraft followed right behind.

"Haven't you learned anything, Chuz?" Phom said. "You have to know how this will end by now."

"Yeah, Phom. I've learned some things," I said and saw something in the map in my vision, but I thought it away. Instead of mapping the tunnels, I gave the implant another mission. "Here's my report, you fuck."

The moment I plugged in, the implant went about harvesting all of my memories since I'd last been connected to the Network. Now, I commanded it to dump all that data to Phom with emergency priority. All the images, sounds, and feelings of my last two days in 99 Town flooded to the front of Phom's consciousness.

Through the Network, we relived those moments together. Phom broke into a coughing fit when the memories of the burning tattoo parlor overwhelmed him. He saw Sammy and Reggie's burnt corpses. He smelled the smoke and felt the burn in his eyes and lungs.

Mickey's dead body in the bail bonds office. The shells on the floor and the holes in the walls. My heart racing and pumping adrenaline through my veins as we searched the shadows of the office for attackers and tripwires.

The explosion at Cheap Hotel. The heat of it. The force that had sent me flying backward into the parking lot. The confusion and disorientation in my head from the concussion. The ringing in my ears.

We gasped for air and felt relief when suddenly the memories were of warm coffee and a star-lit night. A soft bed. Softer skin. Beautiful eyes. Something closer to heaven than he'd ever experienced. I felt Phom's reprieve, and I reprioritized the memories to force-feed him something more recent.

A car wreck. Pain. Confusion.

A rooftop. The same eyes and the same head, but now ripped from her body and dangling at the arm's length of an android. I relived the moment along with Phom. The pain of it hitting me harder than it could have ever hit him. But I suffered it so he could suffer it.

Cut to the courthouse. Phom saw a view of himself as he strolled up to the bar, drew his neural inhibitor, and turned Mister Meade's brains to soup.

"Stop it! That's enough, Chuz," Phom yelled. He focused and fought off the incoming memories. "I order you to stop!"

"Good idea, old buddy," I said and slammed on the brakes.

A hundred meters ahead, the tunnel ended at a brick wall.

All four of the Mustang's tires locked up and cut into the hard-packed dirt surface. The hovercraft, all but unpiloted by Phom and his distractions, smashed into the car. Phom was thrown to the taut length of his harness, nearly onto the car's trunk. The hovercraft careened off the Mustang and collided into the side of the tunnel. Something caught and it twisted around. The bottom of the craft hit the ground and tumbled forward and smashed against the ground and the walls.

As the hovercraft churned into a burning wreckage, the tunnel's dead-end rushed to meet the Mustang's front bumper. The hood crumpled on impact. Any glass left in the car shattered and peppered the wall. Ruby's body flung through the windshield. The lap belt whiplashed me. My forehead smacked hard into the steering wheel. The implant dislodged from my port and went over the dash. Everything blurred.

I wasn't sure if I lost consciousness. I lifted my head off the steering wheel and saw the destruction all around me and the burning wreck of the hovercraft behind me. I saw Ruby's body on the hood, and next to her, a handgun caught in a fold of the crumpled hood, and next to that the implant. I tried my door, but one of the multiple crashes the Mustang had suffered left it sealed shut. I climbed around the steering wheel, through the windshield, and onto the hood. I picked up the implant and the gun. Mike's gun. I turned to the hovercraft.

"Chuz!" Phom yelled. He stood in front of the burning hovercraft, assault rifle still in hand. "I'm not done with you yet."

I stepped over the windshield, onto the roof, down the trunk, and jumped to the floor of the tunnel. The Mustang's taillights and the hovercraft's fire painted the tunnel red and orange. I stopped about ten meters from Phom.

There was a thin trail of blood running down Phom's mouth. His abdomen and right leg were soaked. In the strange light, the blood on the Order whites looked black. Like Indian ink on paper. Phom swayed like a punch-drunk boxer.

"You going to shoot me, Phom?"

"I'm going to shoot you till every last bullet is out of this gun," Phom said. "And if you're not dead by then, I'll haul your ass back to Chicago myself. I'll have justice."

"Justice? You murdered my wife," I said. "Are you going to face justice alongside me?"

Phom tried to laugh but choked instead. "You're a funny guy, Chuz. Sure. I'll stand next to you before the Order, and we'll let them decide who's just."

"How about we finish this right here instead? Me and you. Just like old friends."

Phom gestured to the gun in my hand. "Like old friends, huh?" Phom spat, and a long trail of saliva dangled from his mouth to the ground. "I like that, Chuz."

"Go ahead. Make your move." What more did I have to lose?

I eyed the assault rifle in Phom's hands and felt the heft of the handgun in my palm. I watched through the firelight for the barrel of the rifle to rise up. The heat from the burning hovercraft enveloped us. Smoke filled the ceiling of the tunnel.

The barrel of the assault rifle twitched.

I raised the gun and pulled the trigger. The hammer fell on an empty chamber with a metallic click. Out of ammo. Phom smiled, then wavered and collapsed into the dust of the tunnel floor. The last of his life seeped out of the wound in his abdomen.

Chapter Twenty Five

The maintenance ladder went up to a steel manhole cover, hidden by the black smoke of the burning hovercraft. By the time I climbed up and shoved the lid out of its seat, the fire had reached Phom's corpse and was cremating him.

I pushed up with my shoulder to unseat the lid and dump it off to the side of the opening. As I climbed up to the surface, a plume of black smoke followed me. I coughed and hacked and spilled out of the tunnel like something born from hell. I landed in soft soil and sunlight. The dirt and plants around me smelled like I was alive again. I squinted against the bright sunlight and was confused by the soft sounds of the breeze pushing through rows and rows of corn stalks.

I blinked away the burning from my eyes and saw that I was in a field. The corn was tall, lush, and green, which meant I was on the Order side of the border fence. 99 Town was behind me. I saw the skyline and even a thin stream of smoke from where Rogue's Tattoos still smoldered. Closer to me, the manhole gushed black soot like an old industrial smokestack.

It wouldn't be hard for the Order to find me out here, all by myself, marked by the steady black plume. It would be even easier to find me after I plugged back in.

I looked down at my hands. In my right was Mike's empty service automatic. In my left was the implant. I tossed the handgun into the rows of corn. It was useless. The implant on the other hand… I dug into my shirt pocket and pulled out the slip of paper I'd first found next to my pillow in my Chicago home. Not just *my* home. *Our* home.

In case you still love me.

I turned the paper over and saw the nine digits on the back.

1321345589

The implant. It was the end of everything. The end of the Order's unchallenged rule. Of the uneasy peace between the Order and the Underground. The end of me. Everything came to an end. Another lesson learned in 99 Town.

I plugged the implant into my port and called up the data. Lines and lines of names. Some surely guilty of crimes and corruption. Others, most I guessed, were as innocent as my wife, but dead all the same.

At the end of the list was a short prompt.

Network-wide publication is
restricted to authorized personnel
only. Enter passcode to continue.

: _ _ _ _ _ _ _ _ _

I mentally entered the digits into the blanks. For reasons I didn't fully understand, I tucked the slip of paper deep into a pocket. As soon as the last character was submitted, the implant went to work publishing the data with emergency priority. Everyone under the Order would have it pumped directly into their prefrontal cortex. Everyone would know. People would be upset. Especially those who recognized names on that list. The Order would be furious.

I sat down on the lip of the manhole, exhausted. It wouldn't be long now.

I closed my eyes and already I heard the sound of an incoming hovercraft. Wired into the Network, if I wanted I could follow the flight path of any inbound hovercrafts and implants as they came in for the kill. I decided I'd rather not see it coming. I cleared the information out of my vision. The progress bar of the publishing data too. It couldn't be stopped now. It was done.

The hovercraft drew closer, and while I thought about shutting off audio input to my brain, I decided I'd rather experience my last few moments as naturally as I could. When the downdraft of its rotors started knocking over corn stalks in front of me, I closed my eyes and forced myself to focus on memories.

Sara. Under the stars. The smell of coffee. The flickering light surrounded by moths. The gentle sound of crickets and dried corn stalks at night. The bed upstairs. The thick quilts. The warmth of our bodies pressed together, moving in sync with each other. The mutual ecstasy. A night of sleep more restful than all the nights across this whole life added up. The goose bumps on her skin in the morning sunlight.

I could die with that image in my head, and they couldn't take it away from me.

"Chuz," a voice, sweet but hard spoke to me. Not Sara's voice. Not the voice of the Network either. But familiar and thick with memories and evoked emotions. "Chuz, wake up."

I opened my eyes. A woman stood before me. Beyond her was a black hovercraft humming as it idled on the ground. Machine guns and cannons were bolted to the frame. Red flames had been painted onto the nose. The paint job had been scorched and marred. It looked like a war machine. Nothing the Order would fly. Rough men with weapons and body armor stepped out and flanked the woman.

Her face. Her eyes. Her long brown hair knotted into a ponytail.

"Maggie?" I asked.

"Get in, Chuz," my wife said. "We have a lot to talk about."

About the Author

Joe Prosit writes sci-fi, horror, and psycho fiction. His debut novel is "Bad Brains," followed by the "From Order Series" featuring the novels, "99 Town," "7 Androids," and "Zero City." "Machines Monsters and Maniacs" is a self-published collection of sixteen of his short stories. He has been published in various magazines and podcasts, most notably, in 365Tomorrow, The NoSleep Podcast, Metaphorosis Magazine, and Kaidankai Podcast. You can find it on Amazon or at his website, at www.JoeProsit.com. If you're an adept stalker, you can find him on one of the many lakes and rivers or lost deep inside the Great North Woods. Or you can just follow him on Twitter, @joeprosit.

SCI-FI HORROR PSYCHO FICTION

JOE PROSIT.COM

Prefer to read on your device?

Go to this link and enter in the password: Ru@BadBrain? to download your free eBook version that is included in the purchase of this book.

Made in the USA
Monee, IL
22 April 2024